The Deconstructionist

A Russ Walker Novel

Patrick Jones began his working life serving a five year apprenticeship in engineering, after which life took a dramatic turn when he entered the novitiate of an Anglican Franciscan Order.

Two and a half years later, on deciding the celibate life was not for him, he left to join the police service. After several years, he felt called to train for the Anglican priesthood.

Having been a priest for forty years, he is now retired and devotes his time to writing.

He has an MA in Theology and lives in South East Kent.

Patrick Jones

The Deconstructionist

A Russ Walker Novel

Olympia Publishers
London

www.olympiapublishers.com
OLYMPIA PAPERBACK EDITION

A CIP catalogue record for this title is
available from the British Library.

ISBN: 978-1-84897-566-8

(Olympia Publishers is part of Ashwell Publishing Ltd)

Most of the action in the novel takes place in London and the South East, but
certain liberties have been taken in portraying the towns and villages themselves
and their institutions. This is wholly intentional. The world presented here is a
fictitious one, as are its characters and events. Any resemblance to actual incidents,
or to actual persons living or dead, is entirely coincidental.

Published *in 2015*

Olympia Publishers
60 Cannon Street
London
EC4N 6NP

Printed in Great Britain

This book is dedicated to my loved ones.

Acknowledgements

I'm grateful to the many individuals who have supported me in the writing of this book. I especially thank Jan Limb for tirelessly proofreading the ever-changing script and her encouragement. Thank you also to Dr Gordon Plant FRCP FRCOphth at St Thomas' Hospital, London, for restoring my eyesight and enabling me to see this through. Thanks to the whole team at Olympia for their dedication, and last but not least, to Pam, for being there with me.

Chapter 1

There was a lightness in his step as Russ Walker emerged from Charing Cross Station into the morning sunlight. The exhaust fumes and noise from passing traffic, steering his way through the sheer volume of people - all this might feel like an assault on the senses to an occasional day visitor from the provinces, but for him, it was familiar, comforting. It was like coming home. Yes, there was no denying it; he hadn't realised how much he'd missed it. He'd always enjoyed the sensation of anonymity in the midst of so much frenetic activity. Having caught the high speed train from Ashford to London, circumspect but not unduly anxious, he made his way along Villiers Street to Victoria Embankment, and then left to the Savoy Hotel.

He informed one of the smartly uniformed door porters that he was meeting someone for coffee.

The man smiled. 'Excuse me for asking, sir, but are you Mr Walker?'

Surprised, he nodded, 'Yes, I am.'

'Ah, good. We have a table reserved for you. If you'd care to follow me.'

He led Russ through the cavernous front hall to a table in The Thames Foyer, close to the ornate gazebo under a glass cupola, and held the chair as Russ sat down. Russ glanced at his watch – it was 10.55 a.m. This was surreal. He'd never been to the Savoy before and had no idea who he was waiting for. Relieved he'd chosen to wear his charcoal grey suit, white shirt and tie, he still felt uncomfortable, out of place. This iconic hotel, in the heart of the Capital, catering for the super-rich, had recently reopened after a £12 million refurbishment. As a private investigator, desperate for clients, he lived and struggled in a different universe from the well-heeled who patronised this place. His pragmatic approach to life and work made him less than comfortable with mystery or surprises - but today was different. After yesterday's bizarre phone call inviting him here, he was almost looking forward to this meeting.

'I'm glad you could make it, Mr Walker.' The voice came from behind him.

Russ turned and looked at his watch; it was exactly eleven. Approaching his table was a tall, thin man, the perfect caricature of a civil servant in his white shirt, college tie, navy pinstriped suit and highly polished black shoes. He was in his early sixties, clean shaven, with short, straight mousy-coloured hair parted on the right. He wore half-moon gold framed glasses and carried an attaché case.

With a thin smile he held out his hand. 'Good morning. My name is Shand.'

Russ stood and shook his hand. 'You have the advantage on me, Mr Shand? I don't believe we've met.'

'All in good time; let's sit down and I'll order coffee.'

Shand seated himself opposite Russ, caught the eye of a waiter and nodded. Almost immediately, coffee and a selection of biscuits were brought to the table. The waiter poured the coffee and left.

Shand stirred cream into his coffee. 'You're feeling settled now in East Sussex?'

Russ wasn't sure if it was a statement or a question. 'Yes, thank you, I am', he said impatiently, 'but who *are* you Mr Shand ... and why are we here?'

'As I said yesterday, what we have to discuss is of a highly sensitive nature. Your resignation from the police service is a matter of great regret to us. You served with distinction and achieved some notable successes in the fight against organised crime.' He paused, and took a sip of coffee. 'Of course, the tragic death of your fiancée, Rebecca, last year, was an enormous loss to you...'

At the mention of Becky, he felt a constriction in his chest. *What the hell is this?*

'Look, I have no idea who you are or what this is about.'

Shand looked him squarely in the face. 'Provone – Marcus Provone! We both want to see him brought to justice. Please bear with me, Mr Walker.'

Russ stiffened and looked directly at Shand, waiting for him to continue.

'We are both aware that Provone is head of one of the largest crime syndicates in London and the southern counties. I know too, that your determined investigations into his activities led to the discovery of a large quantity of illegal drugs at a warehouse at Billingsgate. You took the appropriate action and called in the Scene of Crime

Investigators... your late-fiancée, Rebecca was a civilian member of the team.'

Russ swallowed, and his breathing became laboured. He would live to regret that decision for the rest of his life.

As if reading his thoughts, Shand continued. 'There's no way you could have foreseen the tragic events that ensued. That the Crown Prosecution Service hold to the view there is still insufficient evidence to bring the perpetrators to trial, has, I believe, been the major cause of your disillusionment with our legal system, resulting in your subsequent resignation.'

Too bloody true! He didn't need to be reminded of this. Not a day passed without him feeling the pain of separation and loss. The knowledge that Provone and his thugs were untouchable deepened his sense of injustice and anger.

'I hope you're not trying to suggest I've overreacted; that I shouldn't have resigned.' Russ barked. 'From where I'm sitting, there's something badly wrong with a system weighted in favour of murderous scum like Provone!'

Shand's face remained impassive. 'Mr Walker, I'm not here to question your resignation, but I do have a proposition for you to consider. At this present time, we are facing an unprecedented rise in organised crime, terrorist activity, and the associated problems of immigration. To say that the security services and the police are stretched to the limit is, of course, an understatement. The recent disclosures by the media of the enormous weaknesses within the Home Office have surprised no-one. To put it bluntly, Walker, we're in a bloody mess.'

Shand paused. 'As you know, the strengthening of resources for counter-terrorism and national security has left us woefully lacking in our capability to deal with rising crime and anti-social behaviour. In spite of the many successes of the Serious Crimes Unit and other agencies, we are still only scratching the surface. As a result, we often find we have to prioritise. The recent attempt to curb the much-publicized rise in gun-related crime is an obvious example. In addition to the media breathing down our necks, we are plagued by civil liberties groups and other self-appointed watchdogs.'

Russ still had no idea where this was leading. 'You're preaching to the converted, Mr Shand. Why are you telling me this?'

He held up his hand. 'Patience, please. To put it simply, we want you to continue working for us - but as a civilian. Your new venture, as a private investigator living out of London would be an ideal cover for the kind of work we have in mind. Your experience and expertise would be invaluable to us. We would expect you to continue in your business and take on work for clients, but at the same time, make yourself available to undertake covert assignments for us. We are prepared to pay well for your services, offering a monthly retainer, and extra finances as and when required.'

Russ felt a shiver of excitement run down his spine. From as far back as he could remember, all he'd ever wanted was to join the police service and become a detective, and that dream became a reality. Recent events, however, had changed everything. With the loss of Becky and his unwillingness to accept the constraints imposed by the Police Criminal Code, he now believed private investigation was the only option available to him. And yet the proposal Shand appeared to be making was irresistible. He tried hard to not let the excitement show in his response.

'I'm certainly interested, but could you be more specific? Who is the "us" that I'd be working for, and what exactly do you mean by "assignments"?' he said, keeping his voice even.

Shand drained his cup. 'I'll be as succinct as possible, and what I share with you *must* remain strictly confidential. By "us" I mean Her Majesty's law enforcement agencies. If you agree to work with us, I, and I alone would be your point of contact. There would be no written contracts or formal agreements, no conditions of employment and no official recognition of your role. We are not seeking to recruit you into MI5 or any other department. As a freelance detective, you would be freed from many of the constraints that are imposed on orthodox methods of fighting crime.'

Russ reached for the coffee pot and refilled their cups. 'Let's imagine for a moment that I accept your proposition. How would this work out in practice?'

'In practice, Walker, you would be a "deconstructionist", not in the philosophical sense, but in practice. People like Provone have constructed complex criminal networks that reward them with many millions of pounds each year. The time and expense we incur seeking to bring them to the courts for justice are simply not cost effective. Like every other Government department, we are having to make severe cutbacks. Years ago, the old fashioned bobby would give culprits of a misdemeanour a clip around the ears rather than waste time and money bringing them to court. It was described and accepted as having been "dealt with summarily". We would be looking for your help to "deconstruct" specific criminal organisations or activities. If you like to deal with them summarily. In reality, it would be a cost-cutting exercise for our agencies, if you see what I mean.'

He paused and sipped his coffee. 'It could be dangerous, but no more so than your work in the SCU. Whether or not you agree to work with us, you must *never*, I repeat *never* - under any circumstances – reveal the details of this arrangement to *anyone*. Were you to do so, we would, of course, vigorously deny it. So, how do you respond?'

Resisting the urge to bite his hand off, Russ paused briefly before answering. 'Well, I'm grateful for your confidence in me, and I'm certainly interested; but if you're to be the sole point of contact, how would we communicate with each other?'

Shand withdrew a card from the top pocket of his jacket, and passed it to him. 'I can arrange for money to be deposited directly into your bank account, and would contact you by phone or special mail delivery. You would communicate with me through this Westminster Post Office Box number or, in an extreme emergency, by phoning this number. Please commit them to memory; do not write them down.'

This wasn't a problem for Russ. His former colleagues had been envious of his uncommon ability for remembering numbers or addresses without an aide-memoire. He studied the information, filing it away in his mind before handing the card back to Shand.

Russ gave his own business card to Shand. 'I'll post my bank details to you.'

'Thank you, Mr Walker; that would most helpful. From now on, in order to maintain a level of security, please refrain from using the nom de guerre I adopted for this meeting. In all future communication between us, you and I must always use the code name "Derrida".'

The man got to his feet; Russ followed. 'I'm most encouraged by our meeting. Have a good journey back to Rye. I'll be in touch.'

After shaking hands, he turned, and walked briskly to the main entrance. Russ sat and finished his coffee, and checked his watch. Plenty of time to call in on a couple of friends before catching a train back to Ashford to pick up his car.

Chapter 2

For a Monday night, Harbour Rocks was unusually busy.
Behind the bar, the landlord remained self-possessed. If some
of the patrons had to wait, so be it; they'd all get served
eventually. No one seemed predisposed to complain; whether
this was due to their good-humoured patience or because
Elmo Kernow, at six foot three, with his oriental features and
close-cropped hair, bore a striking resemblance to Odd Job, a
character in a James Bond movie, was arguable. He was
dressed in his usual attire – an embroidered black shirt and
boot-lace tie, black drainpipe trousers and grey suede shoes
with an inch of crepe. Expecting no more than a handful of
customers this early in the week, he'd encouraged his partner,
Amy, to take the night off. No sooner had she left to visit her
mother at the nearby town of Rye, Sod's Law kicked in and
a large contingent of a Rock 'n' Roll Club from Canterbury
piled through the door.

Harbour Rocks – known locally as *The Rocks* – is a themed
pub dedicated to the Rock and Roll era of the fifties and
sixties. It was a nineteenth-century white stucco building on
the High Street, between Bowen's Garage and the General
Stores, in the hamlet of Rye Harbour on the East Sussex coast.

When Elmo bought it in 2008, it was The King's Head, a dingy, unappealing village pub patronised by a diminishing handful of irregular customers. At that time it was no longer a going concern, but he was a risk-taker with an entrepreneurial spirit; for years he'd nursed the dream of owning a themed pub. On leaving the army after fifteen years in the Paratroop Regiment, which included active service in the Falklands and the liberation of Kuwait, and against the advice of his accountant, he took a leap of faith and secured a mortgage on the property. Within six months, the dream had become a successful reality.

For some of the locals, it was too much of a seismic shift when he unsubtly had a sign writer substitute the head of Henry VIII for Elvis Presley on The King's Head sign outside the pub. Protestations from the local history society and conservationists, forced Elmo to relent. Eventually a compromise was reached; he would call it Harbour Rocks, with a generic harbour scene on the new sign. The whole interior was refurbished, but as a sop to the protesters, he left the horse-brasses and dried hops on the oak beams surrounding the bar. Most of the wall space was given over to photographs and posters of singers and groups popular in the fifties and sixties. At strategic points in the L- shaped bar, he positioned four large flat-screen TV monitors for the showing of video clips of various artists during Happy Hours. Against the wall, to the left of the open fireplace, he installed a restored 1956 Wurlitzer Juke Box, containing a selection of 200 45rpm vinyl records. Some of the regulars were Rye Harbour locals, but as a testimony to Elmo's marketing skills, the majority of patrons were an eclectic mix from around the county. To an unsuspecting outsider, crossing the threshold of Harbour Rocks was like finding oneself in a time warp.

Interrupting Jim Lowe trying to fathom the mystery of the green door on the Juke Box, Elmo rang a bell and called for last orders.

Sitting at a table close to the main door, Russ Walker pointed to his companion's glass. 'One for the road?'

Sue Westbrook shook her head. 'No thanks; it's time I was tucked up in bed.'

He leaned back in his seat, a wry smile on his face. 'My thoughts exactly. Shall we go?'

Rolling her eyes, she reached for her clutch bag. 'Dream on, big boy, I'm going back to Winchelsea.'

After his meeting at the Savoy, and calling to see a couple of friends on the Isle of Dogs whilst in London, on returning home, Russ had persuaded Sue, his part-time secretary, to join him for a drink at his favourite watering hole. He'd made no mention to her of the real purpose of his trip to London, other than for meeting up with friends. He picked up their empty glasses to return them to the bar as the door to the street swung open. An elderly, frail-looking man trailing an overweight black Labrador on a lead stepped over the threshold.

In a quavering voice he called out. 'Someone call for an ambulance! There's an injured woman outside... I think she's unconscious.'

Elmo reached for the phone as half a dozen spirited rockabillies followed the man out the door, Russ and Sue close behind them. The street was deserted, except for the crumpled figure under the streetlamp on the pavement across the road. The rockabillies gathered hesitantly around the inert woman, staring in morbid curiosity, hoping for someone else to take the initiative and administer first aid. She was face down, her right arm under her body, and the left at a crooked angle to her side. Russ pushed his way through to the front and knelt beside her. It was difficult to gauge her age; she was probably in her thirties or forties, and was wearing jeans, a light blue sweater and missing one of her shoes. Gently moving her long hair away from her neck, he put his fingers on her carotid artery. There was a definite pulse, but it was weak. She smelt strongly of vomit. From beneath her head, a rivulet of blood seeped slowly onto the paving slab.

Aware that Sue was standing behind him, Russ turned his head. 'We'd better not move her. I hope to God the ambulance won't be long.'

Standing up, he shrugged off his jacket and gave it to Sue. 'See if you can slide this under her head; don't worry about the blood. Can you stay with her? I want to talk to the guy who found her.'

The number of onlookers was growing by the minute. Scanning the faces, hoping the old guy hadn't left, Russ eventually spotted him at the back of the crowd and eased his way towards him through what had now become the majority of Elmo's customers. As he approached, he could see the incident had shaken the old boy; his hands were trembling as he stroked his dog for comfort.

'Hey, you okay? Good job you came by when you did.'

The man straightened up; his face drained of colour. 'I didn't know what to do. Will she be alright?' There was a tremor in his voice.

'Don't worry, as soon as the paramedics get here, they'll take care of her. Can you tell me what happened?'

He ran a hand through his hair. 'I was taking Trudy out for a pee before turning in. As we passed the pub, there was a loud scream.' He pointed to the row of terraced houses. 'It came from the one on the end. I stopped, but didn't know what I should do. I mean... If it was a domestic dispute... I didn't know if I should interfere; then the door opened and she came running out. She must have tripped and hit her head on the pavement.'

'Did anyone else come out of the house?' Russ asked.

He shook his head. 'No, just the woman. I went over to see if she was hurt, but she didn't move. Must have knocked herself out... Then I went into the pub to call for an ambulance.'

Russ had a bad feeling about the scream. 'Any idea who lives in the house?'

The man shook his head again. 'Not a clue. Used to be an old lady, lived on her own. I think she went into a nursing home about a year ago. No idea who's there now.'

Russ nodded slowly, patiently, as if conversing with a child. He bent and patted Trudy's neck.

'Well, you did the right thing. The ambulance should be here in a minute. Do you live locally?'

He inclined his head in the direction of the Harbour. 'The road on the left... Walling Close, number 23.'

Russ held out his hand. 'I'm Russ Walker by the way; I live on the Stade. And you are...?'

He shook the hand. 'Trevor Blunt. The wife and I retired here nine years ago.'

Having gleaned all the information he was likely to get, Russ thanked him and gave a reassuring pat to his back. Pushing his way back through the crowd, he found Sue stroking the woman's cheek, talking to her, but getting no discernible response.

Leaning down, he spoke quietly. 'I just want to check the house she came out from... Be back in a minute.'

It was numbered 17. The door was closed but unlocked. Side-stepping a pool of vomit as he entered the hallway, he pulled the door to behind him. He'd always considered he had a strong stomach and could just about cope with most smells, but vomit was the exception; the odour from aliphatic acids always made him gag. Breathing through his mouth he called out, but there was no reply. If there was anyone here, doubtless they would have heard the commotion outside and made an appearance - unless, of course, they were deaf, or immobile.

The lights were on in each of the rooms on the ground floor; they were clean and tidy, no sign of disorder or of an occupant. In the kitchen, he noticed the back door to the garden was unbolted, a mortise key in the lock. He felt a knot in his stomach as he climbed the stairs, taking care to avoid touching the banister rail. From the landing, he saw subdued light coming from the half open door of the front bedroom. A woman's shoulder bag lay on its side outside the door, as if it had been dropped. He called out again and, with the toe of his shoe, pushed the door fully open. Like a punch to the gut, the cold horror of the scene took his breath away. Even from this vantage point, he knew she was dead. She was naked and spread-eagled on her back, her bruised body with its deathly pallor glistening with oil; hands and feet secured by blue nylon rope to the four casters at the head and foot of the double bed. Her eyes, open but lifeless; tape on her mouth. From the expression of absolute terror on her face – death must have been a merciful release. He pulled out his mobile phone and punched 999. He remained at the door to avoid contaminating the crime scene, his eyes registering the details.

The room showed no obvious evidence that a struggle had taken place; there was no sign of a disturbance. The lined curtains at the window were drawn, the bedside lamp switched on. Her clothes were neatly folded on an upright chair; various items of make-up on a small dressing table; the mirrored doors of the fitted wardrobe were closed; a laundry basket in the corner with its lid in place; two pairs of women's shoes in line beside it.

Retracing his steps, Russ returned to the street, relieved to discover the ambulance had arrived and the injured woman was now inside, about to be transported to a hospital. As the ambulance pulled away, the crowd of onlookers, oblivious to the tragedy that had played itself out only yards away, began to disperse. Looking across the road, Russ saw the lights go out in Harbour Rocks. Elmo was locking up.

Sue walked over to Russ. 'They're taking her to The Conquest. They think it's probably concussion and a broken nose. Hopefully she'll be okay.' She held up his blood-stained jacket. 'I'll take this with me; I might be able to get the stains out.'

'Yeah, thanks,' he said abstractedly.

She looked at his sombre face; he was biting his bottom lip.

'What is it, Russ? You look awful; what's happened?'

He frowned putting his arm round her shoulders. He didn't want to say; at least not tonight. He knew she'd be distressed, and living alone, she'd probably be frightened too. 'I'll tell you in the morning, Sue.' He checked his watch. 'It's getting late; time you went home. Thanks for coming tonight. I'm glad you liked The Rocks, I'm just sorry the evening ended the way it did. You were great with that woman.'

She pulled away and looked at him squarely. 'Come on, Russ, don't fob me off. What's happened?' She put her hands on her hips, defiantly. 'I'm not leaving until you do.'

There was no way he could sugar-coat it, so he didn't try. He took hold of her hand. 'A woman's been murdered; her body's upstairs. I've notified the police. They'll be here in a minute. The poor woman in the ambulance must have found her.'

She looked at him incredulously. 'Murdered? A woman? How did she...?'

She couldn't finish the sentence and put a hand to her mouth; her eyes filled with tears. Russ pulled her to him and gave her a long hug.

He held back from sharing the gruesome details, and managed to persuade her to leave before the police arrived. She wasn't a material witness. There was little point in waiting around for hours to be questioned about something she knew nothing about.

Reluctant to leave him in a now empty street, Sue made her way to his home on The Stade to collect her car. Two minutes later, he waved to her as she drove slowly past. As he watched the tail-lights of her Mazda disappearing in the distance, he could make out several vehicles with flashing blue lights approaching at speed from the direction of Rye.

A uniformed Inspector with two police constables was first to arrive. Identifying himself as Inspector Harding from Rye, he asked Russ to sit in the police car until CID officers were ready to question him. Before entering the house, Harding ordered the PCs to take up positions to the front and rear of the premises to seal the crime scene and prevent unauthorised access.

From the car, Russ watched with critical interest as Harding came out of the house and police personnel in an assortment of vehicles pulled up in the street. He observed a number of people wearing white coveralls with hoods, shoe covers and latex gloves enter the house. A pathologist and detectives, he guessed, plus two or three Scene of Crime Officers. Uniformed officers began erecting a frame tent to cover the front door and ground floor window. A sudden weight of depression pressed down on him, and agitation set in. He wanted to get out of the car; it felt all wrong, and unnatural to be excluded. The sense of impotence was almost unbearable. A few months ago and he could have been the lead detective. This was his area of expertise. As a Detective Chief Inspector in charge of the Serious Crimes Unit in the Met, this was his bread and butter. He groaned, expelling the air from his lungs in a huge sigh, shaking his head. This was the first time he'd begun to experience a deep sense of regret, and yet it had been his decision, and his alone. His resignation from the police service had not been undertaken lightly.

His attention was drawn to two men who'd emerged from the building and were removing their protective clothing; one, in his mid-fifties, the other probably late thirties. The older of the two, whom Russ took to be the detective in charge, wore a light brown suit. Smoothing his dishevelled grey hair with both hands, he walked towards the uniformed Inspector. After a brief exchange they turned, looking in Russ's direction and shook hands. The detective walked over to the car, opened the door and stepped aside for Russ to get out.

From his breast pocket, he pulled out his badge, introducing himself as Detective Inspector Baillie, Hastings CID.

'I'm sorry to have kept you for so long; you must be Mr Walker. I understand it was you who discovered the body and made the phone call - is that right?'

Russ nodded. 'Yes, Inspector, I was ...'

Baillie held up his hand cutting him off. 'Just a minute, please.'

He called to the younger detective and beckoned him over. He had the physique of a body builder, his height about five ten, and he was wearing a black leather jacket, white T-shirt, light blue jeans and black shoes. His head was completely bald. As he approached, Russ wondered if he'd shaved it for effect until he realised there were no eyebrows or eyelashes either.

Baillie spoke without emotion. 'This is Detective Sergeant Askew. He needs to ask some questions and take a preliminary statement from you. I suggest you use my car.' He nodded towards a dark blue Mondeo.

Askew deferred to Baillie. 'Right, Guv.' With a George Bush swagger he led Russ to the Mondeo and opened the rear passenger door. 'In there,' he said in an acerbic tone, slamming the door as soon as Russ was inside.

Askew slid into the front passenger seat. From the inside pocket of his jacket, he pulled out his notebook, and turned sideways, looking sourly at Russ. 'Okay, pal, let's start with your name and address.'

Russ felt the hackles rising on his neck. During his time in the Met, he'd had his fair share of subordinates with an attitude problem. Refusing to be intimidated, he kept his voice even. 'Russ Walker. I live at Fisherman's Cottage, The Stade, Rye Harbour.'

The detective made a note in his book. 'Russ? I take it that's short for Russell?' He deliberately pronounced it with a W.

'Oh that's funny, Officer,' he said without smiling. 'No, it's Russ with an R. That's the name my mother gave me.'

Askew made a snorting sound. 'So, how old are you, and what's your occupation?'

Russ straightened in his seat. 'I'm thirty-five and I'm a self-employed private investigator.'

Askew grimaced. 'Well, now, an amateur sleuth; that's a turn up for the books. So how come you were nosing round the house? I'll bet you shit yourself when you found a corpse.'

Russ locked stares with him and leaned forward. 'Listen, smart-arse,' he said caustically. 'I don't know what your problem is; you can either be civil and take my statement *now*, or I'm getting out of this car.'

Askew slowly turned a page in his notebook. 'Until you tell me what you were doing in that house, sunshine, you're not going anywhere.'

Russ couldn't believe this sorry conversation was actually taking place. Fighting the urge to be uncooperative, he sat back in his seat and recounted the chain of events that led to his discovery of the body. He included the name and address of the old man with the dog.

Askew looked through his notes. 'You sure it was The Conquest Hospital they took the woman to?'

'That's what I was told,' Russ replied.

Askew snapped his notebook closed. 'Okay, that'll do for now, but we'll need a formal statement from you tomorrow. We'll want to know what exactly you did in the house and what you touched; we'll also need a copy of your dabs for elimination purposes.'

From his wallet, Russ took a business card and passed it over to Askew. 'You can reach me on one of those numbers.'

As if on cue, DI Baillie opened the front door of the car and spoke to Askew. 'You finished in here, Sergeant? We're going back to the nick; they've picked up Tiltman.' He opened the rear door for Russ. 'Thank you for your help, sir; we'll contact you again tomorrow. In the meantime, I can't stress enough the importance of keeping the details of what you've seen to yourself. We don't want any of this getting out; it could seriously hamper our investigation.'

It had turned one thirty in the morning when Russ, still rankled at the unprofessional behaviour of Askew, let himself into Fisherman's Cottage. Sleep didn't come easily; the shocking image of the dead woman's face flashed in and out of his mind. He tried not to think about the terrifying ordeal she must have endured, but couldn't set it aside. He knew only too well the horror that lay beneath the fact of violent death. He thought of the effect this would have on the family and friends of the victim, and on the woman who'd discovered the body. He knew only too well what murder meant to those left behind.

Chapter Three

The hamlet of Rye Harbour is two hundred years old, having been built on an extension of the shingle beaches progressively deposited by the sea over the last eight hundred years. It has a resident population of around five hundred souls, and is where three rivers – the Tillingham, Brede and Rother - all converge with the sea, making a natural harbour just two miles southwest from the ancient town of Rye. In the harbour there are yacht moorings, a small fishing fleet, some commercial shipping, and a long-established lifeboat station. There is also a holiday village of mobile homes on the edge of the hamlet.

It had seemed almost providential that seven months earlier, on the actual day of his resignation from the Met, Russ noticed the advertisement in the *Evening Standard*; "Get away from it all! Period detached fisherman's cottage for sale at Rye Harbour, a small hamlet on the East Sussex coast. Owner going abroad – offers invited for quick sale." As far as he could remember, he'd never been to the town of Rye, let alone the adjoining hamlet of Rye Harbour, but it seemed far enough away from London to maybe try and build a new life. Becky's death had shaken the very foundation of his existence. For months after her murder, he had felt as if he was walking around in a terrible dream; that somehow he could force himself to wake up and none of it would have happened - that Becky would be alive, and he wouldn't be blaming himself for not having thought of the possibility of a booby trap that would take her from him.

It was two weeks before their planned wedding. As lead detective of a specialist Serious Crimes Unit in London, based on the Isle of Dogs, Russ, with two colleagues, was involved in an operation to bring down a suspected drugs baron when they discovered a large consignment of heroin and cocaine at a warehouse in Billingsgate. He had made the decision to call in the SOCOs to search for forensic evidence. Becky was one of the civilian scene of crime officers, and it was she who triggered the device and was killed in the blast.

Fisherman's Cottage had originally been two semis dating from around 1850; in recent years, it had been imaginatively converted into a single residence and a garage built adjacent to it. The front door opened on to the pavement, and a high fence had been erected down each side of the property and across the rear end of the garden to ensure privacy and a degree of security for the occupants.

The sale of his house at Poplar and the purchase of the cottage had been relatively straight forward, as had been the renting of a small office in the town of Rye, from which to operate a private investigation agency.

The office was on the northern side of the High Street, above Patsy's, a small delicatessen, and opposite the George Hotel. The entrance was in Market Road, a small side-road leading off the High Street, beside which was a parking space for two cars. The door was signed No.1; underneath was an engraved plaque – *Walker Investigations*. The door opened to a flight of stairs. At the top was a small landing where there were three frosted glass panelled doors - one to the office, and the others to a lavatory and miniscule kitchen.

Although small, the office was light and airy, with a large window overlooking the narrow High Street, and another which looked down on Market Road. It was minimally furnished, with two desks set at right-angles, two swivel chairs, a couple of upholstered seats for clients, a small coffee table and a three-drawer filing cabinet with a copier placed on top.

The journey from home to the office was a ten minute drive in his pride and joy, a 1965 metallic bronze Ford Capri. Following what had become his usual morning ritual, he arrived at eight thirty, made himself a cafetiere of coffee, and then settled down with a cigarette and the *Times2* crossword to the backdrop of hits from the fifties and sixties on his CD player. If asked, he would freely acknowledge this was escapism, but what else could he do? To say business was slack was an understatement. He'd made a decision not to get involved in divorce cases unless crime was involved, and yet advertisements in local newspapers seemed only of interest to the lunatic fringe. Fed up with time-wasters and cranks, he was beginning to wonder if becoming a private eye was the biggest mistake he'd ever made. Sitting about killing time was alien to him. It was challenge that stimulated; the cut of the chase that made him feel truly alive.

He glanced at his watch – almost nine. In a couple of minutes Sue would be here, and the ritual would continue.

Like following a script, she'd complain about the noise from her neighbour in the flat above, turn off the CD player, remind him that it's against the law to smoke in the office, look over his shoulder at the crossword and smugly attempt to answer the clues that were left.

The phone rang and startled him. He turned the volume down on the player and reached for the receiver.

'Good morning, Walker Investigations, how may I help?'

She sounded young and upset. 'Oh, hello; do you trace missing people?'

He smiled, hoping she might hear it in his voice. 'Yes, we most certainly do. If you'd like to give me your name and address I'd be happy to make an appointment to come and discuss details with you.'

She cut in quickly, 'I don't want you to come here. Can I come to your office - today if possible?'

He wondered who the patron saint for PIs might be – perhaps he should pop over to the parish church and light a candle to him or her.

'One moment please, I'll just check.' He looked at the blank page in the diary. 'I could fit you in at two this afternoon - would that be convenient?'

'Yes please,' she said softly, and rang off.

He made an entry – 2 pm. Ms Vexed to see Mr Detective - then turned the volume back up on the player; it was Procul Harum's *A Whiter Shade of Pale*.

It took him a moment to switch gears when he heard her unmistakable footsteps on the stairs. Sue Westbrook opened the door and came into the office. As Johnnie Tillotson would say, she was 'poetry in motion'; a beautiful diminutive twenty eight-year-old, wearing a close-fitting pale blue dress that accentuated her shapely body. He was attracted to her, of course he was; any straight guy would be. As she turned to close the door, he happened to notice the definite outline of a thong. Always good to start the day with something pleasant to think about.

He looked up. 'Hey, Sue.'

She smiled. 'Morning, Boss. You're bright and cheerful; don't tell me you've finished the crossword already?' She waved her hand in front of her face. 'You've been smoking again; one of these days you'll have a visit from a Health and Safety Inspector... It'll be your own fault.'

She dropped her handbag on the upholstered chair that still longed for the weight of a client's backside and walked round the desk. From over his shoulder, she looked down at the crossword. 'Oh, dear; you obviously need help?'

He turned the paper over. 'No thanks, smart-arse. Hey, see this! He pointed to the entry in the diary. 'I'm seeing a prospective client at two, this afternoon; something about a missing person.'

She grinned. 'Hey, that's great! I said give it time; it's still early days.' As if it were an afterthought, she continued, 'That'll be a welcome distraction from your usual voyeuristic activities.'

This wasn't a reference to his surveillance skills. Last night in The Rocks he'd been foolish enough to tell her about the clear view he had of guests occupying the bedroom across the road at the George Hotel. He'd mentioned the foreign-looking woman who, on four successive mornings, had drawn the net curtains aside, offering clear proof she was a natural blonde; and of the two occasions he'd seen a naughty young woman getting spanked by her partner.

He grimaced. 'You probably don't draw your curtains either.'

She chose to ignore him and reached for the coffee pot.

'Help yourself,' he said. 'And I'll have a refill, please.'

Cupping her hand round the cafetiere, she pulled a face. 'Not from this, it's cold. I'll make a fresh pot, and then you can tell me about last night.'

She came back from the kitchen and, placing the cafetiere and clean mugs on the desk, reached for the CD player and put an end to Del Shannon wondering why his love had run away.

'I can't hear myself think with that, and I've a rotten headache; I hardly slept last night.'

He rolled his eyes in mock despair. 'Sue, that was Del Shannon. *Runaway* is a classic!'

Feigning disinterest, she pushed the plunger down and poured the coffee. Sliding a mug across to him, she picked up her own and sat on one of the upholstered metal framed chairs. The expression on her face changed.

'So, tell me about the murder; I can't get it out of my mind. What happened after I left?'

Knowing she was the sole of discretion, Russ described what he'd discovered in the house at Rye Harbour and told her about his encounter with the police.

She listened attentively, with both hands cupped round her coffee mug as if she was holding an injured bird. 'If they've picked up someone called Tiltman, it sounds as if they already know who killed her.'

He shrugged his shoulders. 'Could be, and I hope you're right; this killer is one hell of a sick individual. The police obviously know something we don't. I mean, to bring in a suspect right at the outset of an investigation... Maybe we'll learn more when DS Askew calls to take my statement.' He changed tack. 'In the meantime, we've got work to do; we need to be more proactive. If we don't find some clients soon, we're both going to be out of a job.'

He suggested she compile a list of all the solicitors' practices within a thirty mile radius of Rye, and make contact with the senior partners offering his investigative services. Then she could try the large stores and industrial concerns in the area; none of them were immune to problems of theft or security. It was worth a try.

Russ took the mugs and cafetiere to the kitchen to wash them, while Sue went to her desk. She switched on the computer and waited for it to boot up. As she logged on, the doorbell rang. She pressed the intercom button.

'Good morning, Walker Investigations.'

'Detective Inspector Baillie to see Mr Walker.'

'Please come in; the office is at the top of the stairs.' She pressed the catch release button as Russ came back into the office.

Baillie appeared at the open door. Apart from the tell-tale redness around the eyes, for a man who'd probably been up most of the night, he looked surprisingly alert. He was wearing the same light brown suit he'd worn last night. His sober face was narrow and seemed to accentuate his aquiline nose.

Russ held out his hand. 'Good morning Inspector.' He turned to Sue. 'This is my secretary, Sue Westbrook. Can we get you a tea or coffee?'

Baillie shook their hands. 'Black coffee, no sugar, please.'

Russ gestured to the chairs and they sat down, the low table between them. Sue went out to make the coffee.

Baillie seemed reluctant to begin the conversation. 'I didn't recognise you last night, but it came to me later... You were a DCI in the Met. A couple of years ago, I attended a lecture you gave at Bramshill on Offender Profiling.'

Russ smiled and shook his head dismissively. 'Don't remind me, it was a last-minute thing. One of the scheduled speakers couldn't make it and I was press ganged to fill his slot.'

Sue returned with two mugs of coffee, and a small plate of biscuits, placing them on the table. 'I'll have mine downstairs at Patsy's. Call me when you've finished.'

Baillie's eyes settled on her shapely bottom as she moved to the door. After she'd closed it behind her, he smiled appreciatively at Russ. 'Very nice. You should see the old biddy who types my reports.'

Russ laughed. 'She's a real gem, is Sue. Only works for me in the mornings. In fact, she's a freelance physiotherapist; works afternoons at the Rye Memorial Centre.'

Baillie took a sip of coffee. 'Lucky patients! DS Askew filled me in on your conversation with him last night. Terrible business. The victim was a single woman aged thirty-eight, named Elaine Knightley. She was a teacher at Rye Secondary School for Boys. It was her twin sister, a Catherine Forbes, who initially found her; she was the woman who tripped and hit her head when she ran screaming from the house.'

Russ exhaled noisily. 'Dear God! Imagine finding your sister like that... Your own twin! The shock could have given her a heart attack. Any news on how she's doing?'

'Apart from a broken nose and slight concussion, thankfully she's not too bad. They've reset the nose and hopefully she'll be released from hospital later today.' Baillie took a biscuit and dunked it in his coffee. 'According to Catherine's husband, Elaine was supposed to be babysitting for them last night, but didn't turn up. At first they weren't too bothered, although it was unlike her not to phone if there was a problem. They assumed she must have forgotten, but it was no big deal; they were only going out for a drink. Catherine telephoned her sister several times during the evening, but got no reply. Apparently Elaine didn't have much of a social life and hardly ever went out in the evenings. Catherine began to wonder if she'd been taken ill or had an accident, and to put her mind at rest before going to bed, she decided to pop round to make sure she was alright; they only live in Anchor Square. She had a key to the house, and let herself in. The husband is beating himself up for not going with her. The pathologist reckons Elaine was killed sometime in the afternoon – most likely between one and four.'

It pleased Russ to hear him use her name. Clearly for Baillie, she wasn't simply a victim, a statistic, another corpse... She was a person - a person for whom he would want justice. No-one deserved what she'd had done to her, and for Baillie, as with any good detective, that would be the driving force, the overriding motivation for catching the perpetrator and getting a conviction.

'Last night, I heard you tell DS Askew that someone called Tiltman had been picked up. Is he a suspect?' Russ asked.

Baillie put his coffee mug down on the table and brushed imaginary lint from the sleeve of his jacket. 'Look, I want to be upfront with you.' He paused, as if weighing in his mind what he was about to say. 'I've been doing a bit of digging; I know about your time in the Met. I also know why you left the job and I just wanted to say, I'm really sorry.' His eyes took in the room, and he gestured with his hand. 'Even so, I can't believe that with your knowledge and experience you'd settle for a crap job like this – I mean a PI, and here, of all places. I mean... We both know PIs are mostly losers who couldn't make it in the Service, or dreamers who've read too many Raymond Chandler novels and fancy their chances. But why are *you* doing it? I just can't get my head round it.'

'It's a long story. Let's just say, unlike you, I can choose what I do and when I do it; plus, I don't have to answer to desk-bound superiors so obsessed with statistics and league tables, they've lost touch with the real world.'

Baillie frowned. 'Hey, come on; you're getting cynical in your old age.'

Russ shrugged and scratched a non-existent itch at the back of his head. 'Maybe I am ... Or maybe I just wasn't suited to the job and needed a change.'

He was warming to Baillie, but there was no way he was ready to discuss the real reasons for his disillusionment. 'Anyhow, you can't deny the hierarchy seem to be more concerned with massaging numbers to please Home Office Ministers than giving real support to people like you and me.'

There was a softening in Baillie's voice. 'I won't argue with that... But you've got a reputation; you were bloody good at your job and got results, and you've thrown it all away... For this?' He shook his head in disbelief and took another drink of coffee. 'Anyhow, I've been assured by a senior colleague in the Met that you're a man of integrity, that I can trust you. So, about last night; as you're new to the area, you're probably not aware that six months ago a woman was sexually assaulted and murdered at her home in a village called Tilling, six miles west of Rye. Her name was Carol Tiltman. It was the same MO... naked, tied to the bed, covered in oil, sexually abused before strangulation.'

Russ cut in. 'And you didn't get the killer?'

Baillie ran a hand through his hair in a gesture of frustration. 'All the evidence pointed to her husband as the perp... But unfortunately it was only circumstantial.'

He noticed Baillie used the word 'perp', short for perpetrator. It was an Americanism that was beginning to find its way into the English crime fighter's vocabulary.

'We've got a good team at Hastings and the SOCOs are first rate; yet, in spite of their best efforts, we didn't have enough to nail him. No incontrovertible evidence to prove he was responsible. The Crown Prosecution Service deemed most of the evidence as inadmissible in court and refused to agree to him being charged and put on trial.'

'So that's why you picked him up last night.'

'That's right, and guess what? He's got no alibi, reckons he was at home all afternoon... alone. We searched his house... clothes... car, and found... sod all; not a trace of anything to link him with it. Had to let him go.'

Russ leaned forward, his elbows on his knees, hands clasped together under his chin. 'Do you really fancy him for what might be a serial killer?'

He managed a half-smile and shook his head. 'No, not really.' There was no apology in his voice. 'These crimes demonstrate a relatively high level of sophistication and planning that suggests the perp's no stranger to the world of criminal activity. No, Tiltman's too clean; I'd be surprised if he's ever been given a parking ticket... But he's all I've got at the moment.'

Russ reached forward and took two printed sheets of A4 from the top of his desk. 'I've written a formal statement about what happened last night, and signed it. Your affable DS said you'd need my fingerprints. I guess the Met will still have them on file.'

He took the statement from Russ. 'Yes, they have; that's already been dealt with.' He paused. 'Look, I'm sorry about Askew; I gave him a bollocking after you'd left. It was his rest day yesterday and he wasn't thrilled about being called out, plus he's dealing with a few personal problems at home, but that's no excuse. He's a good cop, and I try to make allowances, but that's no justification for his surly attitude, and I won't put up with it. He's been warned.'

He looked at his watch and stood up. 'I must go. I hate to sound melodramatic, but as you know, with a killer as organised and ruthless as this one, every minute counts. I don't want his next victim's blood on my hands if I can possibly avoid it.' He shook Russ's hand warmly. 'Thanks for your time. I'll keep in touch, if that's okay.'

Russ opened the door for him. 'I'd appreciate that, and good luck with the investigation. I know I'm a civvy now, but if there's ever anything I can do to help, give me a call.'

As soon as he heard Baillie close the door downstairs, he phoned Sue's mobile, calling her back to work.

By the time Sue left the office at one o'clock, she had identified and written letters to ten solicitors' practices within the area. Russ slipped down to Patsy's and bought a sandwich and doughnut to take back to the office.

Chapter Four

The woman arrived at five minutes to two. She was older than he'd expected, maybe late forties, early fifties. Her short blonde hair, pretty floral sundress and stylish sunglasses gave her a younger look, as did the slim figure and false Mediterranean tan. When she removed the sunglasses, he could see the tell-tale lines of aging under her heavily made up eyes, and the neck band didn't quite hide an older woman's neck. She exuded enough perfume to knock over an elephant.

He gave her a reassuring smile and shook her hand. 'Good afternoon, I'm Russ Walker; please have a seat. How may I help you?' Russ sat behind his desk.

She didn't so much sit as perch on the rim of the chair, her arms resting across her knees. She played nervously with a small embroidered handkerchief.

'My name is Wendy Drew. Thank you for fitting me in today. I feel a bit awkward... I've never met a private investigator before. I'm not local; I live in Folkestone, but a friend of mine saw your advertisement and suggested you might be able to help - that's why I phoned.' she said, almost apologetically.

He nodded. 'What is it you need help with, Mrs Drew?'

There was a hint of desperation in her voice. 'It's my daughter, Hannah; she's left home and I don't know where she is. Can you find her for me?'

He picked up his pen and turned to a blank page in his notepad. He looked appraisingly at her. 'I think you'd better tell me what's happened. How old is Hannah?'

'She's seventeen, a student in the sixth form at the Foxwood Academy in Folkestone. I ought to tell you she's at a difficult age, a bit of a handful really. For the past six months she's been mixing with a rough crowd of young people; staying out late, drinking too much, sometimes staying out all night.'

Russ interrupted. 'I take it you're not talking about the normal kind of teenage sleepovers.'

She shook her head, 'Most certainly not; I think she's sleeping rough sometimes; I can tell by her clothes... I'm the one who washes them; they're often very dirty and reek of cigarettes and alcohol.' She pointed to the carafe of water and the tumbler Sue had thoughtfully placed on the coffee table. 'May I?' she asked.

'Of course, help yourself.'

She filled the tumbler and took two or three sips. 'Anyhow, two weeks ago, Saturday the 17th, she stayed in bed until about midday; when she got up, Brian, that's my husband, he had a go at her for being out so late the night before. She went ballistic, shouting and swearing at him. He lost his temper and told her that if she didn't stick to the rules he'd laid down, she could go. Without another word to either of us, she stormed upstairs, packed a suitcase and left. We haven't seen or heard from her since, and I'm worried sick. She's our only child, Mr Walker. She and Brian rub each other up all the time. He gets angry with her for the way she behaves, and angry with me for not being strict enough with her. I do try, but... I can't seem to get through to her; she just won't listen to me.'

He made some notes on the pad. 'What about your husband - has he done anything to try and find her?' he asked gently.

She put the glass on the table and dabbed her nostrils with her handkerchief. Her cheeks were flushed, eyes filling with tears. She shook her head and began to cry; tears coursed down her cheeks.

'I'm sorry,' she said, wiping the tears. 'For four days he refused to do anything. He kept saying she'd be home again in a day or two when her money ran out. He told me he'd talked to a policeman he plays golf with who said Hannah couldn't be classed as a missing person, because legally she's no longer a minor and left of her own accord. But I want her home, Mr Walker; I'm frightened she might be in danger.'

He nodded and smiled sympathetically. 'Mrs Drew, hiring a PI is quite expensive; it could take some time to find her, and even then, I couldn't guarantee that she would come home.'

She was pleading with him, 'I want to know she's all right. If I could just talk to her. But I don't want my husband to know I'm hiring you - he'd be angry and say it's a waste of money - but I have my own bank account.'

Russ explained what his fees were and the terms of the contract they would both be entering into. She readily accepted the conditions and signed an agreement, together with a cheque as a down payment.

'I need the names of her closest friends – especially the ones she stayed out late with - and I'd like to have a look in her bedroom too,' he said.

Wendy Drew nodded. 'She has a school friend called Shelly, Shelly Martin, but I've already spoken to her. She says she doesn't know where Hannah is, and hasn't heard from her. She said none of her classmates have any idea where she might be.'

Russ knew that might be true; but there again, they may have been primed to say that. He made a note of Shelly's phone number.

'What about the people she goes out with in the evenings? Do you have any of their names?'

She shook her head. 'We don't know who they are; she refused to talk about them. She used her mobile phone to make contact with them, and she's taken that with her. I've tried phoning, but all I get is an answering machine.'

'Do you have a recent photograph of her I could borrow, and when would it be convenient for me to look at her bedroom?'

She was much calmer now. 'If you come to the house tomorrow morning, say eleven o'clock, 35 Selwyn Avenue, Folkestone... Brian works for British Telecom; he'll be in Maidstone all day. I've a day off tomorrow; I normally work mornings at a nursery school. I'll look out some recent pictures.'

He made a note of the address and Hannah's mobile number. 'That's all I need for the moment.' He gave a reassuring smile. 'I'll see you tomorrow at eleven. Try not to worry, Mrs Drew... I'll find her for you.'

Wendy Drew left the office more relaxed than when she'd arrived. It would probably take no more than two or three days to find the girl, but at least he was in business; maybe his luck was about to change.

Chapter Five

Russ removed the compilation disc, and was about to slip a Jerry Lee Lewis CD into the player when the doorbell rang. He pressed the intercom button.

'Walker Investigations; please come in.' He pressed the release catch button.

Through the frosted glass, he saw a man's outline appear on the landing. The man tapped on the glass and opened the door. He was stylish, mid-fifties, with the appearance of a businessman, wearing a handmade dark blue suit and highly polished black leather shoes. Carrying too much weight, his paunch strained the buttons of his pink shirt; he was shorter than Russ, probably five eight; his round face sporting a neatly trimmed full beard. Behind the rimless spectacles, the dark bags under his eyes gave him a haggard look.

Russ got to his feet and extended his hand over the desk, 'Good afternoon, I'm Russ Walker.'

Closing the door behind him, the man stepped up to the desk and shook the offered hand. Russ gestured to a chair. 'Please, have a seat.'

Without looking directly at Russ, his eyes scanned the office, as if assessing the quality of the furniture and décor; he seemed unimpressed. He sat on one of the clients' chairs as Russ settled back on his swivel chair.

Scratching at his beard, he spoke brusquely. 'Ex-police! What does that mean?'

Russ leaned forward. 'Excuse me?'

'Mr Walker, I won't waste your time or mine. My name is George Tiltman, and I need help – professional help - well-meaning amateurs are no good to me. In your newspaper advertisement, it says you are ex-police; what does that mean?'

Russ didn't believe in coincidence, but what the hell... Tiltman? Was this the suspected perp? Whoever he was, his arrogance touched a nerve.

Russ gave him a penetrating stare. 'It means I was a senior detective in the Metropolitan Police before I resigned and set up as a private investigator. It means if you hire me, you're hiring class. I don't get involved in divorce cases unless crime is involved and I don't go looking for lost pets. Now is there something I can help you with?'

Tiltman was unfazed at the tone of the reply. 'Before I consider hiring you, I need to know why you left the police force.'

Russ kept his face impassive. 'Mr Tiltman, I'm not prepared to discuss personal details, except to say I was head of an elite unit of detectives in London investigating serious crimes. I became disillusioned with the legal system and left of my own volition. If you care to explain why you need help, I'll decide whether or not I can be of assistance, and what it will cost. In the meantime, anything you might share with me will remain strictly confidential.' He reached for a small tape recorder. 'If you have no objection, I'd like to tape our conversation. If you hire me, it could be useful to me, and if you don't... Well, you can take the tape with you.'

Tiltman's façade was of a hard-bitten business man, an overbearing, control freak, yet in an instant it all seemed to change. He sat back in his seat; his shoulders drooped, as if acknowledging defeat.

He spoke calmly, 'Mr Walker, anything I say to you has already been recorded by the police several times. I have nothing to hide, and money's not a problem. Six months ago, my wife, Carol, was murdered, and I'm the chief suspect. Although initially I was arrested, I've never been charged because they have no evidence. I believe the police have given up looking for the real murderer, because they are convinced I did it. Yesterday, a woman was murdered at Rye Harbour; I was pulled in for that one too. The incompetent bastards think I'm a serial killer.'

He looked at Tiltman in silence for a few moments and switched on the recorder. 'I'll be perfectly frank with you, Mr Tiltman. I may be ex-police, but I'm not anti-police. I have no doubt the investigation into your wife's death will have been undertaken thoroughly and professionally. The police have highly trained and sophisticated teams that work steadily through the appropriate actions. I can't see what I could do that hasn't already been done.'

His mouth wrinkled with disgust. 'Prove my innocence, that's what you could do! Listen, Walker, I swear to God, I-did-not-kill-my-wife. No one believes me... I don't know what to do.'

His face reddened as he tried to suppress the tears that brimmed in his eyes. He pulled a handkerchief from his trouser pocket, took off his glasses and wiped his eyes. The glasses still in his hand, he looked pleadingly at Russ. Tiltman's eyes were set close together, and above them his eyebrows, needing a trim, met in the centre. He stuffed the handkerchief into his jacket pocket.

'We'd had our ups and downs, but who doesn't? I loved her; why would I want to kill her?' Again, he took out his handkerchief and blew his nose, making a sound like the horn of a vintage motorcar. He pocketed the handkerchief. 'The police are convinced I did it, and once it became known I'd been arrested, everyone else thinks it too, even my bloody solicitor.' He leaned forward. 'And you know what? Her body is still in the mortuary; I can't even have a funeral and lay her to rest. Look, Walker, I really need your help. I don't care what it costs; please help me prove my innocence.' His arrogance had given way to despair.

There's an innate quality that can never be learned from studying training manuals, or attending refresher courses, and yet it makes all the difference between a good detective and the best, and that's intuition. Some call it instinct, others a sixth sense, and a detective either has it or he doesn't. Over the years, experience had taught Russ to trust his intuition, and there were many villains who had found themselves guests of Her Majesty's Prison Service who might not have done if he'd ignored it. Russ felt a tingle go down his spine, a surge of adrenaline. He picked up a pen and turned to a blank page in his notepad. 'I think you'd better tell me what happened to your wife; let's start at the beginning... How old are you, Mr Tiltman? What do you do for a living?'

'I'm fifty-three. Carol was forty-five. I own a small engineering works at Bexhill-on-Sea; we make ball bearings. I don't know how well you know the area; we – I - live at Tilling, a village six miles west of Rye.' Turning in his seat, he pointed to the location on the wall map behind him. 'The house is called Whitegates in Passmore Lane; that's where she was killed.'

Russ nodded and wrote on his pad. 'How was your wife murdered?'

He looked straight at Russ; his eyes didn't waver. 'It was three days before last Christmas, the 22nd of December; it was a Thursday. I'd been in London all day, and when I came home, I found Carol's body upstairs. She'd been tied up, sexually assaulted and killed. I called the police. They took me to Hastings Police Station and started questioning me. I couldn't believe it; it was a bloody nightmare. They accused *me* of the murder and I was arrested.'

Russ held up his hand. 'Right, we'll come back to that. Tell me about your wife - Carol.'

Tiltman nodded, took a tissue from the box on the table, and wiped his nose. 'She was a local girl, born in Tilling. We met through a local dramatic and operatic society. We started dating and eventually got married. We'd have been married nineteen years next month.'

Russ interposed. 'Was Carol employed by your firm?'

'Good heavens, no; she was a qualified midwife. In the early days of our marriage she worked on the district in this area. After about ten years, she gave up work altogether; then eighteen months ago, she decided to look for temporary work and registered with a nursing agency. They found her a part-time job as a care assistant at an old people's residential home in the village. She worked eight till four on Mondays, Tuesdays and Fridays. She was well liked in the village, and was involved in various activities like the drama group, keep fit, Village Hall Committee – that sort of thing.'

'You haven't mentioned a family – do you have any children?' Russ asked.

He shook his head. 'No, unfortunately; that was the one thing she couldn't really come to terms with. It just didn't happen. I think that's why she gave up midwifery – delivering other people's babies but not being able to have one of her own.'

'Did you ever think of adopting?' he asked evenly.

'Yes, but we decided against it; she always hoped she still might get pregnant one day. But what the hell does all this have to do with her murder?'

Russ forced a smile. 'I'm sorry, but if I'm going to take this on, I need to know everything there is to know about your wife, and about you – and I can assure you, it'll get a lot more personal than this!'

'Yes, of course,' he said in a tone of surrender.

'Mr Tiltman, do you stand to gain anything by your wife's death? Was she wealthy? Did she have shares in your business? What about life insurance?'

He shook his head impatiently. 'It's a preposterous suggestion! She didn't even have her own bank account - we had a joint one; and no, she didn't have shares in the business. Eighteen months ago I did take out an insurance policy on her life to the tune of £250,000; she took one out on mine for the same amount. We did it for the sake of the business. The recession was beginning to bite; we both thought it a prudent thing to do. And before you ask, no, I did not kill her for the insurance pay out!'

Russ looked down at his notes. 'You say you'd been up to London on the 22nd of December. Why was that?'

'There was a trades fair at Earl's Court; I go to it each year. It had been on for three days, and Thursday was the final day.'

'Did anyone go with you?'

'No, I went on my own; I always do.'

Russ nodded. 'Okay. I want you to tell me everything about that day; when and how you travelled, both there and back. What you did while you were there, who you spoke to. Where, and even what, you ate and drank. Were you able to produce any tickets, receipts or literature as evidence that you'd been there?'

Tiltman pressed his fingers beneath his chin as if considering where to begin. He made his decision. 'I left home at seven thirty in the morning and drove to Ashford International Railway Station. I bought a return ticket at the station and caught the eight twenty to London. I went by tube from Charing Cross to Earl's Court and arrived at the Exhibition Centre about ten fifteen. I paid the entrance fee at the door, then spent most of the time visiting various trade stands. I went to the restaurant for coffee during the morning and again at lunchtime, where I had a mixed grill and another coffee. I didn't leave Earl's Court until about three in the afternoon. I caught a train back to Ashford, picked up the car and arrived home at a quarter to seven. The police asked me to produce tickets or receipts but I couldn't.' He looked embarrassed. 'I know it's stupid, but I didn't keep them – I never do. You see, I always put them in my right-hand jacket pocket.' He patted his pocket. 'When I'm in the car, if no one's behind me, I open the driver's window about an inch, and one by one I let them fly out. I convince myself they are biodegradable, and nature will dispose of them. I know it's stupid and I wish to God I hadn't done it, but I did!'

Russ cleared his throat. 'Did you buy anything on the train – tea, coffee?'

'No. I think there was a refreshment trolley being pushed by a man, but I can't swear to it; I didn't take much notice.'

Russ stopped writing; he tapped the pen on his lower lip. 'Okay,' he said. 'What about the exhibitors, can you name any you spoke to, and what about leaflets and brochures they give out - what did you do with them?'

He frowned and paused as if considering. 'I gave the police a list of some of the stands I visited. I'd collected quite a few brochures, they keep thrusting them at you; to be honest, I didn't really want them. Like a lot of people, I simply dumped them in a waste bin near the entrance. I'd only gone for a day out - there was nothing in particular I was interested in.'

Russ spread his hands in a gesture of resignation. 'So, clearly there's nothing to prove you were in London. Let's move on; tell me what happened when you arrived home.'

Tiltman looked miserably at his hands, and then back at Russ. 'As I said, I arrived back home at a quarter to seven. When I pulled into the driveway, I was surprised, because the house was in darkness and yet Carol's Mini Cooper was parked in front of the double garage. The outside security lights came on as usual when I parked my BMW. I let myself in through the front door with my keys, and that was the first thing that unsettled me; we have two locks, a Yale and a mortise, but the mortise was unlocked. I switched on the hall lights and went to key in the code to silence the burglar alarm, but it hadn't been set. That's when I started to worry. Neither of us would ever leave the house without setting the alarm. I called out, but there was no reply. I checked all the ground floor rooms and everything looked normal, except that none of the curtains had been drawn. Then I went upstairs and saw our bedroom door was closed. We never close it, not even when we're in bed, so I knew something was wrong.'

He stopped speaking and covered his face with his cupped hands; he began crying helplessly with huge, shuddering sobs; his shoulders heaved. Thirty seconds passed before he took control of his emotions, reached for another tissue from the box and blew his nose. He continued, a tremor in his voice.

'I went into the bedroom and found her – she was lying on her back, naked. Her hands and feet had been tied with rope to the castors at the four corners of the bed. Her eyes and mouth were open – she was dead.' He paused again and wiped his eyes. 'I touched her face... It was as cold as ice. She looked absolutely terrified. I can't get that image out of my mind. I picked up the phone by the bed and called the police. I didn't know what to do.'

'Apart from touching her face, and picking up the telephone, did you touch anything else?' Russ asked.

'No, nothing,' he said. 'I went straight downstairs, poured myself a large whisky, and sat in a chair waiting for the police.'

'Weren't you afraid the murderer might still be in the house?'

'No, she was so cold. It was obvious she'd been dead for hours; whoever did it would be miles away by then.' He ran his tongue over his lips. 'Would you mind?' He gestured to the carafe of water and picked up the tumbler Wendy Drew had used.

'Of course not, help yourself.' Russ replied, hoping there were no tell-tale smears of lipstick on the rim.

Tiltman poured himself some water; he drank half a glassful.

Russ watched him in silence for a few moments; then he said, 'So, the police arrived. Plainclothes or uniform?'

Tiltman put the glass down on the table. 'Both. It took about fifteen minutes for them to arrive. I explained to the one in charge how I'd found her. He took me out to one of the police cars and they drove me to Hastings Police Station. At first they were very caring. They put me in a small interview room and brought coffee and sandwiches. A policewoman sat with me for a long time. I was in a terrible state; I couldn't understand why no one was talking to me. Every time I asked what was happening, I was told someone would come and see me shortly. I started to get angry and demanded to see the officer in charge. Eventually two detectives came and I was asked if I would like to have my solicitor present. I didn't understand why they asked that, and then the penny dropped; they suspected me... That I'd murdered Carol! They told me I was being arrested on suspicion of murder and gave me an official caution outlining my rights. I went berserk and they put me in handcuffs.'

Russ picked up his pen, and turned to a fresh page. 'I'd like the name of the solicitor.'

'Peter Lant. He's the senior partner of Lant and Davies at Tenterden. I've dealt with them for years. When he arrived, they took off the cuffs and he advised me not to say anything. They switched on a tape recorder and started the questioning, accusing me of murder. Lant kept telling me to be quiet, but why should I? I'm not a murderer; she was my wife, for God's sake! I told them what I've just told you. They didn't charge me, but released me on bail at ten the next morning. I spent Christmas and the New Year at my brother's place at Fleet in Hampshire. It was nine days before they let me go back home.'

A motorcycle with a defective silencer roared by on the High Street; the noise was deafening. Russ paused until it had passed. 'And the name of the officer in charge?'

Tiltman looked exhausted. 'Detective Inspector Baillie – spelt B-A-I-L-L-I-E. He's head of the CID at Hastings. Look, will you help me, Walker, please?'

Russ was calm and measured in his response. 'Mr Tiltman, please understand this; I would never take on a job if I didn't believe I could come up with a result. Before I decide, it's important I speak to your solicitor, and hopefully DI Baillie. I promise you, I'll let you know my decision by tomorrow evening; I'm afraid that's all I can offer you at the moment.' He stood up, walked round the desk and held out his hand.

Tiltman got to his feet shakily, and gripped it. His words were barely audible. 'If you can't help me, my life is finished.' he said.

Russ opened the door for him and Tiltman left.

Russ stood at the window overlooking the High Street. He stared unseeingly at the passers-by on the pavement across the road. God alone knew how much he needed this assignment, but was this need colouring his perspective? He'd seen it all before; tears and the pleading of innocence from many a guilty party; some swearing on the life of their baby, even a Bible – inviting God to strike them dead if they were lying; and yet he'd sensed an authenticity about Tiltman – he was either a bloody good actor, or... Maybe he was innocent. He patted his pocket, pulled out his packet of Benson and Hedges and a lighter. He was trying to cut down, but what the heck, it was only the second of the day. He took out a cigarette, placed it between his lips and lit up. Blowing the smoke upwards, he turned back to the desk, balanced the cigarette on the edge of the ashtray and reached for the telephone directory. He found Lant's number and dialled. The solicitor seemed less than enthusiastic about seeing Russ, but finally suggested he could spare only a few minutes of his precious time at four thirty that afternoon.

Russ made a second call to a number he knew well.

It was answered after two rings. 'Hello, Phil Windsor.'

'Hey, Duke, how are you doing?'

'Hey, super sleuth, not bad; how's yourself?'

Phil Windsor, known as Duke to his friends, was the closest Russ, being an only child, had to a brother; their friendship extended way back to their teens. They first met when they'd enrolled within a month of each other as police cadets in the Met. Having completed their training at Hendon, they were surprised and delighted to discover they had both been posted to the Police Headquarters on the Isle of Dogs. For the past seven years, they had worked together in the Serious Crimes Unit. At thirty-four, a year younger than Russ, Duke stood six feet three in his socks, and weighed thirteen and a half stone. He had been made Detective Sergeant shortly before Russ was promoted to Detective Chief Inspector. He was to have been best man at Russ and Becky's wedding.

Like Russ, he too had resigned from the police service, but for a different reason. Duke had encountered difficulties working with Russ' successor, DI Angus Ternon, a surly, ginger-haired Scotsman from Glasgow. From the word go it had been an acrimonious relationship, which hadn't been helped by Duke questioning Ternon's decisions on several occasions, resulting in a reprimand from the station commander. During their last altercation, Duke had lost control, allowing his temper to get the better of him; he'd pushed Ternon in the chest, which led to Duke's suspension from duty. A disciplinary board found him guilty of assault and gave him the option of demotion to uniform, or his resignation. There was no contest – he'd resigned.

Not wanting to leave London, he'd taken over the lease of a former bakery on Shooters Hill in Eltham, transforming it into an emporium for Army surplus equipment and high-tech security gadgetry. He lived above the premises in a three bedroomed flat.

Russ picked up his cigarette, flicked off the ash, and drew on it. 'Yeah, I'm doing okay, but I could do with some help. Do you have any contacts with CID at Hastings? I need to have a look at the file they have on the murder of a Carol Tiltman that took place on the 22nd of December last year.' He then gave him a brief resume of his conversation with Tiltman.

Duke gave a brittle laugh. 'Bloody hell, Russ, you've picked a good one. You're not seriously thinking of taking this on, are you?'

'I know; I know it sounds improbable, but my gut feeling is that he really might be innocent. I need to know what they have on Tiltman. I hate to ask, but do you think Em could help?'

Duke had lost both parents in a motorway pile-up when he was only seven and was brought up by a maiden aunt at Brixton. He had two younger sisters – Liz, a librarian, married with two children, living at Walthamstow, and Em, a clerical officer, working in an intelligence department at New Scotland Yard. She wasn't married, but lived with a partner called Val at Forest Gate. Like her brother, to whom she was devoted, Em sailed close to the wind sometimes. In the past, if it would help Duke or the SCU with an investigation, she hadn't been averse to a little duplicity to assist them.

The suggestion didn't seem to bother him. 'It's worth a try. I'll have a word with her and get back to you. Ciao.' He hung up.

Russ stubbed out the cigarette and checked his watch; it was three thirty. He picked up his car keys and took his digital camera from the desk drawer; it was time to pay Tiltman's solicitor a visit.

Taking the B2087 out of Rye, he made his way through the villages of Playden and Iden, crossing into the county of Kent. It was a half an hour's drive to the small market town of Tenterden, which stands on the edge of the Weald, overlooking the valley of the River Rother.

The town centre has a long, broad, tree-lined High Street flanked with a number of attractive Georgian buildings, tall Victorian houses, and, like Rye, a host of specialist shops, tearooms, and restaurants giving it a timeless air. The pavements were crowded with shoppers and sightseers. He pulled into a parking space outside the NatWest Bank.

At four thirty, he sat in the cluttered office of Peter Lant, a short, obese individual who greeted Russ with a wet, fleshy handshake. He was in his early sixties, wearing a navy pinstriped suit, the waistcoat bulging just above his trousers. His thin, mousy-coloured hair was greased and combed over, unsuccessfully, to cover his baldness; the double chin hid the knot in his tie. Papers and manila files covered his desk and most of the floor.

Inviting Russ to have a seat, Lant removed his suit jacket, draping it over the back of his swivel chair, and revealing large damp patches under his armpits. Russ could smell the man's body odour. He watched as Lant lowered himself onto his chair, wondering how on earth he could manage to bend low enough to retrieve a file from the carpet.

Taking a business card from his wallet, Russ handed it to the solicitor. 'Mr Lant, thank you for agreeing to see me at such short notice. My name is Russ Walker; I'm a private investigator. I have an office in Rye and I've been approached by a client of yours, George Tiltman who, as you know, was arrested six months ago for the murder of his wife. He's asked for my help in proving his innocence.'

Lant frowned. 'Yes, go on.'

'I understand he hasn't been formally charged with the murder, yet he believes he remains the chief suspect, and the police are no longer looking for anyone else in connection with her death. Before I decide whether or not I can help, I'd be grateful for your opinion about his innocence or guilt, and any other information you have on this case.'

Pushing his chair back with his feet, Lant placed his hands on the armrests and levered himself to a standing position; his expressionless face gave nothing away. He walked round to the left of his large desk and looked down to an untidy collection of files on the floor close to the wall. Steadying himself with one hand on the wall, he went down on one knee, and picked up a file. Pushing against the wall, he swung his weight onto his other leg, stood up again and went back to his seat behind the desk. *Problem solved – that's how it was done!*

Opening the file, he flicked through the papers; his back stiffened. 'Mr Walker, I have a major problem here – one of client confidentiality,' he said imperiously. He tapped the file with his finger. 'I've had a telephone call from Mr Tiltman; he informed me of his intent to engage your services, and yes, he did ask that I cooperate fully with you. However, I explained to him that I am professionally opposed to your involvement, and advised against any action that might have a detrimental effect on the outcome of this case.'

What an arrogant prick! Russ sighed heavily. 'Mr Lant, I'm not here to play games. I'm a professional too, and fully aware of the code of confidentiality. I'm also aware that, as his solicitor, you have to consider what actions may or may not be in his best interests; but damn it all, I need to know where you stand. Do you think he murdered her, or is he telling the truth – that he's innocent?'

Lant's face was shining with perspiration; he was hot and uncomfortable. Leaning back, his hand went to his trouser pocket and pulled out a handkerchief. He unfolded it, and, as if it were hand towel, wiped his face and neck.

'The reason Tiltman is still a free man at the moment is that the police have no admissible evidence of his guilt. Everything points to him being the murderer, but it's all circumstantial. I'm not required to believe in his innocence, but to provide the best legal representation for the circumstances in which he finds himself.'

Russ couldn't let this go. 'But if he hasn't convinced you, how on earth are you going to persuade a jury that he's innocent?'

Barely hiding his irritation, he said, 'If he should be charged and brought to trial, I will be recommending that an experienced criminal lawyer takes over the responsibility of representing him.'

Russ felt a surge of relief. Thank God for that! Lant would be a liability, but at this moment, it was information he needed.

'So, tell me about the circumstantial evidence.'

Clearly agitated, Lant looked down at the file. 'You must be aware he's unable to provide anything, or anyone, to support his alibi that he was in London on the day his wife was murdered. The police found no evidence to suggest an intruder might be responsible. The house was secure, and the forensic officers were unable to find any DNA samples, fibres or fingerprints, other than those matching Tiltman and his wife. Her body had no signs of defensive injury, and they found nothing under her fingernails. Not long ago, he took out a large insurance policy on her life; all rather incriminating, don't you think? I understand the police want to bring Tiltman to trial, but the Crown Prosecution Service insist there's insufficient admissible evidence.' He closed the file and stood up. 'Now, if you'll excuse me, Mr Walker, I have another appointment. Perhaps you could see yourself out.'

Chapter 6

After consulting the Drivers' Atlas, Russ decided to make a detour on his way back to Rye. By following the A28 Hastings road, he estimated he could be at Tilling at about six o'clock. Traffic was reasonably light, apart from occasional groups of motorcycles flashing past at intervals. He switched on the CD player; Ricky Nelson was in full flow about his exploits as a *Travellin' Man* – walking on the sand at Waikiki. If only...!

Eventually he approached a sign, "Tilling welcomes careful drivers". Tilling was a small picturesque village with a number of thatched cottages, an inn dating from Tudor times, a long-handled water pump on the village green, and no doubt featured in magazines such as *Country Life* or *This England*. He began to look for Passmore Lane and found it shortly beyond the village hall on the right - a quiet country road without a footpath. About a hundred yards from the main road, he saw Whitegates on the left. The house wasn't visible from the road. An open five-bar gate painted white gave access to a winding gravel drive with a high rhododendron hedge on either side. He turned into the drive, which led to a large modern detached house with an adjoining double garage. A silver BMW was parked beside a blue Mini Cooper. He pulled up behind the BMW, and made for the now open front door of the house.

George Tiltman must have seen Russ arrive and was walking towards him; a slow smile crossed his face.

'Hello, Mr Walker, I heard your car on the gravel. Do come in.'

Russ followed him into the house. 'I'm sorry to have called unannounced; I hope it's not an inconvenient time. I'm on my way home from a meeting with your solicitor, Lant – just wanted to keep you informed.'

He was shown into a large, airy drawing room in which a grand piano, its lid cantilevered open, and with sheet music ready on the stand, took pride of place. There were large French windows providing access to a paved patio, beyond which was a spacious neatly cut lawn surrounded by shrubs and bushes. Above the fireplace, on the mantle shelf, were two framed photographs.

Tiltman saw they had caught Russ' attention and inclined his head to the nearest one. 'That's Carol. It was taken last year at a Chamber of Commerce dinner.'

Russ reverently took it from the shelf and held it for a moment. He wouldn't have described her as beautiful, but not unattractive either. There was something about her eyes and nose – not unlike Barbara Streisand, he thought. It was a natural shot; sitting at a table, wine glass in her hand, laughing to the camera. Her blue dress, probably a size fourteen, was the sort Becky would have worn, similar to a Laura Ashley design. Replacing it, he reached for the second frame; it was their wedding day, the mandatory pose in a hotel garden. A happy young couple, she in a traditional wedding dress and he in a Moss Bros outfit.

Tiltman picked up a whisky glass from a small table beside an armchair. 'Please, have a seat. I was just having a drink before getting something to eat. Will you join me?'

He declined the offer and replaced the photograph as Tiltman sat down. Russ chose the settee.

'My meeting with Lant was rather unproductive. He made it clear he's unhappy about you hiring me, but I guess that's his problem.'

Tiltman was nervous. He sat upright, holding the glass in both hands, with the facial expression of a Labrador restlessly waiting to hear the word 'walkies'.

Russ continued, 'I wondered... Would you mind if I take a look at the bedroom and then generally around the house?'

Tiltman welcomed the suggestion. 'Not at all. It's still a mess, just as the police left it. I can't bring myself to go in there, not even for my shoes or clothes. I've bought new ones, and sleep in the second bedroom.' He drained his glass, placed it on the table and got up from the chair.

Russ eased himself off the settee. 'On second thoughts, perhaps you could walk me through everything you did the night you arrived home and discovered your wife's body. Could I suggest we begin outside, where you parked your car?'

They left the house, Tiltman locking the door behind them and walked to his BMW. 'Of course, it was dark when I came home. I parked right here, next to Carol's Mini.' He pointed to a security light above the garage door. 'The light came on as normal. I locked the car and walked to the front door.'

He led Russ to the house, and used two keys to open the door, one for the mortise lock, the other, a Yale. 'We always used both keys. I think Carol was more security conscious than me; she'd use both, even if she was outside cleaning her car by the garage. That's why I couldn't understand why I only needed the Yale key.'

They entered the house and he closed the door. He touched the light switch and inclined his head towards the alarm panel in the hallway. 'I switched on the hall lights and called out to let her know I was home, then I went to reset the alarm before it went off, but it hadn't been set; that's when I began to be anxious. She would always set it if she was on her own.'

He walked into each of the ground floor rooms, as if looking for Carol, and said, 'They were all in darkness, none of the curtains had been drawn.'

Russ made a mental note – all the windows and doors were double glazed.

They returned to the hallway. 'I wondered if she was unwell and had gone to bed, so I went upstairs.'

Russ followed him up to a large landing, with doors to a bathroom, a separate WC and four bedrooms. All the doors were ajar, with the exception of one.

Tiltman glanced uncomfortably at the closed door. 'That was our bedroom.' He pointed to one next to it. 'I'm sleeping in there now. When I came upstairs, our bedroom door was closed; that's when I really knew something was wrong, because we never closed the door, day or night.'

Russ smiled disarmingly and put a steadying hand on his shoulder. 'Would you mind leaving me to have a look in the room? Perhaps you might like to go and finish your drink. I won't be long.'

He waited for Tiltman to go down the stairs before opening the bedroom door. The room smelt musty; the windows were closed. The king-sized double bed had been stripped to the bare mattress – no sign of pillows. The bed was set into a gap between fitted wardrobes, with cupboards above it. The cream-coloured doors still showed the tell-tale patches of black powder left by the SOCOs - like smoke damage after a fire. They'd certainly been thorough; everything had been dusted, even the walls. He stood quietly for a moment. Such a lovely room defiled by malevolence. *Carol, what really happened here?* With his digital camera, he took shots of the room from various angles. The police and SOCOs would have been meticulous in their search, but he wanted to know more about Tiltman and his wife; how they lived, their likes and dislikes, even their taste in clothes. The contents of cupboards and drawers revealed expensive taste – plenty of designer labels in their clothes and shoes. Carol had a liking for sexy lingerie – there were two drawers full of matching bras and panties, black and red basques, and a selection of thongs. The top drawer of her bedside cabinet contained a Catherine Cookson novel, an unused notepad, paracetamol tablets and a tube of KY jelly. The other drawers were full of stockings and tights.

Tiltman's underwear proved to be a little more sober - jockey shorts, sleeveless vests and some un-sexy Y-fronts. A selection of books on the window sill contained nothing more sinister than thrillers by Harlan Coben, Patricia Cornwell and Ian Rankin. He wondered if the police had found any sex toys or porn.

He'd seen enough. Closing the door behind him, he made his way downstairs.

Tiltman was in the kitchen preparing a salad for his supper. He looked at Russ expectantly.

'Walker, will you help me - help prove my innocence?' He was desperate for an answer.

Softly, Russ said, 'I'm afraid I have to get back to Rye, but I'll let you have my decision by tomorrow evening.'

He handed Russ a business card, and said, 'I'm not going in to work for the next two days. I'll be here waiting for your call.'

Fifteen minutes later, Russ was in Rye, climbing the stairs to his office. The light on the answering machine was flashing; there was a message from Duke telling him to check his fax machine, and reminding him that he owed Em big time.

He made a mug of instant coffee and gathered up the papers from the fax machine. He flicked through them as he lowered himself onto the swivel chair.

Grinning, he said aloud, 'Em, you're a gem! You're bloody brilliant!'

There were several photographs of the crime scene at Tilling, DI Baillie's full report, the pathologist's findings from the post-mortem, full details from the SOCOs and a complete list of those who'd been interviewed, including some of the statements.

He looked first at the photographs. There were three general shots of the bedroom. His eyes were drawn to the naked woman lying on her back, spread-eagled on the bed. Blue cord or rope from her wrists and ankles was tied to the castors under the four corners of the bed. There were no pillows; she was on a pale green sheet. Her body appeared to be wet, reflecting the flashlight from the camera. He studied the background; as far as he could tell, the room looked exactly as he'd seen it earlier. He would check that later against his own photos. The close-ups of the body were horrific. The expression on her face was of sheer terror. Her staring eyes, wide open, filled with fright, and her mouth contorted as if she was screaming. There were signs of bruising on both sides of her neck. The genital area showed signs of injury – bruising and blood – with something protruding from her anus. *Dear God, what had this poor woman been subjected to?* The post-mortem report made for grim reading. The body was coated with oil and had been subjected to a severe sexual assault. There was external bruising around the vagina, and internal injuries indicated repeated insertion of a large object, the size of an adult male's fist. Evidence of condom lubricant was found in both the vagina and anus. No trace of semen. A plastic vibrator had been inserted and left in the anus. There was bruising on both breasts. There were no signs of defensive injury. The cause of death was strangulation, estimated to have occurred between 2pm and 4pm on the 22nd of December 2014.

Forensic examination revealed traces of an adhesive substance on and around the mouth, suggesting the victim's mouth had been covered with duct tape pre-mortem. No evidence of drugs, alcohol or other toxic substances were found in the body. The chemical constituents of the oil on the body were identical with those of any common brand of baby oil available from most chemists and supermarkets. Fingernail scrapes provided no evidence.

The Scene of Crime report was surprisingly brief. Examination of the nylon sheet on which the body was found revealed no DNA evidence, other than body hair and blood from the victim. A protracted and detailed search of the bedroom found no evidence of hair, skin, fibres, or fingerprints to suggest anyone other than the victim and her husband, George Tiltman, had been in the room on the day of the murder. A search of the house and grounds was unable to locate a container for baby oil, the fragment of duct tape or a used condom. A packet of condoms had been found in a bedside cabinet, and one was missing. Examination of the drainage pipes and sewage system revealed no trace of disposed evidence. A partially used roll of grey duct tape was found in the garage.

There were no signs of forced entry at any of the doors or windows of the property. The home computer and discs belonging to George Tiltman, the husband of the victim, were removed from the house and later examined by technicians. No incriminating evidence was found. There was no evidence of pornographic material in the house.

The transcript of DI Baillie's interviews with George Tiltman offered no more than what Tiltman had already told him. There was a list of some fifty people who had been interviewed; they were neighbours, friends and work colleagues of Carol Tiltman. Not one of them had anything helpful to contribute.

DI Baillie's report to the CPS outlined all the evidence of the pathologist and forensics, suggesting that it removed any doubt that Mr George Tiltman, the victim's husband was responsible for her murder. In addition to this, Mr Tiltman was unable to provide evidence to support the claim he was in London at the time of the murder.

The response from the CPS indicated they too were inclined to believe George Tiltman killed his wife, but considered there was insufficient evidence with which to initiate proceedings against him.

Russ squared up the papers and laid them to one side. He pulled his laptop towards him and booted up. Opening Microsoft Word, he typed a heading:

'How did the perpetrator gain access?'

1. Carol knew the perp and let or invited him/her in.
   (Certainly a possibility)
2. Carol didn't know the perp but was tricked into giving access.
   (Someone with false credentials of a meter reader, telephone engineer etc? – And yet the body showed no signs of resistance)
3. Carol opened the door and the perp made a forced entry.
   (Again a possibility but why no defensive injuries?)
4. A window or door was insecure and the perp broke in.
   (a possibility)

5. Someone (other than Tiltman and his wife) had keys and let themselves in.
   (Cleaning lady; Gardener; friend or relative?)
6. Tiltman came home and let himself in.
   DID HE MURDER HER?

Going to a new page, he typed another heading:

'Why was Carol Tiltman murdered?'

1. It was marital sex-play that went wrong.
   (A not uncommon scenario)
2. A secret lover lost control.
   (Again a possibility)
3. A premeditated crime by a sexual predator – known or unknown to the victim.
   (Are any known sex-offenders living in the area, and have they been eliminated? Why no evidence of resistance by victim?)

On a third page he wrote:

'Why is George Tiltman hiring a PI?

1. He really is innocent and desperate to prove it.
   (A distinct possibility)
2. He is guilty, and it will help him to appear innocent.
   (A possibility - He knows no further evidence can be found)
3. He is guilty and mentally unstable.

(Unlikely but possible - only a professional shrink could prove or disprove this)

After printing copies, he gathered the papers together and put them in his empty filing cabinet. It was time to call it a day. Taking his laptop he locked up and went to his car.

He enjoyed cooking, but it was a spur of the moment thing; at the Kettle of Fish roundabout, he pulled into the car park, and from the fish restaurant bought cod and chips to take back to the cottage.

Settled in front of the TV, he ate his takeaway. Tuesday evening viewing was always a disappointment and tonight was no exception. After a particularly boring documentary about a crofter's life in the Outer Hebrides, he was further irritated by yet another advertisement exhorting the benefits of digital television. 'All you need,' said the cheerful announcer, 'is a receiver - an inexpensive little box to plug the aerial into.' They always forgot to mention that in some areas of the country, such as Rye Harbour, the signal was too weak for anyone to receive it. Surfing through the four terrestrial channels available to him, he found nothing to dissuade him from calling it a day and going to bed.

Sleep wouldn't come; there were too many images floating in and out of his mind; his conversation with the man calling himself 'Shand' at the Savoy, the discovery of the body here at Rye Harbour, DS Askew, Wendy Drew, George Tiltman and his murdered wife. He slipped down stairs and brought his laptop to the bedroom. He climbed into bed, his back to the headboard, opened his laptop and booted it up. He Googled the name 'Shand', and found himself trawling through countless websites of businesses using Shand as a brand name. He typed in the word 'Derrida' and immediately struck gold. According to The Stanford Encyclopaedia of Philosophy, *"Jacques Derrida, (1930-2004) was a <u>French</u> <u>philosopher</u> born in <u>Algeria</u>, who is known as the founder of <u>deconstruction</u>. His voluminous work had a profound impact upon <u>literary theory</u> and <u>continental philosophy</u>."* Russ read on, hardly understanding a word until he came across two sentences – *"deconstruction works towards preventing the worst violence. It attempts to render justice. Indeed, deconstruction is relentless in this pursuit since justice is impossible to achieve."* He smiled to himself. Shand was using the philosopher's name and his philosophical theory out of context, but nonetheless Russ saw the parallel in terms of fighting criminality. He switched off the computer; it was time for sleep.

Chapter 7

The gulls woke him at six; their plaintive cries seemed especially loud that morning. Russ sat up in bed, propped against the pillows. Through the diamond panes of the leaded window, he watched the sunlight dancing like a myriad of fairies on the calm shimmering water in the harbour. It was high tide; most of the fishing boats had left their moorings and were now out at sea. Half a dozen leisure craft were berthed by the low harbour wall. Overhead, the high vapour trail of an aircraft drew a thread across the cloudless blue sky. He was in good spirits. He'd slept well, and awakened refreshed, not only physically but mentally and spiritually too. His lean dark features were excited, his eyes gleaming. A sense of purpose had returned to his life; at last he felt motivated. He was in business and eager to get started.

He donned his tracksuit and trainers, and set out on his morning jog down to the Point, then through the nature reserve, taking the path that ran parallel with the sea to Winchelsea Beach. It was mid-June; the forecasters had predicted yet another scorching day. If this heat wave was the result of global warming, apart from the Southern Water Company, not many in the South East were complaining and neither was he. An hour later he had returned home, showered and had breakfast.

By eight fifteen he was in Rye, heading for the office. From Cinque Ports Street, following the one-way system, he turned right, driving through the Landgate Arch into the High Street. He remembered the thrill he'd experienced when he first came to this medieval gem; he'd felt like a time-traveller stepping back a few hundred years, as he explored the quaint cobbled streets and alleyways of the citadel. He was surprised to discover a beautiful twelfth-century church, which could probably seat around four hundred worshippers, and a picturesque Strand Quay offering a safe haven to the local fishing boats and leisure craft. He remembered thinking Rye must be one of England's best kept secrets. He couldn't believe how quiet it was compared to London, and as for the air – it was like breathing pure oxygen!

Rye has a sleepy down-to-earth charm despite its vast number of visitors and the proliferation of gift shops; yet it was a real town, a place where people live and work the year round. From a book on local history in the town library, he'd been surprised to discover that the name Rye is derived from ancient descriptive words which generally mean an island and a somewhat desolate one at that! Apparently, variations such as Atter eye, Attereye, Ria, la Rye and Rye were, by the end of the sixteenth century, finalised as Rye. Bit of irony, he'd thought... from the Isle of Dogs to the Isle of Rye – neither of which is a real island!

Rye town stands on a sandstone promontory, as does its sister town Winchelsea, five miles to the east; twin headlands of the old coastline of pre-marsh days. The whole of the coast from Eastbourne to Folkestone has changed since Roman times, particularly the area from Fairlight near Hastings, to Hythe in Kent. The main enemy was, and still is, the up-Channel drift carrying beach from promontory to promontory, forming lagoons and banks which, with the silt brought down by the rivers has formed marshlands.

Turning right into Market Street, he pulled into the office parking space. Five minutes later, he sat at his desk, a mug of coffee in his hand, the Tiltman file open in front of him. He pored over the details page by page, making notes in his pocket book. It was a sickening crime. From the accumulation of evidence before him, he had to concede George Tiltman looked the most likely perpetrator, but his intuition said otherwise. Baillie and his team had been thorough, but what had they missed? Idly, he chewed on the end of his pen; questions he couldn't answer crowded his mind. This was fast becoming a cold case, yet he was convinced it was there - someone or something held that vital clue - still waiting to be uncovered; it sent a rush of adrenaline through his veins.

Russ was a pragmatist. Theorising and double-guessing undoubtedly had their value and could point to possible leads, but for Russ it was in the dogged scrutiny of facts - in the examination of minutiae – the answers were more likely to be found. He pulled out the photographs and placed them side by side. His eyes focussed on the livid bite marks on her breasts and bloody ones on the genital area. He took a deep breath and let it out slowly. He re-examined the notion he'd earlier dismissed out of hand – that the perp was simply an opportunist who'd struck lucky; that Carol was a random choice. But it was too neat, too well thought out. Preceding her death, Carol Tiltman had been subjected to a sadistic and protracted assault. The evidence suggested not a frenzied attack out of sexual rage, but one that was slow and deliberate, possibly lasting for anything up to an hour. The murderer had brought oil, rope, duct tape and a vibrator; it was clearly premeditated. He'd expected her to be at home and alone, to have sufficient time to carry out his warped intention without fear of being caught. But why target Carol? Was he privy to the Tiltmans' arrangements for that day?

He shook his head slowly. *Carol, I'm going to nail this bastard, but I need your help.*

From the file, he drew up a list of those who had known her well: colleagues at the residential home where she'd worked, the chairman and secretary of the drama group, and members of the Village Hall Committee. That's where he'd start. Through them, he would learn more about Carol - the real Carol. He wanted to know what had made her feel truly alive, what excited or depressed her, her hopes and dreams, who liked her, and who didn't.

Sue breezed in at nine, wearing a white summer top, light brown three-quarter length trousers and open-toed sandals. She grinned.

'Morning, Boss, my, you look busy!' Walking around the desk, she looked down at the papers spread out in front of him. 'What's this, no crossword?' She reached for the player on the windowsill, and lowered the volume of *It's Now or Never.*

He looked up, eyebrows raised in mock surprise. 'Aha, so you're an Elvis fan after all; there's hope for you yet!'

Grinning, she went to her desk, sat down and switched on the computer. 'So how did it go yesterday with the mystery visitor?'

He told her about Wendy Drew and that he'd been hired to find her missing daughter. Her mouth fell open when he went on to tell of the unexpected visit of George Tiltman.

'I'm going to Folkestone this morning and Tilling this afternoon; there are one or two people I want to talk to before I contact Tiltman again.' After a slight pause, he said, 'Tell you what, if you're free this evening, how about supper? If you're prepared to risk it, maybe I can impress you with my culinary skills and bring you up to speed with the Tiltman situation.'

A slow smile crossed her face. 'That sounds good. I promised Mum I'd see her at six; is seven thirty okay?

'Seven thirty it is.' He gathered the papers together and passed them over to her. 'Could you file these, please? I ought to be going.'

The A259 was heavy with farm tractors, learner drivers, caravanners and HGVs. It was a slow, frustrating journey that took almost an hour to Folkestone. Situated at the foot of the North Downs, the town has stunning views of the surrounding countryside; even the coast of France was visible. As with most British holiday resorts, Folkestone had suffered much deprivation since the end of the Second World War. The rise in cheap package holidays to foreign destinations helped to seriously damage Folkestone's tourism business. The closure of the ferry services between Folkestone and

Boulogne and the opening of the nearby Channel Tunnel hastened the town's demise. It was hard to believe that a hundred years ago, this town was a Royal holiday destination, a fashionable resort playing host to the high and mighty, and those who were desperate to be numbered among them.

It was just before eleven when he drew up outside 32 Selwyn Avenue, a 1960s mock-Georgian terraced house in a quiet, middle-class neighbourhood. Wendy Drew was watching at the window as he locked the car. Before he reached for the bell-push, she opened the door and invited him into a small hallway. Closing the door behind him, she ushered him into the lounge. It was a large room, with a dining area at the far end. Several photographs of her daughter were spread out on the dining table, two or three of her in school uniform, and the rest informal snaps, taken in the garden or on holidays. He tapped a postcard-sized print of a sultry looking teenager, with black spiky hair.

'How recent is this? Is it a good likeness of Hannah?'

She picked it up and gave it to him. 'Yes, that was taken last month at her cousin's wedding. As you can see, she's into the Gothic look. It was so embarrassing, Brian was livid. She absolutely refused to dress up.'

'I'll make a copy and let you have it back.' He slipped it into his document case. 'Now, if I could take a look in her bedroom, please.'

She led him to the foot of the stairs. 'It's the one next to the bathroom. Help yourself. I must warn you, it's an absolute tip.'

For a teenager's room, it was tidier than he'd expected. Posters of Goth Bands he'd never heard of covered the walls

- Killing Miranda, Kindred Spirits, Kismet. Black Sabbath was the only name he recognised. The black duvet cover and pillowcase on the single bed added to the heavy, depressive atmosphere. On an impulse, he crossed to the table beside the bed, the top cluttered with school books and CDs. Checking everything on it, he wondered if she kept a journal or diary that could provide a key to the mystery. The covers of her school exercise books were covered in scribble and drawings. None of it made sense to him; the letters DIZ seemed to have been used over and over. He checked the cupboard, wardrobe and drawers, hoping to find letters or cards from a boyfriend, searched through pockets in her clothes, in her handbags and under the pillow and mattress – nothing! Back at the desk, he flipped through the pile of CDs. None of the bands or singers were familiar to him. On the back of a CD case, written with a black felt pen were the words, 'Want it back. DIZ!' He slipped it into his pocket.

He came down the stairs to find a tearful Wendy Drew sitting at the dining table, looking at the photographs of her daughter. Russ pulled out a chair beside her and sat down.

'Do the letters D-I-Z, DIZ, mean anything to you?'

She looked confused. 'No, should they?'

He explained about the doodles on the schoolbooks, pulled the CD cover from his pocket and held it up. 'Presumably it's the nickname of someone she knows, I'll have to ask around... And if I could have her friend Shelly's address, that would be helpful.'

She'd already written it on a slip of paper which she handed to him.

He looked at his watch, pushed his chair back and stood up. He gave her a reassuring smile. 'Try not to worry, Mrs Drew. I hope to have news of her in a day or two. How would you like me to contact you?'

She gave him the telephone number of the nursery school where she worked. 'You can get me at this number, but only in the mornings. Please don't phone the house unless it's absolutely necessary.'

Russ eased the Capri out of Selwyn Avenue and at the next junction followed the signs for the town centre. He left the Capri in a multi-storey car park, and made his way to Bouverie Place, the in-town shopping centre. Folkestone had been seriously damaged during both world wars, and like the neighbouring town of Dover, due to its proximity to the French coast, had suffered considerable shelling in the Second World War, which gave rise to the name of "Hellfire Corner". He noticed there had been significant physical redevelopment in the town centre, clearly in a bid to revive Folkestone's fortunes.

As Russ had expected, the shopping centre was bustling with activity, and had its fair share of young hoodies wandering aimlessly, wearing low-hung jeans revealing the elastic bands of their underpants; hardly the type Hannah Drew would be drawn to. Rap would be more their scene, rather than heavy metal or Gothic. He pulled out his Benson and Hedges and lit a cigarette. From behind him, a woman shouted, 'Just stop it.' He turned guiltily, wondering if this was a no-smoking area, that the words had been directed at him. He was in the clear; it was a young mother shouting at a little boy.

'It's not fair!' he whined, his eyes brimming with tears. The curly-haired toddler kicked the wheel of the buggy. 'It's just not fair; Dad said I could!'

The care-worn young woman reached for his arm and jerked him to a standstill. She was close to tears herself. She bent down and turned his face to hers. 'I don't care what he said; you're not having one. Now get into the buggy!' Russ noticed she had a butterfly tattooed on the upper part of her right breast.

In defiance, the boy shrugged off her hold and refused to move. 'It's not fair!' he repeated.

In exasperation, she picked him up and deposited him unceremoniously into the seat. To prevent his escape, she tilted the buggy onto its back wheels, and as they moved away, there was bitterness in her voice. 'Life isn't fair, and the sooner you realise that, the better!'

Russ followed them with his eyes until they'd turned the corner. He dropped the cigarette butt and ground it out with his foot. A lump had formed in his throat. The kid was right; it's not fair! If his dad said he could, then it wasn't fair. There again, his mum was right too - life isn't fair, and the sooner the kid realised that, the better. But what difference will it make? How will it help him when things don't work out the way they should? What is fairness, anyway? From cradle to grave, we are exhorted to honour moral obligations; to strive for justice, equity, and even-handedness in our dealings with others - well, that's fairness! And what *of* those others - don't we have a right to expect it of them? And yet, why doesn't it work when applied to fate, destiny or God? Cancer isn't fair. Disability isn't fair. Becky's death wasn't fair.

He shook his head; this wasn't helping. He thought about the butterfly tattoo. He'd never understood why people felt the need to have them. Then it occurred to him... Goths loved tattoos!

Looking around, he noticed a young couple peering at the window display in River Island. The young man was wearing a white T-shirt and had tattoos on both arms. Russ sidled over to him and asked if there was a tattooist in Folkestone. The man directed him to a tattoo and body-piercing parlour in a side street near the seafront.

It was a small, scruffy shop with blacked-out windows. The door was open, and as Russ entered, the tattooist, leaning on the counter and reading a newspaper, looked over his John Lennon glasses and smiled. His eyes were dark and quiet in their intelligence. He was in his late thirties and was wearing a sleeveless vest tucked into his jeans. His long brown hair was pulled back in a ponytail. Russ was surprised not to see any tattoos or body-piercings on *him*, and even more astounded at his cultured accent.

'Good afternoon, sir, my name is Terry – what can I do for you?'

The walls of the room displayed numerous tattoo designs, from simple Oriental symbols and flowers to dragons and warriors, with an area reserved for explicit sexual images and enlarged photographs of pierced body parts.

Russ approached the counter. 'Oh, hi. Sorry, I'm not after a tattoo, but information. I'm trying to locate a young man who may be a customer of yours. He's known as DIZ; he's into things Gothic.'

The smile disappeared from Terry's face. 'You should try the police station; he's certainly one of *their* regulars. Trouble is, they keep letting him out. He's a very nasty piece of work.'

Russ raised his eyebrows. 'Not a valued customer, I take it. Do you know where I might find him?'

Terry pushed his glasses higher on his nose. 'He's in a squat on the seafront - but not for much longer, thank God. There's a terraced row of derelict houses due to be pulled down for redevelopment. He and his equally unsavoury mates are in the end one on the right; but I wouldn't advise you to go there - certainly not on your own. He's a vicious sod.'

'What can you tell me about him?' Russ asked.

'Nothing much, other than he's an extremely unpleasant thug. I've given him a few tattoos and facial piercings for the privilege of not having my own face disfigured and the shop trashed.'

He felt concern for Terry. 'So it's scum I'm after! I appreciate your help. Who knows – maybe I can persuade him to modify his behaviour.'

Terry wasn't convinced. 'Hey, just be careful – and for God's sake, don't let him know *I've* spoken to you.'

Russ held up his hand. 'Don't worry, I won't. Thanks, Terry.'

He followed the pedestrian signs for the harbour. Expecting the romantic scene of colourful fishing boats and yachts bobbing at their moorings, he was disappointed. It was low tide, and the harbour was almost devoid of water. There were a handful of fishing boats and small yachts propped up on the wet mud, amongst discarded shopping trolleys and lumps of wood the size of railway sleepers. Holiday makers in shorts and vests ambled beside the harbour wall with their ice-creams and plastic tubs of cockles and whelks.

How different a scene from the one in 1915 when, during the First World War, Folkestone was the main embarkation point for soldiers leaving to fight in the trenches of France and Belgium. He tried to visualise the hundreds of thousands of soldiers, including many Canadian troops, who left from Folkestone, having marched from the town to the harbour along the route now called the "Road of Remembrance".

He stood for a while at the fish market and watched a young man in his rubber apron and Wellington boots hosing the concrete floor where the morning sales had taken place. Herring gulls and common terns swooped and fought with each other for the morsels swept away in the gulley that ran into the harbour.

Heading west along the front, he passed the Burstin Hotel, and came to the sad remnants of an amusement park. The stalls and attractions had been boarded up or partially demolished; a prime but desolate site awaiting redevelopment. Across the road opposite were neatly kept lawns and flowerbeds, beyond which stood an Edwardian crescent of derelict houses. The ground floor windows and doors to the front were secured with sheets of four-ply. On closer inspection, he discovered a small service road giving access to the rear of the buildings. The house on the end showed no sign of illegal entry; boards covering the rear door and windows were still in place. The adjoining house, however, was less secure. The windows remained blocked, but the rear door had been forced open and left slightly ajar.

Checking that he couldn't be seen, he climbed the three steps and slipped quietly inside. For a full two minutes he stood motionless in the dark, listening for signs of activity. Using the mini-torch on his keyring, he began a search of the ground floor, carefully avoiding broken glass and detritus. Having found no evidence of squatters, slowly he took the stairs to the first floor. Pausing halfway, he became aware of a humming noise, not unlike the sound made by a vacuum cleaner. The stench of excreta filled his nostrils as he reached the landing. He pulled out a handkerchief, held it over his nose and mouth, and directed the beam of the torch into a large room to his left. There were several plastic buckets filled to the brim with human waste, and piles of it on the floor. He'd found the source of the noise – hundreds of blow-flies. The next room was an equally revolting latrine area, but in the third, he found what he was looking for - a hole, large enough to crawl through, had been made in the wall, giving access into the end house. Peering through, he could see the room was empty, but there were voices coming from somewhere deep in the house. It was impossible to tell how many were there, or what they were saying. Quietly, he retraced his steps back to the ground floor and slipped out through the door into the bright sunlight.

He'd reached the main shopping area before the smell finally left him. He phoned Duke on his mobile, bringing him up to speed on the Tiltman case, and his search for DIZ.

There was concern in Duke's voice. 'Russ, don't go to that squat again on your own. Do you want me to come down? I could be with you in an hour and a half – and hey, I could do with of a bit of excitement!'

'No, it's okay, but thanks for the offer. I'm cooking a meal for Sue this evening, but I might ask Elmo if he fancies coming with me after closing time at The Rocks. Don't worry, I'll be careful. I'll call you tomorrow and let you know how things went.'

They talked for another ten minutes, before Russ rang off and made for the multi-storey car park.

Chapter 8

The coastal road from Folkestone to Rye was still heavy with traffic. As he drove through the small town of Hythe, the road ran parallel with the Royal Military canal, built in 1809 as a third line of defence against Napoleon. The canal stretches for 28 miles, hugging the old cliff line that borders the Romney Marsh from Hythe in the northeast to Cliff End in the southwest. Some fifteen minutes later, he had passed through the village of Dymchurch and was on Romney Marsh, a sparsely-populated wetland area covering a hundred square miles. The road was full of bends, two or three almost at right angles; on both sides, sheep grazed on lush below sea-level grassland. The few trees he saw were almost at right angles having yielded to the strong winds blowing across the exposed landscape. In the distance to his left stood a monolithic structure he assumed was Dungeness power station. He smiled to himself as he recalled the conversation he'd had with Sue about Dungeness. She had described it as the most depressing place on earth, with nothing but pebbles, sea cabbage, fishermen's shacks, a lighthouse and an ugly power station. After a short pit stop for a burger and coffee at the Little Chef at Brenzett, thirty minutes later he was back in his office at Rye.

Sue had left a note on the desk, "See you at seven thirty".

He switched on the laptop, opened a new page on Microsoft Word and typed 'Derrida', followed by his bank details. He printed it off on a plain sheet of paper and sealed it in a stamped envelope, addressed to the Westminster Post Office Box number he'd memorised.

From the filing cabinet he took a list of the names and addresses of people at Tilling he intended to interview. Locking the office, he dropped the envelope in a post box on the High Street and made for his car.

He left Rye on the Udimore road. Turning left onto the A28 at Broad Oak, within a few minutes he was in the village of Tilling.

He had no difficulty locating Beech Lodge Retirement Home. It was in a prominent position in the centre of the village, set back from the main street in its own grounds. A large red-bricked building with a pretentious portico at the main entrance afforded it the grandeur of a large manor house. Pulling into the driveway, circling a neatly-mown lawn in the centre of which stood a giant copper beech, he parked on the left by three other cars. The owners were Mr Keith Prince and Ms Jacquie Toland.

He rang twice before the door was opened by a member of staff wearing a red tabard over her white blouse and navy trousers. She was an Asian girl, probably in her mid-teens. He asked if he could speak to Mr Prince or Ms Toland, and was told neither was available, but Jenny the matron might be able to help. He was led along a corridor to a small office at the end. A middle-aged woman wearing a nurse's dark blue uniform and butterfly buckle on her belt, sat at her desk and appeared to be working on duty rotas. She stood up and introduced herself as Jenny Pierce. He noticed a wedding ring as he shook her hand.

'Good morning, Mrs Pierce. My name is Russ Walker. I was hoping to have a word with Mr Prince or Ms Toland, but I understand neither is available.'

She picked up a ballpoint pen and wrote his name on the pad by the phone. 'Yes, I'm sorry, they're not here very often; one of them usually comes in on a Friday morning. I'm the Matron; is there anything I can help you with?'

She removed boxes of tissues and packs of toilet rolls from a chair and gestured for him to sit down.

He sat and smiled disarmingly. 'I wanted to talk to them about Carol Tiltman; I understand she worked here before she died. Did *you* know her?'

She put her hand to her mouth. 'Oh my God, poor Carol! Yes, she was here for about a year, such a lovely person. She was temping through a nursing agency to begin with, but Mr Prince persuaded her to stay as my deputy. We hit it off straightaway and became good friends.' A sad smile crossed her face. 'You've no idea how much I miss her.' Her eyes flickered, unsure. 'Are you a policeman?'

He handed her his card. 'No, I'm a private investigator. Would you mind if we closed the door for a moment?'

She got up, removed a doorstop, and closed the door. Returning to her seat, she lowered her voice. 'I suppose you're all trying to understand why he did it.'

'I assume you mean her husband. Do *you* think he did it?'

She sighed, shaking her head mournfully. 'Well he was arrested for it, wasn't he? For the life of me, I can't understand why he's still walking about. It's all so strange; I mean he never struck me as the sort of man who could ever do such a thing. You just never know, do you?'

He tried his best conspiratorial tone, 'Did Carol ever talk about him, or their marriage?'

She gave a slight shrug of her shoulders. 'She used to say he was boring, but don't get me wrong; she thought he loved her in his own way, but said there was no romance any more. All he thought about was his work and socialising with other business people – you know, Rotary, Chamber of Commerce, that sort of thing.'

'But they did *do* things together, didn't they... Like the drama group, for example?' he urged.

She gave a sad smile. 'In the earlier years, yes, but he hasn't been involved in *anything* in the village for years. She carried on with the drama group, but he didn't want to know. It hurt her that he wouldn't even put himself out and go to the performances. Two years ago, she had the lead part in 'My Fair Lady', she was Eliza Doolittle – he never even went to that! She was devastated!'

Russ frowned. 'Did they argue very much?'

She gave another shrug. 'I don't think so. Carol kind of gave up really. She used to say, "If you don't expect, you don't get disappointed," but I know she was.'

There was a knock on the door; it was opened by the young Asian, asking for the key to the medicine cabinet. Jenny Pierce took it from a row of hooks on the wall above the desk and gave it to her.

'Ask Jane to check the dosage, and don't forget May's eye drops.'

He waited for the carer to close the door. 'Carol obviously shared a lot with you. Did she ever suspect her husband might be having an affair?'

She laughed at the absurdity of the suggestion. 'Never! I asked her that once. She said she half-wished he would; it might liven him up a bit.'

Again there was a knock on the door; the carer was back with a problem. Clearly this was not a good time; Jenny confirmed it with a shake of her head and an apology,

'Look, I'm sorry. I really haven't time for this at the moment. I mean, the police did interview me at the time, but if you think I can help, do call again.'

Russ stood up. 'I quite understand. Thanks for your time; perhaps another day.' *There was no perhaps about it. He'd be back, and soon.* Jenny Pierce asked the carer to show him out.

Russ returned to the car and consulted the list. His next port of call would be to Jeremy Wadsworth, a bachelor, aged fifty-six and chairman of the drama group. According to the file, Wadsworth was a local entrepreneur who owned a general store known as Tilling's Mini-Market, a video and DVD rental shop and the village garage and petrol station. He gunned the engine, slipped into first gear, drove slowly round the drive, and turned left onto the main street. Leaving the Capri in a parking bay outside a launderette, he set off on foot for the garage he remembered passing as he entered the village.

On the forecourt, a balding middle-aged man, dressed in a beige safari suit and holding a clipboard was checking the meters on the pumps.

Russ approached him. 'Good afternoon,' he said genially. 'Forgive me for interrupting, but are you Jeremy Wadsworth?'

The man ignored the question and continued writing on his clipboard. He took another glance at the pump meter, frowned and checked his sheet.

Russ tried again. 'Excuse me, are you Jeremy Wadsworth?'

Safari man rubbed the glass on the meter; his chin came up in a challenge. 'Who wants to know?'

He placed his card on Wadsworth's clipboard. 'My name is Russ Walker, I'm a private investigator. I wonder if you could spare me a few minutes. It's about the late Carol Tiltman.'

Wadsworth looked at the card and stiffened. 'I never talk to private investigators. Anything I might want to say about Carol Tiltman, I've already said to the police. Now, if you don't mind, I've a business to run.' He pulled away abruptly, turned his back and walked away.

What a tosser! This was another of those times when he felt naked and powerless without his police badge and warrant card. He followed Wadsworth with a stare, cursing under his breath and silently marked him down for further attention.

A woman in an estate car hooted; he was blocking her from pulling up at the pump. He mouthed the word 'sorry' and moved out of the way.

Returning to his own car, he sat for a while, smoked a cigarette, deciding who to visit next: Ms Janice Austin, aged forty-two, secretary of the drama group, living at 11 Church Road. Locking the car, he decided to walk.

Her home was a whitewashed prefabricated detached bungalow; the entire front garden had been paved. There were a dozen earthenware pots of varying sizes containing shrubs and flowers arranged under the front windows and on either side of the front door.

The door had no bell, so he tapped firmly with the brass squirrel knocker. No one answered so he knocked again; still no reply. Thinking she might be in the rear garden, he tried the gate to the left of the bungalow. Lifting the latch, the gate opened with a loud creak. Closing it behind him, he followed the concrete path that ran beside the bungalow, bringing him to a vast expanse of lawn, secluded by a high laurel hedge on either side.

He took a sharp intake of breath. She was sunbathing on a blanket, lying on her stomach, reading, her head supported by the heels of her hands propped up on her elbows. The bikini top hung on the arm of a wicker chair beside her; if she was wearing the bottoms, it wasn't obvious. He was about to make a discreet exit when she looked up. Smiling, she pushed her sunglasses onto her forehead.

'Oh hello! Are you looking for me?'

She was an attractive woman with long, black wavy hair, and a lithe, lightly-tanned body.

He cleared his throat. 'Look, I'm sorry to intrude... I did knock... but there was no reply. My name is Russ Walker, I'm a private investigator. I was hoping to have a word with Janice Austin.'

She pushed herself up and sat on her haunches, her hands on her thighs. 'Ooh, how exciting. I'm she. Come and have a seat.' There was a girlish upper-crust affectation in her voice.

She saw him hesitate. 'We naturists have to make the most of what little sunshine we get in this country, and there won't be much more of it today. If it doesn't bother you, it certainly doesn't me.' She pointed to a tray which held a jug and two glass tumblers. 'Have some iced lemonade. I'm expecting a friend, but I can soon get another glass.'

She reached over, took her bikini bottoms from the seat of the chair and placed it with the matching top on the arm.

Feeling distinctly over-dressed in his T-shirt and jeans, he crossed the lawn and sat in the chair beside her.

She lowered her sunglasses to the bridge of her nose, picked up the jug and poured lemonade into the tumblers. Replacing the jug, she took a tumbler and offered it to him. Reaching to take it, try as he might, he couldn't avoid stealing a glance at her breasts. They were beautiful: full and round, the light brown areolae surrounding her proud erect nipples.

'Are you here to investigate *me*, Mr Walker?'

He cursed himself inwardly, averted his eyes, and focused on the melting ice-cubes in the tumbler. He cleared his throat. 'Not at all.' *Doesn't bother me love; I see breasts like that every day!*

He took a sip from the glass and swallowed hard. 'I believe you knew Carol Tiltman; I'm told she was a member of your drama group.'

She straightened. 'Oh, it's about Carol! What a terrible, terrible, tragedy. It was such a shock to all of us. Poor George – what on earth could have possessed him to do such a thing?

I know one shouldn't speak ill of the dead, but it couldn't have been easy for him. I mean…Why not just leave her. People get divorced all the time.'

He took another sip of lemonade, his voice relaxed, as if the answer didn't matter. 'Why do you think it couldn't have been easy for him?'

She gave a hollow laugh. 'Oh, come on! They say prima donnas are never easy to live with. I guess they get addicted to centre-stage and can be quite demanding. But don't misunderstand me – Carol was a darling. We all loved her and miss her enormously - especially Jeremy, our producer.'

'You mean Jeremy Wadsworth?'

'Mm, yes; it really shook him.'

He looked at her face. 'I've always imagined a special kind of intimacy develops between members of a drama group; her death must be a great loss to all of you. How did Jeremy cope with it?'

She placed her hands behind her on the blanket and leaned back on her arms, pushing her legs out in front, slightly apart; she made no attempt to cover the curly black triangle of pubic hair. Shifting her weight onto one arm, with her free hand she took off her sunglasses and thought for a moment.

'I know it really shook him. He's said very little to any of us, I think he's internalised it. He used to be quite demonstrative with his hugs and kisses particularly with Carol, but since it happened, he's sort of withdrawn. He was always such a fun person to be with.'

He noticed there was less affectation in her voice and sensed something of the real Janice Austin was coming through.

'How about you, Janice? Were you close to Carol?'

She gave a slight frown. 'We used to be... Until I took over as secretary. She could be a bit bitchy sometimes. I think it was jealousy because I was seeing more of Jeremy than she did. It was stupid really. I mean, it wasn't as if he had the hots for her, or anything like that. In fact, he was embarrassed by the attention she was showing him.'

Russ heard the side gate open and close. Turning his head, he saw Jeremy Wadsworth, with a rolled up towel under his arm, walking towards them.

Janice looked up, a broad smile on her face. 'Jeremy, darling, come and meet Russ Walker. Would you believe, he's a private investigator?'

Wadsworth glowered. 'We've already met, Jan. I'll come back later.'

Standing up, Russ forced a smile, 'No, please, it's alright, I was just about to leave.' He turned to Janice Austin, 'It's been good to meet you. Thanks for the chat and the lemonade. I hope to see you again sometime.' He handed her his card, and made his exit.

Russ returned to his car and set off for his last visit of the day.

Chapter 9

Pulling into the drive at Whitegates, he found George Tiltman by the garage, washing the windscreen of his BMW. Russ switched off the ignition, grasped his document case from the passenger seat, and got out of the car. Tiltman was walking towards him, drying his hands on a duster. He greeted Russ warmly and led him into the house. As they entered the lounge, Tiltman offered him a drink. Russ asked for a beer and sat on the settee. Tiltman went to the kitchen and returned with an uncapped bottle of Heineken and a glass. As Russ filled his glass, Tiltman poured himself three fingers of Glenfiddich from a bottle already beside him on a small oval table.

Russ chose his words carefully. 'Mr Tiltman, I'll be perfectly frank: I'm now aware of the evidence the police have uncovered during their investigation into your wife's murder, and I have to agree it strongly points to you as the prime suspect. However... it hasn't convinced me. In fact, I believe you may well be innocent, and the murderer has yet to be caught.'

Tiltman covered his face with his hands and began to sob. He tried to speak, but could only shake his head. The floodgates were open; his shoulders shook as he continued to cry. He fought to compose himself.

'Thank God!' he said heavily. 'In all this time, you're the only person...They all believe I killed Carol. You're the only one who's said I might be innocent!'

Taking out his handkerchief, he dried his eyes. He picked up his whisky, took a large mouthful and swallowed with a gulp, wiping his lips with the back of his fingers. He looked pleadingly at Russ.

'Will you do it...? Please? Will you help me prove my innocence?'

Russ nodded. 'Yes, if that's what you really want, but you must understand, it will take time, and could be expensive. I think the only way to prove your innocence is to find the actual murderer, and that won't be easy. I don't have access to all the resources available to the police, but that doesn't mean it's impossible. There will be times when I have to pay for information and for extra help. And be sure you understand this - if I've got it wrong, and uncover proof that you did in fact murder your wife, it will be given to the police immediately.'

Tiltman made no attempt to hide his relief. 'Of course... But you won't... You can't... I didn't do it! Please find the killer. I can give you a cheque now...Is there anything I have to sign?'

From his document case, Russ produced a contract form and ran through the details. Tiltman was only too happy to add his signature. He insisted Russ accept a cheque for £8,000 as a down payment, explaining yet again that money wasn't a problem.

Russ slid the papers and cheque in his case. 'Mr Tiltman, you'll have to bear with me. I'll be pestering you quite a bit over the next few days; there are still a lot of questions I need to ask.'

'Of course, of course, any time. You have my landline and mobile numbers.'

*

Russ returned to the office and spent the next hour on his laptop updating the Tiltman file. He scanned a dozen copies of Hannah Drew's photograph, and decided to call it a day.

On his way home to the cottage, he called at Budgens, Rye's only supermarket, bought two fresh rainbow trout, the ingredients for a salad and a lemon brûlee.

On reaching Rye Harbour, he put the car in the garage, leaving the parking space free for Sue's Mazda. The cottage always felt welcoming; it was a good place to call home. Spreading the shopping on the worktop in the kitchen, he began to lay up two trays; they could relax with them on their laps in the lounge. To the accompaniment of an Everly Brothers CD, he donned an apron, and set about preparing the trout. With a sharp knife, he cut off the fins and the heads and slit along the backbones, carefully easing out the bones. He washed and dried the fillets, brushed them with oil and sprinkled lemon juice, salt and pepper over them; they were ready for grilling. The salad took less time to prepare, leaving him with at least an hour in which to shower and change before Sue was due to arrive.

He spent some time trying to decide what to wear. Limited for choice, he settled for the chinos, suede shoes and a dark blue shirt. He looked at himself in the full length mirror on the wardrobe door. At thirty-five, he was still in reasonable shape; six foot two, and his weight hadn't changed over the last five years – twelve and a half stone, thanks to the daily run and occasional work-outs' at the gym.

He poured himself a glass of white wine, switched on the TV and sat in the armchair to watch the news on Channel Four.

The doorbell rang. Russ got to his feet, switched off the TV and went to let her in. As he opened the door, the sight of her took his breath away. She was wearing a rust coloured two-piece skirt and waistcoat. The skirt was a three-quarter length with a slit up the front; her white blouse had a high collar, reminding him of a choirboy's ruff. The top three buttons were undone, revealing just enough cleavage to make his temperature rise. The waistcoat was secured at the front with a small gold coloured chain. Her auburn hair shone as it bounced on her shoulders; she wore just a light touch of make-up. His heart soared – what a sight!

He'd never seen her with a headband before. It was about two inches wide across the top of her forehead, disappearing at the sides beneath her hair. She had long, delicately ornate earrings that showed through her hair. Taking her through to the sitting room, he relieved her of the shoulder bag and placed it on a chair. Reaching for her hands, he took a half step back and looked her up and down.

'Sue, you look wonderful,' he said, and kissed her lightly on each cheek.

Slipping off her shoes, she made herself comfortable on the settee, curling her legs under her, while Russ went to the kitchen and put the trout under the grill, setting the timer for five minutes.

He came back into the room with two glasses of Chardonnay; he gave one to Sue and sat on the arm of the settee.

'Supper won't be long.' He raised his glass. 'Cheers,' and took a sip. 'So how are the sick and infirm at Rye Memorial?'

She laughed and briefly told how her afternoon had gone. Hearing the bell on the timer, he went back to the kitchen and turned the fillets, setting the timer for a further five minutes.

Having agreed not to talk shop until after they had eaten, they enjoyed a relaxed meal, comfortable in each other's company. Sue was complimentary about his cooking and its presentation, confessing that she'd expected a home-delivered pizza. He refilled both their glasses and took the trays to the kitchen to be dealt with later.

He came back into the lounge and she patted the cushion beside her. 'Come and sit with me; there's something I want to share with you.' He joined her on the settee, putting his wineglass on the coffee table.

There was excitement in her eyes. 'Russ, I've been turning something over in my mind, and I've come to a decision; I want to go back to Uni and work for an MA.'

He looked surprised. 'Hey, good for you, I think it's a great idea. But ...' he paused briefly, 'Does that mean you'll be going back to Nottingham?'

She shook her head and smiled. 'No, you're not getting rid of me that easily. I've been offered a place at Christchurch University College at Canterbury. It's a two year part-time course starting in September. As it's non-residential, it just means driving over to Canterbury for evening lectures once a week, and for occasional tutorials. Most of the coursework consists of essays and a dissertation.'

'I think you should go for it, Sue. But what about the finances? Can you afford it?'

She took a sip of her wine and placed the glass on the small table beside her. 'I think I might qualify for a grant to cover the fees, but if I don't it's not a problem; last year, my grandfather died and I inherited a sizable bequest. I was his only grandchild; we had a wonderful relationship.'

She shifted slightly as if preparing herself for what she was about to say. 'To give myself time to study, I'm going to have to give up one of my jobs.' His heart sank; he tried hard not to let it show. 'I've decided I want to give up physiotherapy for the time being, and carry on working for you.' He took a breath to respond but she held up her hand. 'Let me explain; I mean... If you continue to employ me for mornings only, what I'd really like to do is stay on for the afternoons too, but on a voluntary basis. We're hardly snowed under with work at the moment, and when it's quiet, I could study in the office just as easily as at home. Besides, wouldn't it be more business-like if you have a real person answering your phone instead of a machine? What do you think?'

He laughed, shaking his head in disbelief. 'You're amazing, Sue... I mean... That would be wonderful, if that's what you really want. For one awful minute, I thought you were going to quit Walker Investigations.'

'I couldn't do that,' she said. 'I love working with you.' She leant towards him and lightly kissed his cheek.

He went to kiss her cheek in response, but she turned her head and their lips met. It was light kiss at first, but as she didn't pull away, his lips remained on hers. She put her hand behind his head pulling his face into hers. She parted her lips, their tongues touching and exploring. He slid his hand under her waistcoat, cupping her breast; he could feel the firmness of her nipple. Her eyes were misty with pleasure.

It came as a surprise, that warm, curling sensation deep in his chest. It was something he hadn't felt in a long, long time, but he was too strongly, essentially masculine not to recognise it for what it was – desire. The primitive male in him was responding to a beautiful female, stirring that dormant need inside him.

She pulled back, took off her waistcoat and let it drop to the floor. A thread of guilt drifted through him; he sat back with a sigh. Becky would have wanted him to get on with his life. She wouldn't have wanted him to shut himself off from people the way he'd been doing. His self-imposed celibacy had closed him off from sharing such intimacy. He took her in his arms again; they kissed hungrily, his hand caressing her breasts. He groaned as his blood stirred hot in his veins. He felt himself harden behind the confines of his chinos, desire aching throughout his body.

As if sensing his inner turmoil, she tilted her head back and looked into his eyes. 'I know it's been a long time since... Well, you know. Just understand this - I'm happy for us to take it a day at a time without any pressure. Just know I'm here for you, Russ; we're both free spirits. Let's enjoy what we have with no strings attached.'

He held her tightly, his cheek against hers. 'Thank you, Sue.' He struggled to find the right words. 'You're unique, you know that? I'm so grateful to have found you.'

He released her, and they both sat back on the settee.

Russ gathered his thoughts. 'I promised I'd tell you about the Tiltman case, and the visits I made this afternoon.'

He laughed at her reaction as he described his encounter with Janice Austin. Other than making a grunting sound when he suggested he might take his own towel on his next visit, she listened intently to everything he said, which included the details of the missing young woman from Folkestone, but excluded his visit to the squat.

She became quite animated. 'Russ, I'm so glad you're going to help them; I mean, who else could they turn to? You know I'll do anything I can to support you... But it's scary, isn't it?'

They talked for a while until Sue decided she ought to go home. After a goodnight kiss, she set off for Winchelsea.

Russ picked up the phone and called Elmo, briefly explaining the situation at Folkestone. As he'd anticipated, Elmo was more than happy to go with him to the squat after closing time at The Rocks.

Chapter 10

It was nearing midnight when Russ and Elmo reached the seafront at Folkestone. Russ drove the Capri slowly past the squat, and left the car two hundred yards away in an empty public car park. Taking a torch from the glove compartment, he noticed Elmo take a wooden pencil from the breast-pocket of his shirt, and begin sharpening it. Russ shook his head in bewilderment.

'Are you planning on taking notes, or something?'

Elmo grinned as he held up the pencil and sharpener. 'I was never a Scout, but I like to be prepared.'

The seafront was deserted as they walked casually back towards the squat. From the service road at the rear, they entered the door of the second house. Inside, they stood quietly in the dark for a full two minutes. Russ gave Elmo the torch, and slowly led the way upstairs, using the light from his keyring. The stench was overwhelming as they reached the landing. Directing the beam from the torch onto his own hand, Russ pointed to the open door of the room that would give access to the squat. As he entered the room, from behind the door a hand reached out and lightly touched his right shoulder. The fractional moment of panic, if that was what it was, passed instantly as he turned and shone the light into Duke's face. Duke put his finger to his lips. Elmo, aware that something had happened, slipped past Russ to his left, and stood in the darkness, his back against the wall.

Illuminating his face, Russ mouthed to Elmo, 'It's okay, he's a friend.'

Duke made signs for them to go back to the landing. In a whisper, Russ introduced Elmo and Duke to each other. They bumped fists. With his fingers over the glass, Duke switched on his torch, allowing a narrow shaft of light through the fingers. He kept his voice low.

'I've had a look around. I reckon there are five or six blokes and two girls in the house next door - front room, downstairs. There's no-one upstairs. They're using hurricane lamps for light and from the smell, they're smoking joints.'

Duke shrugged a small rucksack off his back, and from it produced three ski-masks. 'It's better to remain anonymous and it'll scare the shit out of them.' He then pulled out latex gloves. 'If there's blood, we don't want to catch anything.'

After donning the masks and gloves, Duke led the way back into the room and through the hole into the end house. Russ followed with Elmo bringing up the rear. They moved slowly down the stairs along a hallway, until they reached the closed door to the front room. The three looked at each other and nodded. Elmo raised his right leg and kicked at the door beside the handle. It flew open and they rushed in.

Duke shouted, 'Nobody move!'

All the occupants were in a state of undress, either sitting or lying on sleeping bags scattered around the room. The air rich with body odour and cannabis. Two young girls and two youths were naked and having sex, while four other men wearing only boxer shorts looked on. One of the men, heavily built, with a short-cropped Mohican hairstyle, quickly slipped his hand under a pillow and stood up. He was about thirty, wearing off-white jockey shorts; he had a machete in his right hand. The letters D.I.Z. were crudely tattooed across his chest.

'Who the fuck are you? The fucking SAS?'

Russ, Duke and Elmo stood in the centre of the room with their backs to each other. The three other men jumped to their feet, holding smaller but equally menacing knives.

It all happened in a flash. Elmo was facing the man with the machete. He took a step towards him, and as the man raised his weapon to strike, in a flash, Elmo brought his shoe up between the man's legs, crushing his gonads. He gave an explosive grunt, dropped to his knees, sucking for air. The machete fell from his hand. As a follow up, Elmo smashed his knee into DIZ's nose, sending him backwards to the floor.

A short ginger-haired youth lunged with a kitchen knife at Russ's stomach. He sidestepped, grabbed ginger's wrist with his left hand, and slammed his right fist into the side of his jaw, felling him with the one blow.

Elmo turned to see the two other youths pointing their knives at Duke. He took the pencil from his shirt pocket, and stepped towards the nearest one.

'Hey, prat, you see this?'

Keeping the knife pointing at Duke, he turned his head. Elmo rammed the sharpened end up the young man's nose. He screamed, letting the knife fall to the floor as both hands tried to release Elmo's grip on the pencil. The more Elmo pushed, the higher on his toes he went, blood pouring from his nose. Elmo then downed him with a sucker punch.

Duke called out his thanks as the last man standing bent to pick up the knife his friend had dropped.

Calmly, Duke put his hand in his trouser pocket, and evenly said, 'I wouldn't bother, if I was you!' He pulled out a stun gun, 'Do you know what this is?'

He quickly dropped the knife.

The two youths had disentangled themselves from the girls and sat open mouthed, not daring to move. The girls huddled together, terrified.

From his rucksack, Duke produced a reel of duct tape. Handing the stun gun to Elmo, he helped Russ remove the men's underpants, sitting them in a cross-legged position with their arms folded. They were trussed up like frozen chickens with their mouths taped. The girls were told to get dressed before they questioned them.

They were local girls, one aged fourteen and the other fifteen. Both admitted knowing Hannah Drew but had no idea where she was. They hadn't seen her for a couple of weeks.

Sitting them at a distance from the men they turned their attention to the now fully-conscious DIZ. Russ pulled the tape from his mouth, expecting a torrent of expletives, but he remained silent.

He squatted in front of him. 'Okay, DIZ, it's time to talk. What's your real name?'

DIZ ignored him.

Duke came over and sat on his haunches. 'Listen to me, dickhead. Every time you refuse to answer, or give a wrong answer, I'm going to break one of your toes – understand?'

Taking hold of the left foot, Duke gripped the smallest toe, and began to bend it upwards. 'I didn't hear you answer me.'

DIZ closed his eyes, and said, 'Yes'

Russ nodded. 'That's better. Now, tell me your name; the one your mother gave you.'

'Shane Disby.'

'Right, Shane. Where can I find Hannah Drew?'

DIZ remained silent; Duke applied pressure to the toe.

'I don't know! I think she's in London.'

Duke bent the toe upwards until there was a crack; DIZ screamed.

'She's working at a club in Limehouse.'

Russ continued. 'Okay, so what's the name of this club?'

'I dunno; just some club.'

Duke broke the second toe.

Diz tried to stifle another scream. 'It's called The Bijou, on Hamilton Road.'

'How did Hannah know about this club?' Russ asked.

'How the fuck should I know?'

Duke took hold of the smallest toe on the other foot.

DIZ panicked. 'All right! All right! She was looking for a job in London and I told her about the club; my brother runs it.'

Russ raised his eyebrows and looked at Duke. He nodded in acknowledgement. This was bad news. The Bijou was one of three clubs in Limehouse that the Serious Crimes Unit had under surveillance. They were believed to be owned by none other than Marcus Provone, the half-Italian, half-English mobster and leading figure in the London underworld. Russ and Duke had spent many an hour investigating the activities of Provone.

Russ stared at DIZ. 'What's your brother's name?'

'Vince Disby.'

'So where's Hannah sleeping? I want the address.'

The pain was excruciating. 'I don't know the number. It's a big house in Redmond Square; I've only been there once. Got a blue front door; a lot of Vince's girls live there.'

Russ put the tape back over his mouth and turned to the girls. 'We're not going to hurt you, but we're going to have to take you into the hallway and tie you to the banister rail. It won't be for long; the police will be here in a few minutes.'

Russ, Duke and Elmo went back upstairs and made their way out through the hole in the wall. Before leaving the building, Duke put the ski-masks and gloves into the rucksack.

Elmo handed him the stun gun. 'Where the hell did you get this?'

As he packed it away, Duke smiled. 'You don't want to know. Let's go!'

Russ tried to persuade Duke to stay the night at Rye Harbour, but he insisted he had to get back to London. They returned to the Capri, and after dropping Duke off at his own car, Russ found a public call-box and made an anonymous call to Folkestone Police Station directing them to the squat, where drugs and under-age sex were taking place, and they would find Shane Disby, aka DIZ.

As they left Folkestone on the A259, Elmo was animated. 'Hell, I haven't had so much fun in years; and your mate Duke – he's something else! But listen, Russ, if you'd been on your own, it would have been goodbye!'

'Elmo, trust me, I wouldn't have gone on my own; but thanks, you were great. I liked the action with the pencil.'

Elmo laughed. 'Believe it or not, I caught an Argie in a fox-hole a mile from Port Stanley and walked him back to HQ on the end of a pencil. But hey, tell me about Duke; what is he, SAS or MI5?'

He listened intently as Russ entrusted him with a condensed account of their time together in the Met, coloured with a few anecdotes. By the time they reached Rye Harbour, Elmo had learnt a lot about Becky too. The Rocks was in darkness; Amy and her sister had gone to bed. After a couple of beers, Russ decided to head back to Fisherman's Cottage.

Elmo was still fired up. 'We made a great team tonight; don't forget, any time you need back-up, just give me a shout.'

'Thanks, Elmo. I appreciate it.'

At eight thirty the next morning, Russ pulled into the office parking space next to a black Lexus. The driver, wearing a chauffeur's uniform, put down the newspaper he'd been reading and got out of the car. He had a carrier bag in his hand.

Russ locked the Capri and approached him. 'Good morning – can I help you?'

'Good morning, Mr Walker. I've been instructed to deliver this package to you before your secretary arrives.' He handed the carrier bag to Russ. 'Have a good day sir.'

Non-plussed, Russ took the bag; its weight surprised him. 'How do you know who I am?'

'It's all right sir, I know who you are,' he repeated. 'Have a good day.'

With that, he got back into the Lexus, fired the engine and drove off.

He let himself into the office. Sue wasn't due in for another half hour. From the bag he pulled out a cardboard box sealed with tape. He was about to open it when the phone rang. He looked at the display - the caller's number was withheld.

'Good morning, Walker Investigations, how may I help you?'

He recognised the voice of the man he'd met at The Savoy.

'Good morning, Derrida; I take it you've received my package and are alone in the office?'

'Yes, I am; I was just about to open it.'

'Ah, good. Be assured this is a secure line, but we must remain on our guard. It was good to meet with you last Monday and that you were able to accept our offer. For your information, the financial arrangements are now in place, and the first assignment concerns your nemesis, M.P. His considerable network is in dire need of deconstruction and we would expect, within the next two months, to see signs that you are making inroads to this effect. I don't have to remind you it will be dangerous work – you must therefore take all possible precautions. There may well be occasions when you need assistance; we have no objections should you wish to recruit the services of your friend and former colleague. However, under no circumstances must he or anyone else become privy to our arrangements. In the package you have received, you will see the enclosed tool is similar to the one used in your previous existence and is untraceable. It is to be used sparingly and only when absolutely necessary. Goodbye, and good luck.' The line was disconnected.

Russ replaced the receiver, the adrenaline coursing through his body. Inside the box wrapped in brown grease-proof paper was a Glock 17 pistol, an attachable silencer, two spare magazines, shoulder holster and two boxes of 9mm ammunition. Hearing Sue's Mazda pulling into the parking space, he quickly put everything back into the carrier bag and locked them in the bottom drawer of the filing cabinet.

As Sue entered the office, she looked at the CD player but made no attempt to silence Roy Orbison. Grinning like the proverbial cat, she gave him a peck on the cheek.

'Morning, Boss! Hey, you're looking flushed – you okay?'

He smiled. 'Morning, Sue. Yes, fine. Probably over did it with the rouge.'

The phone rang – it was Duke. 'Hey, super sleuth, how's tricks?'

'Hey Duke, I'm fine. Thanks for last night. Can I phone you back about that? By the way, Sue's here, looking as lovely as ever.'

'Lucky you! Hey, give her my love and if you dare... Tell her I've found out what's worse than a male chauvinist pig. It's a woman who just won't do as she's told! I'll catch up with you later. Ciao!' He rang off.

He stole a glance at Sue as he put the Tiltman file into his document case; she was staring at him with a quizzical look.

'So what was all that about? I mean, about last night!'

He nonchalantly shook his head and checked his watch. 'Oh, nothing much. Look, I'm a bit pushed for time; I think I'll skip coffee. I'll tell you about it when I get back from Tilling. See you later.'

As he drove, he considered the issues he needed to address. The police had found no evidence to suggest Carol Tiltman was having an affair, and yet she had told Jenny Pierce that her husband was boring and there was no romance in their marriage. Janice Austin seemed to suggest Carol had, or would like to have had, a relationship with Jeremy Wadsworth; was that why he'd refused to speak to him? He wondered if he was known to the police - if he had any form. He pictured Wadsworth with the towel under his arm, and the iced lemonade that was waiting for him. If he strips off with Janice Austin, did he do it with Carol too?

There was no mention in the file about telephone calls. Did Carol receive or make a call on the day of her murder? He knew the detectives would have checked the records of the house phone and her mobile, if she had one. He wondered about Tiltman himself...Was he involved with someone else?

He pulled out his mobile and dialled Tiltman's home number, but disconnected when an answering machine kicked in. He tried Tiltman's mobile; another answering machine. He left a message to say he would be calling at Whitegates during the latter part of the morning.

Chapter 11

Twenty minutes later, as he drove through Tilling, he noticed a café with empty tables outside. He left the Capri in a parking space in front of the parish church and walked back in search of a coffee and doughnut. There was just one customer inside, an elderly man reading a newspaper at a table by the window. The two middle-aged women behind the counter seemed delighted to have another customer and vied with each other for the opportunity to serve him. A compromise was found - one took his order and the other his payment. In unison, they asked him to take a seat and said his order would be brought to him. He sat at a table outside, enjoying his newly found celebrity status when one brought his coffee and the other a doughnut on a plate.

After they'd left him, he took out his mobile and called the garage. A woman answered in a monotone voice, 'Good morning, Tilling Motors, Rachel speaking, how may I help you?'

He asked if he could speak to Jeremy Wadsworth. She told him Mr Wadsworth wasn't available, but he could speak to the foreman.

Explaining that it was a personal matter, he asked how he might contact Wadsworth.

She enquired who was calling. When he gave his name, she was quick to reply, 'Mr Wadsworth has left instructions that he doesn't wish to speak to you. Goodbye.' The line went dead.

He dialled the number for Tilling's Mini-Market. Again, a woman answered with the same response. 'Mr Wadsworth has left instructions that he doesn't wish to speak to you.'

He finished his coffee, put the remnant of the doughnut into his mouth, wiping the sugar and jam from his fingers with the serviette. As if from nowhere, the two counter assistants appeared, one each side of him; one took the cup and saucer and the other the plate. He wondered how they would deal with the 25 pence he'd left for a tip.

Four doors along from the café was the video and DVD rental shop. A bell rang as he entered the shop. A young man wearing jeans and a navy sweatshirt pushed his way through a curtained doorway and stood behind the counter.

Russ gave him a cheery smile, 'Hi, nice morning! Is Jerry about?'

The youth smiled back. 'I'm afraid not. Can I take a message?'

Russ picked up a DVD case from the counter, casually looked at it and put it down again. 'No, it's okay. I've got something he's been waiting for.' He looked at his watch. 'If I get time, I'll try and catch up with him later.'

There was concern on the young man's face. 'Well, if it's important, you can leave it with me. I'll make sure he gets it.'

Russ winked and dropped his voice. 'It's... kind of personal. Don't worry about it; it might piss him off, but he'll just have to wait.'

Following suit, the youth lowered his voice. 'If he asks, who shall I say called in? Are you a friend of his?'

'Oh you can tell him Rob dropped by. Jerry and I go back a long way.' *At least twenty four hours!*

He looked relieved. 'Well in that case, he's up at Broadmead; said he'd be at home all morning.'

Russ thanked him and left the shop, sidestepping two youngsters barging their way in.

On his way back to the car, he met an elderly couple, holding hands, for love or mutual support, walking towards him. He asked if they knew of a house in the village called Broadmead. He waited patiently while they argued and contradicted each other, until eventually they agreed it was the house with a lych-gate at the end of Common Lane.

It was a ten-minute walk to the attractive double-fronted detached house, roofed and part-walled with Kent peg tiles, built probably at the turn of the last century. There was a neatly-mown lawn in front and a gravel drive to the right leading to a garage. He couldn't tell if Wadsworth was aware of his arrival, as there were net curtains at all the windows. Keeping to the edge of the lawn to soften his footsteps, he reached the front door. Placing his finger over the spy-hole, he rang the bell.

Wadsworth opened the door; a cordless phone to his ear. He switched it off, glowering at Russ.

'That was my assistant at the shop, Walker. Get off my property, you're trespassing.'

Russ quickly stepped onto the threshold. 'You're a difficult man to have a conversation with, Wadsworth, but now that I'm here, perhaps we could have a little chat?'

Wadsworth held his ground, 'You slimy bastard, I've got nothing to say to you. Get out of my house, or I'll call the police!' His finger hovered over the keypad of the phone.

Russ smiled and kept his voice even. 'Now, that would be interesting, wouldn't it? After all, the police and I are working to the same end, but I'm not sure they are aware of the games you played with Carol Tiltman.'

His fingers were white as they gripped the phone. 'Fuck off! You're talking shit!'

Hmm, touched a nerve there. With both hands, he pushed Wadsworth in the chest, catching him by surprise. He stumbled backwards trying to keep his balance, but failed, falling unceremoniously onto his backside.

Russ stepped into the hallway and closed the front door. 'Get up, Wadsworth – we have things to talk about.'

He struggled to his feet, the phone still on the parquet floor. 'You bastard!'

He threw a right punch, aiming for Russ's solar plexus. *Not very bright!* Russ quickly sidestepped, grabbed the arm, bending it at right-angles. He then levered the fist down at the wrist and applied pressure. Wadsworth screamed in pain as Russ tucked the elbow into his own side just above the hip joint, keeping tension on the wrist. Wadsworth was completely immobilised, and in agony. At each attempt to free his arm, Russ simply pressed down on the wrist.

'Stay cool, Wadsworth. With one little push, I could break this.'

Keeping the pressure on, he waited for Wadsworth to quieten down. 'Let's talk about Carol, shall we? You can begin by telling me how long you'd been screwing her!'

Wadsworth ignored the question until Russ applied more pressure. He gasped.

'You're breaking my fucking wrist!'

Russ kept up the pressure.

'Okay, okay! So we had something going for a couple of years; so what? For God's sake, let go!'

Russ had total control. 'Not yet, Wadsworth; tell me about this something, as you call it.'

'It wasn't serious – just a bit of mutual fun.'

'So where did this bit of fun take place?'

Wadsworth was in agony, convinced his wrist was about to snap. 'Sometimes here, and sometimes at her place. Look... I didn't force her into anything... She made it clear she was up for it. Her old man wasn't interested, and I gave her what she needed.'

Russ laughed. 'How very philanthropic.' His expression changed. 'So, what happened then; did it all get out of hand? Did you lose your control, or was she begging for more?'

Wadsworth quickly responded. 'For God's sake, man, don't be ridiculous. I didn't kill her – it was her old man. The last time we had sex was two weeks before she died.'

Russ exerted more pressure, causing Wadsworth to scream in pain. 'I swear to you I didn't do it; why would I?'

'You were both into kinky sex, weren't you? And we all know that can be dangerous.'

There were beads of perspiration on Wadsworth's forehead and top lip. '*She* was, you mean. She used to say she fancied being tied up, and liked it in the arse. The bondage thing never appealed to me...We never did it...Just the arse bit sometimes.'

'Who else was she having sex with?'

'How the hell would I know? She didn't tell me.'

Russ applied more pressure. 'Think again, pal. That's not the answer I'm looking for.'

His voice went up an octave. 'I really don't know. She once said she'd met someone who was into S & B, but I don't know who he is, or if they ever got it together.'

Russ smiled gently. 'Well done, Wadsworth, you're doing better now. How long ago did she mention this someone? I want his name.'

'I've told you, I don't know shit. She never said; it was about a month before she died, I guess.'

He let go of Wadsworth's arm. 'I might want to talk to you again, but let's make it easier next time.'

Leaving him trying to rub life back into his wrist, Russ let himself out.

Back on the High Street, business was brisk in the cafe. Through the window, he counted seven senior citizens with their coffees or Complan. One of the assistants noticed him and nudged the other with her elbow; they both smiled and waved. He waved back.

He set off in the direction of Beech Lodge. After their brief conversation yesterday, he felt sure Jenny Pierce was Carol's confidante. What she knew could be vital to the investigation. He rang the bell and the young Asian opened the door. He asked if he might have a word with Jenny the Matron, and was invited in.

Jenny Pierce was in her office and greeted him warmly. Offering him a seat, she closed the door.

'I'm sorry about yesterday. Wednesdays are always hectic, and we were a member of staff short. Thankfully it's much quieter today.'

He gave her an engaging smile. 'Not at all; I was grateful for the time you gave me. There was just one little thing I wanted to ask – I hope you don't mind. You said you and Carol were close friends. I guess that means she felt able to confide in you.'

Jenny crossed her legs and leant forward. 'Bless her; we all need someone we can talk to, don't we? I was glad to be there for her.'

'Did she ever talk to you about Jeremy Wadsworth?'

She paused. 'Well, yes; but I.... I don't think I want to talk about that. I mean.... She trusted me.'

He smiled again, and lowered his voice. 'It's all right, I understand. But of course she's at peace now, and nothing you tell me can hurt or embarrass her, and it could help to tie up a few loose ends.'

She seemed to relax. 'Well, she did tell me about their relationship. I could never understand what she saw in him; she was infatuated. I told her everyone in the village knew he was a womaniser, but she wouldn't believe it. She thought she was the only one he was seeing. It went on for several years, you know... Her husband never knew.'

He nodded. 'Poor Carol. I can't imagine what she saw in him either. If she needed some excitement or romance, surely she could have done better than with him. Did she ever mention going with anyone else?'

She shook her head. 'Not really. I remember her saying she'd met someone she liked, but she didn't elaborate. She could have been seeing him regularly, but I don't think so; I'm sure she would have told me.'

'Can you remember how long ago it was that she mentioned it?'

She closed her eyes for a moment. 'I'm trying to think.' She opened them, nodding her head. 'Oh yes! It was Bonfire Night. We'd been to the Scout's firework display at the playing field, and called in for a drink at The Bell before going home. It was a bitterly cold night. On the way to the pub, I said something like, "I need warming up. I wouldn't say no to a cuddle under the duvet with Piers Brosnan!"' She coloured up and shrugged. 'It was silly girls' talk. We were laughing, and Carol said she'd met someone recently who could warm her up. I egged her on, trying to find out who it was.' She paused, as if lost in thought. A sad smile crossed her face. 'She wouldn't tell me. I think we'd arrived at the pub by then, and nothing more was said about it.'

He knew this was significant and pressed her gently. 'You'd said the name Piers Brosnan; did she give the name of the person she'd met?'

She hesitated. 'I don't think so ... no, wait a minute ... I'd said Brosnan, and she said... I think it was a short name that also began with a B.'

He prompted her. 'Ben? Brian? Barry...?'

She shook her head. 'No, it was shorter... Like... Bo! That was it! Bo! It made me laugh; I said it didn't sound very macho.' She screwed up her face. 'You know, I'd forgotten that. For a day or two afterwards, it was like a private joke. If

I saw her alone in here or the kitchen, I'd pop my head round the door and say "Bo!" and we'd laugh.'

He grinned as if in collusion. 'I'm glad she had you for a friend. Did she ever indicate if Bo was local, or say how they met?'

She was serious again. 'No – she never mentioned him again. I do miss her, you know.' She paused, her eyes filled with tears. 'I know it doesn't sound like it, but she wasn't really promiscuous. She just wanted to be loved.'

Russ sighed. 'Don't we all?'

She pulled a tissue from a box and wiped her eyes. 'It's been good to talk. I haven't shared any of this with anyone else; I mean, I couldn't, could I?'

He conceded this with a slight nod of the head. 'Jenny, I'm really grateful. I wished I'd known her.'

He got to his feet and held out his hand. 'I'd better let you get on with your work. Thanks again for seeing me.'

Dolefully, he made his way back to the car. He checked his watch and decided to skip his other intended calls and drove to Tiltman's house in Passmore Lane.

He was shown into the sitting room, and declined the offer of a drink, taking the chair opposite Tiltman, who had already poured himself a whisky.

He leaned forward, pulled his notebook from his back trouser pocket and opened it. Softly, he said, 'Mr Tiltman, there are one or two things I need your help with. Some of my questions may seem intrusive and extremely personal but they can't be avoided, I'm afraid.'

Tiltman was composed. 'It's alright, Walker, just ask away.'

'I need to know about the physical side of your marriage. How often did you and Carol make love, and would you say it was satisfying for both of you?'

For a fraction of a second, he didn't react to the question, as if his attention had wandered and he hadn't heard it. But then he answered firmly. 'To be truthful, over the last two or three years we hardly ever had intercourse. It wasn't like that in the beginning, and especially when we were trying for a baby. Carol always had a higher sex drive than me; but don't get me wrong, we both enjoyed it, and there was nothing wrong with our marriage.'

He expected Tiltman to object to the next question. 'But what happened? Why did it become so infrequent?'

If he was uncomfortable, he didn't show it. 'I'm not sure really. I think we were getting so engrossed in our respective interests – Carol with her drama, and other organisations, and me with Rotary, Chamber of Commerce...and all that; we began to see less and less of each other. We didn't often go to bed at the same time; the love-making sort of petered out.'

Russ maintained eye contact. 'Forgive me, but I have to ask. You said Carol had a higher sex drive than you. Did she like to experiment with alternative ways of love-making...? Bondage or dressing up – that sort of thing?'

He took a large sip of whisky. 'We never really talked about things like that. I think we were too embarrassed. Sometime last year we'd watched a programme on Channel Four about fetishes and what turned people on. Afterwards, Carol said *we* ought to be more adventurous, but I thought she was joking.'

Russ looked at his notes. 'I understand the police found a packet of condoms in your bedside cabinet, and one was missing. Why did you use them if Carol couldn't conceive?'

'The police asked me that. I don't think they believed me, but I told them the truth - Carol had bought them. She wanted me to try anal sex but I didn't want to, at least, not without wearing something. We only did it the once.'

Russ changed tack. 'I believe you know Jeremy Wadsworth. How do you get on with him?'

He frowned. 'I've never liked him. He's a local businessman; fancies himself as a budding Richard Branson. Carol had more to do with him than me – he runs the drama club she belonged to. Used to come here sometimes to see her about whatever production they were working on, but I kept out of the way.'

'Did Carol like him?'

'Oh, yes. She thought he was the best producer they'd had.'

Insouciantly, he said. 'Someone mentioned the name Bo to me yesterday. Does that mean anything to you?'

He shook his head. 'Bo? No, I don't think so. Should it?'

'Not particularly, I just wondered. Now, there's something else I need to know, and whatever you may or may not have told the police, I need a truthful answer. Are you, or have you been, having an affair with anyone else?'

Tiltman looked pained. 'No – I swear to God! I won't deny I've been tempted, and apart from a one-off visit to a massage parlour in Southampton about three years ago, I've never been unfaithful to Carol.'

Russ pocketed his notebook. 'While I'm here, would you mind if I take a look in your garage, and at Carol's car? Oh, and another thing – do you have a copy of your telephone bills for last year, including Carol's mobile, if she had one?'

'Yes, of course.' He stood up. 'The police took copies of them too – the house phone, that is. Carol's mobile was a pay-as-you-talk, so there aren't any bills for that.' He made for the door. 'I'll unlock the car and garage and leave you to it while I photocopy the bills.'

Outside Tiltman opened the garage door, giving Russ the keys to Carol's car.

The garage was relatively tidy, with the exception of several piles of newspapers at the far end, some of which had collapsed and spread across the floor. They were mainly copies of *The Independent*, the *Rye Observer*, and local free newspapers. There were also two large cardboard boxes full of empty bottles.

Tiltman nodded towards them. 'Ignore the mess. Carol wouldn't have liked that. Every Saturday, without fail, she would take the papers and bottles to the recycling bins at the library car park. It was almost an obsession.'

He left Russ and went back into the house.

He found nothing of significance in the garage or Carol's Mini Cooper. She'd kept it spotless; not even a sweet-paper in the ashtrays, let alone on the floor. Apart from an AA Road Atlas on the back seat, the car was empty. In the glove compartment, he found the car maintenance manual, a torch, a purse with five £1 coins, a folded free newspaper dated the 15th of October, and a small packet of tissues.

He locked the car, closed the garage door and returned to the house. He handed the keys to Tiltman and, in exchange, received copies of the phone bills, plus Carol's mobile phone. He asked Tiltman if he could borrow the phone and charger, promising to return them in a day or two. He had no objections.

Assuring Tiltman that he'd be in touch, Russ left Whitegates and headed back to Rye.

Chapter 12

He bought a Cornish pasty from Patsy's and took it up to his office. Sue had gone, leaving several letters for Russ to sign and post. He made a cafetiere of coffee. Holding the pasty in a serviette, he stood at the window overlooking the High Street; he ate as he people-watched. The day before, there had been yet another article in *The Times* about the problems of obesity, suggesting England was top of the European league for the highest number of overweight people. It seemed a high percentage of them were visiting Rye.

Something caught his attention in his peripheral vision. The natural blonde was back at The George. She had drawn the net curtain aside, giving him an unobstructed view of her assets. He turned away, sorry to disappoint her, but there was work to be done.

He sat at his desk and attempted to switch on Carol's mobile. As expected, the battery was flat. Connecting the charger, he tried again; it came to life. He went into 'Menu' and scrolled down the list of names and numbers she had entered into its phonebook. There were thirty-two in all, with obvious ones like her husband's office and mobile, the dentist, library, doctor, garage, agency, Beech Lodge, and various businesses; the others were mostly first names of people. Jeremy was listed, but there was no record of a Bo. He checked the list of calls received. There were none for the 22nd of December, the day she was murdered. Of the five that were listed, two were from Tiltman, two from Jeremy and one from Beech Lodge. All had been received several days before her death. He checked for missed calls, but there were none. In the list showing the last five dialled calls she had made, the last was to Tiltman's work's number on the 21st the next, to the hairdresser on the 20th, and the Agency on the 19th. She had called Tiltman's mobile that same day, and Jeremy on the 18th. There were no records of text messages sent or received.

Hearing the doorbell, he pressed the buttons for the intercom and release catch simultaneously and said, 'Walker Investigations, please come in.'

DI Baillie entered the office.

Russ got to his feet, and moved round the desk. 'Morning Inspector. I've just made coffee, would you like a cup?'

Baillie nodded. 'Black, please, no sugar; and it's Alex, by the way.'

Without waiting to be asked, he sat on one of the upholstered chairs.

Russ pushed down the plunger, filled two mugs, placed them on the coffee table and sat opposite him.

Baillie took a sip of coffee. 'I was wondering – what were you doing last night?'

Russ feigned a puzzled expression. 'Last night? I was at home; Sue and I had supper together. Why do you ask?'

Baillie's face darkened momentarily. 'To say there was a bit of trouble at Folkestone last night would be something of an understatement. You see, there's some dispute as to whether the SAS were involved, or well-intentioned vigilantes. After a tip-off from an anonymous phone call, Folkestone CID found six unsavoury characters trussed up like chickens in a squat down at the seafront. Apparently, three masked guys scared the shit out of them; they were relieved to be taken to the nick and are now singing their hearts out. The DCI thinks it's Christmas – you've no idea how many crimes they're going to clear up as a result. There are several warrants outstanding for one of them; including one for armed robbery. Two young girls were with them, they are now in a place of safety.' He paused and looked directly at Russ. 'Ring any bells?'

Russ shrugged his shoulders. 'Sorry, Alex, but I have no idea what you're talking about.'

Baillie raised his eyebrows, and smirked. 'No, I guessed as much; but that's not my problem – Kent will have to sort that one.'

He took several more sips of coffee and placed the mug on the table. 'Okay,' he said, 'I was in court yesterday and bumped into Peter Lant; he tells me you've been hired by George Tiltman. Is that right?'

Russ felt uncomfortable. He didn't want Baillie to think he'd betrayed his confidence. 'Look, Alex, I couldn't believe it; he just turned up out of the blue. He'd seen my advert in the local paper. I didn't let on I'd already spoken to you.'

Baillie gave a slight nod of his head. 'Go on.'

'He told me about his wife's murder, and that he's the chief suspect, and that you're trying to pin Elaine Knightley's death on him too. He's desperate and wants me to help him prove his innocence. I'll level with you. I've interviewed him several times and I've been nosing around the village, talking to a number of people. I've spoken to Lant, of course. I can't dispute that everything seems to point to Tiltman as the perp, but my gut instinct is that he didn't kill her. As far as I know, you haven't released details of how Carol Tiltman was killed, which means Elaine's murder can't be a copy-cat, and there's one hell of a sick bastard still out there who thinks he's unstoppable.'

Baillie nodded in agreement. 'That's my gut feeling too... But unless we get a breakthrough, we're nowhere near collaring him.' He got to his feet. 'I must go; but if you uncover anything that could help our investigations... Just so we understand each other... I'll expect your full cooperation. Keep me in the picture, will you?' As a rider, he added, 'Oh, and if I were you, I'd stay away from Folkestone for the time being.'

Russ stood up and held out his hand. 'You can trust me, Alex; I'm not working against you. Good luck with the investigations.'

They shook hands and Baillie left.

Russ made himself another coffee, and rang Tiltman's home, but an answering machine cut in. He began to leave a message: 'Mr Tiltman, it's Russ Walker. I've just spoken to DI Baillie. Could you give me a...'

Tiltman picked up the phone and interrupted. 'Yes, I'm here. What did that incompetent excuse for a detective say about me?' He was hyperventilating.

'Hey, calm down! You know as well I do, they had to take you in. I would have done the same. But listen to me. They're not really looking at you anymore; they've got a full scale investigation on the go for what looks like a serial killer. I just want to check where that leaves *us*... I mean, you don't really need me now.'

He jumped in quickly. 'Oh, yes I do! If it's the same pervert that killed Carol, they won't find any evidence at Rye Harbour either. I'll always be a suspect until you find him.' He pleaded. 'You will do it, won't you?'

'Okay. I just wanted to check that's what you really want. If you're sure, then I'll see it through.'

Tiltman assured him that it was, and ended the conversation.

Russ rang Duke to thank him for his help the previous evening, and told him about Baillie's visit.

Duke was amused to hear of the outcome. 'Fun, wasn't it? If that jerk DIZ lives long enough to settle down and have children, I wonder if they'll ever play 'This Little Piggy Went to Market'?' Hey, I'm impressed with your friend Elmo – I'm glad he was on *our* side! The pencil trick was a new one on me... Something else for the rucksack.' His tone changed to one of anxiety. 'Russ, tell me I heard it wrong? Diz has a brother, Vince, running the Bijou?'

Russ reached for the framed photograph of Becky he kept on his desk; he took a deep breath. 'That's what he said,

Duke, and that makes Vince Disby a puppet of none other than...'

Duke cut in. 'Yeah, Provone! And that means your runaway is in serious trouble. Tell you what – I'll go and have a sniff at the house in Redmond Square at Limehouse, and I'll see what I can find out about Vince Disby. I assume you'll be coming up to London; the guest room's ready whenever you want it. Mean-while, I'll try and find out what Hannah Drew has got herself involved with.'

'Thanks, Duke, I appreciate it. I'll be up tomorrow if that's okay?'

'No problem; but what about the Tiltman case? If he's out of the frame, does he still want you to find the perp?'

Russ repositioned the photograph. 'Yes, I've just spoken to him. He doesn't have much confidence in the local plod.'

Duke snorted. 'Not surprised, poor sod. So what are we going to do?'

Russ was taken aback. 'What do you mean, *we*?'

'Look, I've a smart little guy called Glen who's helping to run the shop. He's perfectly able to look after things here for a while. How about I join you in Rye on Sunday evening, and stay for a day or two – sort of like a working holiday? To be honest, I miss the action. Be an opportunity to give the T-Bob a good run.'

Although he had a Scoda Fabia for day to day use, Duke had a passion for classic motorbikes. His latest acquisition was a 1500cc Ducati, designed and built by Roger Allmond, one of the country's top designers. It was the envy of his fellow enthusiasts in the biking fraternity.

'Cheers, Duke, I could sure use some help.'

'Ciao, see you later.'

Russ took the Tiltman file from the cabinet, spread the photos of Carol across the desk and began to scrutinise them. He concentrated first on the background details; there was no sign of disorder to suggest a struggle had taken place. On the bedside cabinet, the lamp, clock and box of tissues appeared to be undisturbed. Her clothes had been neatly folded and placed on an upright chair. Again, he studied the victim. The lack of defensive injuries suggested her possible compliance in being undressed and bound spread-eagled. If the perp had threatened violence to gain her cooperation, he would have needed both hands to tie the knots, offering an opportunity for some resistance, and yet it seemed there was none. Traces of condom lubricant had been found in the anus. It seemed unlikely that a perp with an average-sized penis would have positioned the victim on her back for anal penetration; again, this suggested she may have been a willing participant and had agreed to a more appropriate position prior to being tied to the bed. Her body had been covered with baby oil, but why? Although some might use oil to heighten stimulation, he guessed its main purpose was to prevent leaving flakes of dry skin that could provide DNA evidence. But why no trace of body hair other than the victim's? Maybe the perp had shaved his head and body? It appeared nothing had been left to chance. Thankfully there had been no mutilation, but had he taken a trophy, as is often the case in sexually motivated crimes – underwear, a photograph or video?

Russ was encouraged by the plethora of evidence, but deeply troubled too. Something began to gnaw at him – a doubt; a doubt that Carol Tiltman was the perp's first victim.

He thought of the adage "practice makes perfect," yet this was almost *too* perfect; *too* well planned and executed for there not to have been an earlier victim. Maybe a killing, less well thought out, that whet his appetite; that set him on the road to serial murders. He added these observations to his notes.

As he returned the file to the cabinet, his thoughts turned to Elaine Knightley's murder. He wondered if the SOCOs had found any additional clues that might give a lead to Baillie's team. Baillie had mentioned Elaine's sister was Catherine Forbes; he'd said 'she only lived round the corner in Anchor Square'. A search in the telephone directory showed only one Forbes for Anchor Square, a W. Forbes at number 5.

After stopping for petrol at a BP garage on the Winchelsea Road, Russ drove back to Rye Harbour.

It wasn't so much a square but horseshoe shaped. The houses were brick-built, semi-detached, probably from around the 1950s; from their design, Russ guessed they were former Council-owned houses. A light blue Vauxhall estate was parked outside number 5.

He rang the bell. The door was opened by a round-faced woman with sticking plaster covering her nose. She was wearing jeans, a pale blue blouse and sandals. Her hair and build matched that of Elaine. From the puffiness around her eyes, he could see she had been crying.

Russ offered his card. 'Mrs Forbes, I'm so sorry about Elaine's tragic death. My name is Russ Walker; I'm a private investigator. I realise this is a very difficult time for you, but I wonder if you could spare me just a few minutes of your time?'

She looked at the card with puzzlement. 'I've been with the police all morning... Why do *you* want... ?' Then the penny dropped. 'Oh, forgive me; I've been told it was you and a friend who looked after me on Monday night, until the ambulance took me to hospital. Thank you.'

He smiled sympathetically. 'You had us worried.' He touched his own nose. 'Sorry about your nose; I guess it's pretty painful.'

'I never much liked the shape of it anyway, perhaps this'll improve it.' She stepped back. 'Please come in.'

He was led into a front room which was obviously used as a small study, cluttered with books, papers and magazines. She invited him to sit in an upholstered winged back chair, while she took a wooden upright chair in front of a gate-legged table which doubled as an office desk. He glanced at the bookshelves which covered two of the walls from floor to ceiling; in the main, they were books on Theology and Philosophy, with one section devoted almost entirely to John and Charles Wesley, and the Evangelical Revival.

'I hope you won't think me rude, Mrs Forbes, but is your husband a Methodist Minister?'

She forced a smile. 'No, he works for the Inland Revenue; I'm the Minister at Rye Methodist Church.'

'Was Elaine a member of your church?'

She frowned. 'Please, everyone calls me Catherine. No. She found faith a bit of a struggle. She was a Christian when she went up to university to read Theology, but came back an agnostic with an Honours degree. What about you, Mr Walker? Are you a Christian?'

It was a question he'd not anticipated. 'Erm, yes, I'm a struggling Anglican. I'm okay with God – it's the Church I have problems with, I'm afraid.'

She smiled. 'I guess we're all struggling these days.' The smile disappeared. 'The police told me you went into the house after me and found Elaine. I still can't believe it's happened.'

'I don't know how much the police have told you, but it appears Elaine may not have been the first victim of whoever killed her. Six months ago, another woman was murdered in almost identical circumstances. I've been hired by her husband and, like the police, I'm trying to find the person responsible.'

She nodded her head, pulled a tissue from the cuff of her blouse, and wiped her nose and eyes.

He took out his notebook. 'I understand Elaine was supposed to have been babysitting for you Monday evening.'

'Yes, that's right. It was nothing important; we were only going out for a drink. Elaine had offered to look after our toddlers for a couple of hours.'

'I know she was single, but was she in a relationship with anyone? Did she have boyfriends?'

Catherine carefully blew her nose. 'None that I know of. She used to be friendly with another teacher at the school - they'd go out together sometimes, but nothing serious. He moved away about two years ago – to Devon I think. She was a bit of a lonely soul really – it used to worry me. Although we were twins, and quite close, she was fiercely independent, and would resent any interference from me. My husband and I had tried to do a bit of matchmaking in the past, but nothing ever came of it; she really wasn't all that bothered about finding a partner.'

The front doorbell rang. Catherine excused herself and went to answer it. Russ could hear the conversation; it was a church member calling to offer support. He decided it was time to leave.

She returned with an elderly woman. Russ stood up and shook Catherine's hand. 'Thank you so much for seeing me, Catherine. Maybe I could call again when it's more convenient? I'll be holding you and Elaine in my prayers.'

She thanked him and showed him out.

Chapter 13

It was six thirty on Friday morning and the sea mist hung like fog as he ran through the Nature Reserve to Winchelsea Beach and back. Before going in for a shower, he leaned on the harbour wall. It was almost high tide; the water, calm as a mill-pond, looked cold and black. From the direction of the open sea, came the deep chugging of a diesel engine and the cry of gulls. He turned to the sound as the ghostly outline of two fishing boats began to materialise through the wall of mist and made their way into the harbour. He watched as the fishermen in their yellow waterproofs tied up at the moorings, and began to unload their catch. He had no doubt these were hardworking, law-abiding men, but it occurred to him how relatively easy it would be to smuggle people or drugs into the country through little harbours like this.

After a shower and breakfast, he packed a hold-all and was in the office by eight thirty. The light was flashing on the answer-phone, the LED indicating there were four calls. He pressed play, but no-one had left a message. He made a cafetiere of coffee and, giving it time to brew, stood at the window overlooking the High Street. There'd be no entertainment this morning; the curtains were still drawn across at The George. He sat down at the desk, reached for the player and pressed 'Play'. Encouraged by Cliff Richard urging him to "Move It", he made a start on the crossword.

Chuck Berry was well into "Johnny B. Goode" when Sue arrived and switched him off. 'What in heaven's name was that? Don't you ever listen to real music? We'll have a bit of culture next week – I'll bring some of my classical CDs.'

'If it's culture you want, you should have waited. His next song would have been *Roll Over Beethoven?*'

She shook her head. 'I'm beginning to worry about you!'

For the first half of the morning, he caught up with overdue correspondence. He rang Wendy Drew at the nursery school to give her a progress report. He told her he had an address in London where Hannah was believed to be staying, and he hoped to make contact with her over the weekend. He could hear the relief in her voice as she thanked him.

Sue left at midday for a dental appointment, and Russ decided to have an early lunch. He locked up and walked along the High Street to The Mariners, which had become his favourite restaurant in Rye. It was run by a registered charity providing employment to people with learning disabilities. A delightful young waitress with Down's syndrome handed him the menu and stood, patiently waiting for his order. He decided on cheese omelette, French fries, and a black coffee. Sylvia, the manageress, was teaching a young man to work the till. She looked up and gave Russ a wave.

He drove to The Stade and parked by the harbour wall. There was an ache in the pit of his stomach, a churning of emotions inside. He felt sadness and anger for what Carol and

Elaine had been subjected to, compassion and sympathy for their loved ones, and a deep rage was building against the perpetrator. He needed to take a long walk before setting off for London.

It was almost four when he turned off the East India Dock Road and parked outside the church in Newby Place. He walked to a florist's on Poplar High Street, bought a spray of freesias and another of lilies of the valley and made his way back to All Saints. Beside the west door was an area designated a Garden of Remembrance, where Becky's ashes had been interred. Placing the sprays next to her memorial stone, he stood for a while. He read the inscription: 'Rebecca Jane Saunders, aged 30, precious daughter of Clara and John and beloved fiancée of Russ. Taken from us 20th August 2011, now safe in God's keeping'.

He sat on the wooden bench that had been placed in front of the fifteen or so graves. Oblivious to the thunderous roar of traffic on the East India Dock Road, images of Becky filled his mind. They were on holiday in Majorca – she was splashing him in the hotel swimming pool – so vibrant, so happy. He saw her dancing, giggling as she attempted the actions to "The Birdie Song", and then the homemaker, wearing an apron in his kitchen. Their last Christmas together in the bedroom, so thrilled at the negligee he'd given her. *Darling Becky, I love you and miss you so much.* The clock in the tower chimed the half hour; he lifted his wrist to check his watch, but couldn't read the numbers. He wiped the tears from his eyes with the back of his hand – it was four thirty; he had plenty of time. His eyes were back on the stone – 'Rebecca Jane Saunders....beloved fiancée'. He closed his eyes and could see her again. They had just made love; he was on his back, and she, lying on her side, snuggled up under his arm, her head on the side of his chest, her leg pulled up across his. As she played with the hair on his chest, quietly and seriously she had said, "If anything should ever happen to me, I wouldn't want you to be lonely. I would hope you might meet someone else you could love, and be happy with."

He remembered chiding her, "Don't say things like that – there could never be anyone else."

But she had insisted, "Promise me, you'll remember I've said this."

He'd said, "Okay, I promise, but the same applies to you, if anything happens to me." He made her promise too.

The tears were flowing; he *had* forgotten – until that moment. He sat for another ten minutes, and went into the church and lit a candle.

It was the beginning of the rush hour, and it took almost as long to get to Duke's place on Shooters Hill as it had to come up to London from Rye. He left the Capri in the customer car park, and stood outside the shop. It was single-fronted with the entrance door to the right. In the widow was a display of electronic gadgetry, from security lighting to surveillance equipment. The sign above the shop read Windsor's Emporium. On the door was a notice that gave the opening hours – Mon to Sat, 11am to 8pm. A bell rang as he entered, and a small, thin man in his early fifties appeared from behind the counter. He had weasel-like features, with short curly ginger hair. He wore blue jeans and a short-sleeved navy shirt with 'Windsor's Emporium' embroidered on the breast pocket.

Russ offered his hand. 'Hi, I'm Russ, a friend of Duke's.'

He shook the hand firmly. 'Hi, I'm Glen; come through to the back. Duke's out on a job, shouldn't be too long. He was talking about going to the Lions game tomorrow. I think he's going to ask if you want to go. I told him not to bother – they're crap! If they lose, and they probably will, they're gonna be relegated.'

Glen led him into a room that doubled as a workshop and storeroom. 'I was just about to make a coffee; fancy one?'

'Please. So how did you come to meet Duke?'

Glen picked up a jar of instant coffee from the table. Opening it, he put generous spoonfuls in two mugs. 'Oh, I've known him for years. I got into a bit of bother once – well, a long time ago now; could've gone down for it. Duke helped me sort it out – even got me and the missus back together. I made a new start after that and never looked back. He phoned and asked if I was interested in working with him here. I live locally, but was working for an electronics firm at St John's Wood; I was fed up with the travelling so I jumped at it – I mean, working with Duke, and I can be home in five minutes. I've never had it so good!'

They had been chatting for about half an hour when Duke returned to the shop. 'Hey Russ, good to see you. How's tricks?'

They shook hands. 'Good to see you too, Duke. Sue sends her love. Pretty impressive set up you've got here.'

Duke grinned. 'Not bad, is it?' He nodded at Glen. 'Shame about the staff, but beggars can't be choosers.'

Glen shook his head. 'Ignore him. He knows I'm the only poor sod he could find who's thick-skinned enough to put up with him.'

After a few minutes of friendly banter, Duke took Russ upstairs to the flat. Russ dropped his holdall in the guest bedroom, made a quick trip to the bathroom, and joined Duke in the lounge.

Duke looked uneasy as he passed a can of beer to him. 'I'm worried about your runaway... She's in it up to her neck!'

This was definitely bad news, but not unexpected.

'Oh hell! That's what I've been afraid of. What's the score?'

Duke took a slug of beer and wiped his mouth with the back of his hand. 'She's definitely at the house in Redmond Square, number 30 – so are several other girls. I made a phoney ID card and called on one or two of the neighbours; told them I was from the Highways Department, reassessing the parking restrictions in the Square. I asked about their own parking requirements and then got them talking about the other houses. Most of them claimed they didn't know anything about number 30, although I did find an elderly couple who are convinced it's a brothel – but it has to be more than that.'

Russ frowned. 'What do you mean?'

'Last night I did a stake out! They don't have clients go to the house... The girls are picked up by a driver and driven away. Sometime later, they're brought back by the same bloke. I saw the girls go out and come back several times; one of them was definitely Hannah Drew. The Gothic look was gone. She was dressed like a tart and crying, but it was definitely her.'

'So they're being taken to punters by a minder, and obviously they're not happy about it!'

'That's right. They don't even walk to the car on their own; the minder holds their arm till they're in the car or back in the house. The other girls look even younger than Hannah. I had the feeling they're not English.'

Russ felt a knot in his stomach. 'Is it always the same minder?'

Duke shook his head. 'No, there are two. One is white, about twenty-five, clean shaven, looks like a body-builder, but not very tall – five eight, I guess. He's an ugly looking sod, wearing jeans, a red sweatshirt and a black baseball cap, drives a black Mercedes. The other is black, with short hair, a bit older – thirty-ish. He's well built, and wears a light-coloured suit. He's got a little tuft of hair under his lower lip. He drives a black 4x4. I doubt they've got keys to the house, 'cos they always ring the bell when they pick up the girls or drop them off. I did a check with the DVLA on their licence plates; both vehicles are owned by a property developer called Joseph Prior, whose address, believe it or not, is The Bijou, Hamilton Road, Limehouse.'

Young girls smuggled into Britain for prostitution, especially from former Eastern Bloc countries, is an extremely lucrative business; wealthy clients pay well for perverted sex with them. During Russ and Duke's time in the SCU, they had achieved only limited success; a number of girls had been rescued through raids on premises, and several arrests were made, but at least two large syndicates were still believed to be operating in the capital.

Russ took a sip of his beer. 'Any idea who looks after the girls in the house?'

Duke's shook his head. 'None at all. I had a look around, but I don't think there's any way of gaining access to the rear of the houses on that side of the Square; although they do back onto the properties in Millais Road - might be worth having a look from there. What do you reckon?'

Russ rubbed his chin with the palm of his hand. 'Part of me thinks we should hand this lot over to the SCU, but if they raid the place, there's no guarantee Hannah Drew will be there – she could be out with a punter, and that would put her in even more danger.' He kept his eyes on Duke. 'What are your plans for tonight?'

He smiled. 'Not a lot. I had thought we might go up to the West End for a bit of excitement.... Or, there again, we might just bust that place and get Hannah and the others out of there. What do you think?'

He grinned. 'Thanks, Duke, I like it.'

Glen was sent out for three portions of cod and chips, while Duke packed his small rucksack, and made two phone calls. The first was to a friend called Don Platten, asking for the loan of his empty white transit van, and the second to Captain Elsie Flack, the warden of a Salvation Army refuge for battered women, at Shoreditch. He'd known Elsie for many years, a plump sixty-year-old matriarchal woman with a heart of gold. She had lovingly cared for a number of vulnerable women he'd taken to her during his time in the police service. She was one of the few he had written to when he'd resigned, and she'd made no secret of her deep disappointment when she wrote back, begging him to reconsider.

Duke and Russ ate their meal upstairs as they watched the news on CNN. Over coffee they made their plans. Duke drew a sketch of Redmond Square and explained that it had a one-way clockwise traffic system, around a fenced off square of grass, in the centre of which was a thicket of shrubs and trees. This would mean having to travel three-quarters of the way round before reaching number 30.

They were both experiencing a rush of adrenaline as they discussed various options for getting into the house. Making plans and preparation – it felt good, just like the old days.

As the excitement grew, Duke flippantly said, 'I've got it! If we wear suits, we could knock on the door and pretend we're Mormons.'

'That wouldn't work – we don't look young enough, and your beer belly would give us away!'

'Okay, so how about this?'

Duke outlined a straightforward way of getting to the driver of one of the cars before he arrived at the house, and for Russ to exchange places with him. They went over the details several times, making contingency plans should anything go wrong.

It was just before ten when Duke, wearing his small rucksack, drove the transit van into Redmond Square, with Russ in the passenger seat beside him. Although it was dark, the Square was reasonably well lit by street lamps at the four corners. The parking bays reserved for permit-holders were full. Duke parked on yellow lines across the Square opposite number 30, which was obscured by bushes and trees in the centre. Releasing the catch, he jumped out and raised the bonnet before getting back in the van. He and Russ wore thin leather gloves and baseball caps over ski-masks rolled up to their foreheads. They had a clear view of the entrance to the Square, the wait seemed interminable. There were two or three false alarms when smaller cars turned into the Square, the drivers looking for parking spaces – before driving out again.

Eventually, a black Mercedes pulled into the square.

Duke said, 'Bingo! Here we go!'

He started the engine, pulled out a couple of yards from the kerb and switched it off, blocking the road. They jumped out and with their heads under the bonnet, unrolled the ski masks. As he approached, the driver of the Mercedes impatiently gave two blasts on the horn. Keeping his head under the bonnet, Duke raised his arm and gave him two fingers.

The driver got out of the car and walked aggressively towards Duke. 'Hey dickhead, you're in my way. Move it!'

As Duke turned to face him, the driver stiffened at the sight of the mask. He noticed the barrel of a handgun poking from beneath an oily rag in Duke's hand. Before he could react, Duke pushed it into the man's chest.

'Take it nice and easy, pal. Don't say another word or you'll be breathing through your nipple. Put your hands together on your chest, linking your fingers, as if you're saying your prayers.'

He did as he was told as Russ came up from behind and searched him. He found a Smith and Wesson revolver tucked in the waist band of his jeans in the small of his back.

Duke pushed harder with his Magnum. 'Right, I want you in the back of the van, now!'

Russ opened the back door and Duke followed the man inside. It took less than thirty seconds for him to be cuffed with nylon loops and his mouth covered with tape. Russ heard a loud thump followed by a groan.

As he climbed out, Duke grinned. 'He's having a little sleep.'

They rolled up the ski-masks. Duke lowered the bonnet and moved the van back onto the yellow lines. Russ slipped into the driving seat of the black Mercedes, drove round the Square and pulled up outside number 30. Keeping his head down, with the peak of the cap obscuring his face, he walked to the front door. By the time he rang the bell, Duke was in position, their ski- masks rolled down again. As the door began to open, Russ gave it a hard kick and rushed in, closely followed by Duke. The door had smashed the nose of the dark-skinned young man now lying in the hallway. He was in his late teens, with thick, greasy hair combed straight back.

Closing the door with his foot, Russ pointed the borrowed revolver at the man's crotch. 'Don't move an inch, or I'll separate you from your trinket set.'

He looked terrified. 'Please, you no shoot! I no trouble!'

Duke pushed past Russ and went into a room to the left; it was an office. A hard-looking woman with a short black ponytail was sitting at the desk, about to make a phone call. Reaching across, Duke pulled the 44 Magnum pistol from his waistband and held it to her face, as he gently took the phone from her hand and replaced it in its cradle.

She started to mouth obscenities, but he pushed the snub nose into her mouth. 'I don't like shooting women, but if I have to, I will. Don't say another word.'

He saw her right hand move to open the top drawer of the desk and quickly brought the gun down, breaking her fingers. She was certainly a tough one; her face was screwed in agony, but she didn't cry out. In an instant, he was round the desk, holding the woman in an arm lock. With his free hand, he removed a Beretta 92 pistol from the top drawer.

It took only a few moments for the young man and the woman to be secured with nylon cuffs and their mouths taped. Sitting them on the floor, with their backs to each other, from his rucksack Duke produced a length of nylon cord and bound them tightly together.

Before leaving the office, he disconnected the telephone.

A search of the ground floor revealed two empty en-suite bedrooms, a lounge, and a kitchen. On the first floor, with the exception of the bathroom and a separate toilet, all the rooms were locked. Returning to the office, Russ picked up a bunch of keys that were lying on the desk. In the first bedroom, they found two terrified young girls huddled together on a double bed, their faces heavily made up and wearing cheap seductive clothing. The window had been boarded up, and apart from the bed and a set of drawers, there was no other furniture. In the corner was a plastic bucket covered with a tea-towel.

Russ sat on the end of the bed. 'It's alright; you don't have to be afraid – we're not going to hurt you.'

One of the girls started to cry, and the other said something in a foreign language.

He tried again. 'Do you speak English?'

It was obvious neither of them did. He stood up and made signs for them to follow, as he and Duke went out to the landing. Unlocking another bedroom, they found two more young foreign girls in an equally disgusting room. The first two ran in and hugged them. That was when they heard the doorbell.

Duke held up the palms of both hands towards the girls and touched his lips, indicating they were to be quiet; one of them nodded.

He and Russ went down to the hallway. The bell rang again and, as Russ slowly inched open the door, the black man began to push his way in. From behind the door, Duke pushed his gun into the side of the man's head. 'Come on in; it's party time.'

They pulled him into the hallway and closed the door. Duke held the gun to the man's head while Russ searched him and relieved the man of his gun from a shoulder holster. He too was placed on the floor in the office, his feet and hands were bound, and his mouth was covered with tape. Duke secured him to a radiator.

They returned to the girls who were still in the second bedroom, frightened and confused. Leaving them together, they went to the third bedroom, where they found Hannah Drew, alone and crying. She screamed when she saw the ski-masks.

From the doorway, Russ quickly tried to reassure her. 'Hannah, it's okay. We're not going to hurt you - we're friends. We're going to get you out of here. Get your belongings together, it's time to go.'

She didn't move. 'Are you the police?'

'No, but we're working with them. Come on, we have to go.'

Duke helped her put some clothes into a black plastic bag. Back on the landing, he unlocked the last bedroom – it was unoccupied. Clearly the room was used for storage. Hannah Drew saw her suitcase and retrieved it.

The girls were led downstairs and made to wait in the hallway. Russ went back to the office. He picked up all the papers he could find, plus a laptop computer and left, closing the door behind him. Russ removed his mask, while Duke rolled his up to his forehead. Duke left the house and ran back to the van, and swore; it had only been illegally parked for fifteen minutes and had been clamped!

He ran back to number 30 to find two men getting out of a pick-up, about to clamp the Mercedes and the 4x4. It took a lot of persuasion and a generous tip for them to change their minds, but the van stayed clamped; they didn't carry a release key.

They waited for the men in the pick-up to leave. Duke locked the house and took the foreign girls with him in the Mercedes, while Hannah Drew travelled with Russ in the 4x4. They drove in convoy along Commercial Road to Shoreditch; Hannah Drew was clearly in shock, and remained silent throughout the fifteen minute journey.

The Women's Refuge was an anonymous three-storey building in Hanbury Street on the corner with Brick Lane. Russ stayed in the car with Hannah, while Duke placed the four girls into the care of Captain Elsie Flack. It was agreed Elsie would notify the police in the morning about the four young girls who had been mysteriously placed in her care by a stranger the night before.

Returning to the car, Duke pulled out his mobile and phoned his sister Liz. As expected, she was more than happy to look after Hannah Drew for the night.

It was agreed that Russ would take Hannah to Walthamstow and leave her with Liz, while Duke returned to Redmond Square to deal with the man they'd left in the van.

Traffic was light on the Bethnal Green Road. Russ glanced in the rear-view mirror and saw Hannah's empty eyes looking back at him. He smiled.

'Hannah, you're safe now; it's all over. I'm taking you to a friend's house... Just for tonight.'

She stared blankly at him.

'Her name's Liz; you'll like her. She'll take good care of you. Tomorrow, we'll take you back home to Folkestone.'

She started to cry; quietly at first, then the floodgates burst and she sobbed uncontrollably.

Cutting across Cambridge Heath Road, he kept to the side roads as he made for Stratford and Leytonstone.

She spoke in a timid voice. 'Who are you?'

He looked into the mirror. 'My name is Russ. I know your mum. She's been so worried about you.'

She leaned forward and grabbed hold of the back of his seat. 'Please don't take me back to Folkestone. I can't go back. They've got friends in Folkestone.... They said if I ran away, they'd get me... and hurt my mum.'

'Listen, Hannah. DIZ and his friends are no longer there. They've been arrested by the police; you won't be seeing them again. You can forget them.'

She was astonished. 'How do you know about DIZ?'

'It's a long story, Hannah. You'll just have to trust me.'

He pulled up outside a modest semi-detached house in Peake Drive. He turned in his seat and smiled. 'Hey, we're here. Liz and Geoff will look after you; they're good people.'

By the time Russ left, Hannah had taken a long hot bath and was wrapped in a towelling bathrobe, sitting at the kitchen table eating a makeshift meal of beans on toast.

Russ set off for Poplar and the Blackwall Tunnel. Through the tunnel he cut across to Lewisham and parked in the High Street. In the glove compartment, he found an envelope containing £5,000, presumably punters' money, which he slid into his pocket. He opened the window of the driver's door, and left the ignition key in the lock before walking to Lewisham Centre, where he picked up a cab.

Chapter 14

Redmond Square was deserted when Duke pulled up behind the transit van. With the ski-mask in place, it took less than a minute to transfer the now conscious young man from the van to face down on the floor in the rear of the Mercedes. He rolled up the mask, locked the van, and pocketed the cellophane envelope that had been left under the wiper by the clampers. He drove round the Square and out onto White Horse Road. Once through the Blackwall Tunnel, he picked up the A206 to Woolwich. Within ten minutes, he was parked in a dark, secluded cul-de-sac on an industrial estate close to the river.

With his face covered again, he switched on the interior light and searched the car. It was empty, with the exception of a wallet containing over £3,000 in the glove compartment. He slipped the wallet into his rucksack and turned his attention to the young man on the floor behind him. He got out and opened the rear door. Leaning in, he began by removing the man's shoes and socks, and then the tape covering his mouth. He was a tough nut to crack. He had to break three toes on each foot before he had the answers to all his questions.

Back in the driving seat, he removed the mask, before slipping back onto the A2. He left the locked Mercedes and its reluctant passenger by the wrought iron gates at the entrance to the Maritime Museum at Greenwich, and walked a mile into Kidbrooke before calling for a taxi on his mobile phone.

It was a few minutes after midnight when Russ let himself into Duke's flat. He took a cold beer from the fridge in the kitchen, took it through to the lounge and switched on the television. It was a novelty being able to surf the satellite channels, but the events of the last two hours had left him too wound up to concentrate, and he switched it off. He went to the window and drew back the curtains. Watching the traffic on Shooters Hill, he wondered what Duke would do with the man in the van. Ten minutes later, a taxi pulled up; he was relieved to see Duke alight and pay the driver.

He came into the lounge. 'Hey Russ, how's that poor kid?'

'Thanks for tonight, Duke. Thank God she's safe now, but she'll need some help coping with all of this. The sooner she's back with her parents, the better I'll feel.'

Duke went to the kitchen and returned with two cans of beer. He tossed one to Russ. 'Have a refill.'

He caught and opened it. 'Cheers. So, what happened with the guy in the van?'

Duke took a slug from his can. 'His name's Wayne Glassman, and he's lying on the floor in the back of the Merc, outside the main entrance to the Maritime Museum. Apart from his toes, I didn't really hurt him.'

Russ frowned.

Duke threw up his hands in resignation. 'Hey, don't go soft on me Russ - they're scum! You know what he told me? They've got at least four houses in London that he knows of, where, in all, they're holding about twenty-five kids! And that's what these girls are – just kids!

'Of course I do, but...'

Duke cut in. 'But nothing! Do you think he was happy to give me the addresses? Do you think he would have told me who's paying him, and who's behind this filthy business? He got off lightly, because I wanted to break his bloody neck!'

'Hey, okay! So what did he tell you?'

Duke was ebullient. 'There's a house in Bermondsey, one in Peckham and the other in Camberwell. He claims that Vince Disby supervises the overall running of these, and the one we've just busted. It's well organised. There's a flat in Harbinger Road which they use as an office. A bloke called Smithy is in charge of it, and he's the one who takes the bookings from punters. His assistant is a woman called Shani – she contacts the houses and tells the bastards looking after the girls which one to have ready, and when. She then contacts the minders and gives them instructions on which house to pick up from, and where to take the girls.'

Russ crossed his legs and balanced his beer on his knee. 'Did he know who's bringing the girls into the country?'

Duke shook his shaven head. 'He has no idea. He's just a small tiddler in a big pond. I did get a few names and addresses of punters he takes the girls to; and, listen to this - one of the addresses is a warehouse, where he's taken two girls on different occasions but never picked them up again.'

Russ stood up and walked to the window. 'Dear God! Got to be Snuff videos! We have to give all this to the SCU.' He sat down again. 'They'll bust the three other houses and get the girls out, and they might be lucky with forensics at the warehouse, but I doubt they'll find much evidence to link any of this to Vince Disby.'

He nodded in agreement. 'I'll put it all down on paper. Obviously there'll be no mention of Hannah Drew or of our involvement, but I'll make sure they get all the details – including the whereabouts of Wayne with the sore toes. When they go to Redmond Square, my guess is they'll think we're a rival gang trying to put a competitor out of business.'

'But what about the van? We'll have to move that first.'

Duke foraged in his rucksack and pulled out the leaflet left by the clampers. 'No problem! Tomorrow morning, I'll give this to Glen; he can sort it. Once the van's released, he can drop my letter off for the SCU at Millwall nick.'

'That's good; remind him to wear gloves – we don't want his prints on the envelope.'

Russ stifled a yawn, and stood up. 'I think I'll turn in. I'm going to have to give the game a miss tomorrow – sorry, but I want to get young Hannah down to Folkestone as soon as I can.'

Duke pushed himself out of his chair, walked across to his computer and switched it on. 'Of course; I'll ask Glen if his eldest lad would like to come. I'll phone Liz and Geoff and suggest they bring Hannah here in the morning, about eleven – that okay? We can have coffee together before you leave.'

He shook Duke's hand. 'That's great. Thanks again.'

Russ woke to the welcome smell of fried bacon, and the sound of Duke moving about in the kitchen. He'd slept fitfully; images of what those young girls had been subjected to plagued his dreams. He threw back the duvet and placed his feet on the carpet. He sat for a moment on the side of the bed and thought about Hannah. He knew she would need professional counselling to help get over her ordeal, and hopefully return to school.

Duke tapped on the door and opened it. 'Morning Russ, It's just after nine, bathroom's all yours; breakfast will be ready in fifteen minutes.'

After ablutions, he joined Duke at the breakfast table and looked at his plate in astonishment. 'Just think what this is going to do to my cholesterol level. How often do you have this kind of breakfast?'

'Only at the weekends. Are you trying to tell me I won't be getting this at Rye Harbour next week?'

'Sorry, mate, it'll just be cereal and a slice of toast.'

Duke held a piece of fried bread on the end of his fork, and pointed it at Russ. 'You're getting soft, you know that?' He popped the fried bread into his mouth. 'Glen's collected the van and dropped the envelope for the SCU. He's on his way back, as I speak!'

Russ was relieved. 'That's brill! Hey, look what I found in the car before I dumped it.' He took an unsealed envelope from his pocket and placed it in the table.

Duke reached for his rucksack, took out a wallet and laid it beside the envelope. 'Snap! The punters pay well, don't they? How about I parcel them up and send it to Elsie Flack as an anonymous donation for the wonderful work she does?'

Russ was in total agreement.

While Duke went downstairs to open the shop, Russ cleared away the breakfast things and packed his holdall.

It was just after eleven when Glen returned with the van and took over minding the shop. Two minutes later, Liz and Geoff arrived with a subdued Hannah carrying her suitcase. They went up to the flat; Russ was in the kitchen making coffee. Liz carried the tray of cups into the lounge where they sat and made small talk until Duke joined them.

Soon it was time to leave; as Russ picked up Hannah's suitcase, Liz turned and held out her hands to say goodbye to her. Hannah stood up and threw her arms round Liz and held her tightly.

Quietly, she murmured, 'Thank you.'

Russ caught Duke's eye and signalled with a nod of his head towards the kitchen. Duke followed him in.

He gave Duke a slip of paper. 'This is Hannah's home telephone number. Would you give her parents a ring and tell them we're on our way home? You might warn them to go easy on her. If there's a problem, or you can't get hold of them, call me on my mobile.'

He slipped the note into his pocket. 'Fine. I'll see you Sunday evening at the cottage.'

They shook hands and joined the others in the lounge.

Having said their goodbyes, Russ and Hannah went downstairs and out to the Capri. With her suitcase in the boot, Hannah sat in the front passenger seat. They drove in silence as Russ took the A207 and turned onto the A2 heading toward the M25.

Russ took a breath to say something when Hannah spoke. 'They were really kind to me.'

'Who do you mean, Hannah?'

She turned her head; there were tears on her cheeks. 'Liz and Geoff. They didn't tell me off or anything; they treated me like I was their daughter.'

He smiled. 'I knew they would – they're good people.'

She was still looking at him. 'How do you know DIZ, and how did you know where to find me?'

He told her he was a private investigator and had been hired by her mum to find her. He gave an abridged account of his meeting with DIZ at the squat, and of how he'd forced the address out of him.

'He's a nasty piece of work, Hannah, and so are his friends, but you won't be seeing them again – they're all in police custody.' He paused and then continued. 'Hannah, I need to know what happened to you - all of it!'

She shifted nervously in her seat. 'We had another row at home and I left. I wanted to go to London, and DIZ told me his brother Vince would look after me. He said he would give me a job as a barmaid or waitress at his club and find me somewhere to live. I thought that would be brilliant – give me a chance to sort out what I really wanted to do with my life.'

He wanted to keep her talking. 'But it wasn't like that, was it?'

'No. Vince gave me a lot of money and told me to go up to the West End with another girl, get my hair done and buy clothes and make up. He let me sleep in a spare room in the flat above the club. In the evenings I had to put on my new clothes and make-up and go down to the club, collect the glasses and do the washing up.'

'For how long were you doing this?'

'About a week. But then he turned nasty. He said I owed him a lot of money - for the clothes he'd bought, my food and the rent for my room. He said I owed him a thousand pounds, and I'd have to pay it back.' She began to cry. 'I didn't have any money, I couldn't pay it back. He said if I didn't pay, he'd hurt me, and get DIZ to do the same to my mum; and if I ran away or went to the police, they'd still do it to my mum. I didn't know what to do.'

It was a variation on a theme he'd heard many times in the past.

'So he decided to be kind and offered you a way of paying it back?'

'Yes. He said I'd have to earn the money by having sex with men, but it wouldn't be for long. That's when they took me to the house where you found me.'

'How long had you been at the house?'

She lowered her voice. 'Not long - only a few days, but it was terrible! It was like a prison. I wasn't allowed out of my room – only when they took me to have sex with someone. A horrible woman at the house brought food to my room and would take me to the bathroom and watch while I had a shower or went to the toilet. I knew there were other girls there, but I didn't see them until you and your friend came.'

'Hannah, I have to ask you this; did you have unprotected sex with any of the men?'

'Yes, but it's alright, I've been on the pill for about a year.'

He was surprised at her naivety. It hadn't occurred to her that she'd been exposed to the danger of sexually transmitted diseases, let alone HIV.

'Did any of the men hurt you?'

'Yes.' The tears began to flow again. 'They were all older men, and made me do horrible, disgusting things. They made me bleed sometimes.'

The poor girl had experienced a living nightmare. It would take a long time for her to heal, not just physically, but mentally and emotionally.

They were on the M20, approaching the Maidstone Service Station and Russ suggested they stop for a drink and a doughnut.

Hannah asked for a Diet Coke, but he needed a coffee. While she went to find the toilet, he bought the drinks and doughnuts and carried them to an empty table outside in the smoking area. She joined him at the table as he took out his cigarettes.

'Sorry, I can't offer you one; you're not old enough.'

She smiled. 'No thanks, I don't smoke. I don't have any...' She blushed, and covered her mouth with her hand.

He winked at her. 'Vices? You most certainly don't! Come on; let me see you eat that doughnut without licking your lips.'

It was just before two when they arrived at Hannah's home. She looked apprehensive as she released the seatbelt and got out of the car. She waited as Russ took her case from the boot, and together they walked towards the house. The front door opened, and Wendy and Brian Drew rushed to greet Hannah. For a few moments, the three of them huddled together in a tearful embrace.

Russ ushered them into the house and closed the door. Wendy took Hannah upstairs, while Russ explained to her father the situation she'd been in, suggesting Hannah should see her doctor for a medical examination and tests. It was clear to Russ that although deeply distressed, Brian Drew was a sensible man who loved his daughter and was desperate to do the right thing.

He waited for Hannah and her mother to join them in the lounge before taking his leave and setting off for Rye Harbour.

Stopping for petrol and to buy a newspaper, Russ eventually arrived at Fisherman's Cottage at a quarter to four. It had been a warm, sultry day when he'd left London, but now the sky was overcast as if a storm threatened.

He checked the phone for any messages. There was just one; Sue inviting him for supper on his return from London. He phoned her back, accepting gratefully.

Sue lived five miles from Rye in the neighbouring town of Winchelsea. Her two-bedroomed flat was on the ground floor of a purpose built block of six, situated in a side road, off Church Square, with a parking area at the front. She greeted Russ at the door, wearing a floral patterned wrap-around silk blouse, and below her bare midriff, beige coloured cotton leggings. She wore heeled sandals that exposed her painted toenails.

'Hi, Russ, your timing's perfect; I'm just about ready to dish up. Help yourself to a drink.'

She knew Coq au Vin was a particular favourite of his, and had casseroled the chicken with red wine and mushrooms and served it with gratin dauphinois and a tossed green salad. She opened a bottle of Merlot. As they ate and drank, Russ told her Hannah was safe and reunited with her parents. He gave her an edited account of Hannah's rescue.

Sue was clearly shocked. She dropped her cutlery, reached across the table, grabbing his hand. 'Russ, you could have been killed! Thank God you had Duke with you. But what about the police? What if they find out it was you?'

He grinned. 'There's no way they can connect us to it. They'll think it was a rival organisation trying to put Vince Disby out of business.'

Sue had been experimenting and made her first crème caramel. It looked delicious, and tasted even better. After they'd eaten, he offered to wash the dishes, but she insisted they simply pile everything up in the kitchen, and close the door. Refilling their glasses, they settled down on the settee. Sue snuggled up to him.

'Duke's coming down tomorrow evening to help with the Tiltman investigation. He'll stay at the cottage for a few days. So... from Monday morning, we'll be a team!' he said.

Sue turned her face and put her lips to his. He could taste the wine on her soft tongue as she gently pushed it into his mouth. He felt himself hardening; he wanted her so much. Slipping his hand behind her, he undid the tie of her blouse, pulling it open at the front; she wasn't wearing a bra. This was the first time he'd seen her breasts; they were more beautiful than he'd imagined. Groaning in ecstasy, he kissed them. His mouth closed over her erect nipple, and he teased it with his tongue. She stroked the back of his head as he gently kissed and sucked on each nipple.

She cupped his face in her hands and tenderly put her lips first on his forehead, then his eyes, and the tip of his nose. Smiling, she said, 'You make my whole body tingle.'

As he took a breath to respond, there was an ear-shattering blast of music from the flat upstairs.

He pulled back. 'That does it! You don't have to put up with that!'

He got to his feet and made for the door; Sue re-tied her blouse. 'No, Russ, please. I can live with it, I hate confrontation. I don't want any unpleasantness.'

As he opened the door, he called back, 'Don't worry, it'll be alright.' He went out to the hallway, put the catch up and closed the front door behind him.

Sue got up and went to the hallway, opening her door a fraction to listen. He must have taken the steps two at time; he was already on the next landing. She heard his sharp knock on the door, but the music drowned any conversation. About five seconds later, there was a blissful silence; the music had been switched off. Hearing the door slam shut upstairs, she closed her own, and quickly returned to the settee.

When he came back into the room, she looked anxious. He inclined his head and smiled. 'Don't worry, I didn't hurt him. He said to tell you he's sorry for being so inconsiderate, and it won't happen again.'

She adopted a wounded look. 'What did you say to him?'

'Hey, I've told you not to worry – it's alright, honestly!' He sat beside her, took hold of her hand and grinned. 'Talk about bad timing! What about another drink.'

Sue pushed herself up from the settee, pulling him with her. 'I've a better idea.' She led him to the bedroom.

She drew the curtains and lowered the ceiling light with a dimmer switch. They stood, nervously, unsure, facing each other; his cheeks were flushed. She began unbuttoning his shirt, pulling it out of his waistband.

He reached behind her, fumbling as he tried to undo the knot on the tie of her blouse. 'Were you a Girl Guide or something? It feels like a reef knot.'

She sniggered and untied the knot for him. He took off his shirt as she slid out of her blouse. Going down on one knee, she unbuckled his trouser belt and unzipped him. Slowly she eased his trousers down, her hand brushed the bulge in his boxer shorts. He slipped off his shoes, removed his socks and stepped out of his trousers. He picked them up, his hands trembling as he searched for his wallet.

She knew what he was looking for. 'It's okay, Russ, I'm on the pill; I take them to help with my periods.'

She stood up; he hooked his thumbs into the top of her leggings and slowly pulled them down. His heart was thumping so loudly he thought she would hear it; she was wearing a red silk thong. She kicked off her sandals and removed the leggings.

He slipped out of his boxers, leaned forward, picked her up and carried her to the bed. Gently laying her down, he climbed onto the bed beside her. They kissed hungrily, his hands caressing her breasts. He looked into her face; her eyes were misty with pleasure. For the first time in a long time something was soothing the ache in his heart. He didn't dare wonder why. His own body, so long denied, was screaming for release. He began to kiss her breasts, first one then the other. His mouth closed over her nipples, gently sucking on them. She made a murmuring sound of pleasure. He moved to a kneeling position; she raised her hips as he began to ease her thong slowly down her legs and over her feet, letting it fall on the floor. She sat up, opened her legs, then laid back, pulling him on top of her. Reaching down between them, she guided him into her. She was ready for him – soft, warm and moist. He felt her vaginal muscles contract, caressing and pulling him deeper into a chasm of ecstasy. Their love-making was slow and gentle until, unable to restrain himself any longer, he arched his back and made the final thrust, delirious and tearful in the explosion of ecstatic release.

He'd lost all sense of time as they laid quietly in each other's arms. Eventually, he eased himself up onto one elbow, placed a kiss lightly on her lips and pointed to the clock on the mantelshelf.

'I hate to say this, but I think I should get dressed and head back to Rye.'

Chapter 15

The plaintiff cries of herring gulls woke him at six o'clock. As he threw back the duvet, he suddenly remembered it was Sunday. Pulling it back over him, he snuggled down for another two hours.

By nine thirty, he had been for a five mile jog, showered and had breakfast.

He drove into Rye and parked the Capri by the office. St Mary's church bells were calling the faithful to worship. He stood and listened to their cadence. He knew next to nothing about campanology, and wondered if they had a full peal at St Mary's. He remembered Becky asking Father Mosley if the bells could be rung for their wedding at All Saints Poplar, but he'd said they only had one call bell, and it would be inappropriate for a wedding. She had giggled, realising what he meant. It was tolled for her funeral.

He went up to the office, updated the report on the Hannah Drew case, and made out an invoice for his fees and expenses for Sue to deal with. He then re-read the file on Carol Tiltman's murder and the notes he'd made of his own visit to the crime scene. He picked up a pencil and on the pad he wrote, 'Why Carol? Why Elaine Knightley? – there had to be a connection?' He was unhappy with the notion they had been targeted arbitrarily; the methodology of the perp was too complex. He must have known the victims would be alone; that there would be adequate time to accomplish his objectives. But how did he know? Russ could only think of two possible scenarios; the perp had stalked his victims over a period of time and become familiar with the pattern of their movements, or he and the victims had made prior arrangements to meet for sexual liaisons. The link between Carol and Elaine couldn't be determined without more information on Elaine Knightley and the crime scene at Rye Harbour. But something else was bothering him. He knew murderers didn't usually set out to become serial killers. Contrary to fictional portrayals, serial killers don't suddenly become vicious predators, picking on vulnerable women; they frequently have criminal backgrounds that can include burglary, theft, drug-dealing or violence. They often evolve through various stages of criminality, and by far the biggest influence on their unfolding violence is getting away with their first murder.

For some, especially sexual predators, the first kill brings a twisted satisfaction or excitement, and after a period of time, having avoided detection, the perp enjoys a sense of superiority at having outsmarted the police. But later, that sense of power and exhilaration begins to fade, and they develop a growing hunger to recapture the experience.

Russ tapped his teeth with his thumbnail. Instinct told him this perp had killed before; that Carol Tiltman was not his first victim – but who and where? He had no doubt DI Baillie would have followed the normal procedure of running a check through HOLMES2, the Home Office Large Major Enquiry System. This investigation management system was available to all UK police forces and held a data bank for all major incidents, including serial murders. He wondered if Baillie had considered looking beyond the UK. Maybe Duke could ask Em for another favour; her department would have contact with Interpol.

The phone rang, interrupting his train of thought. 'Good morning, Walker Investigations – how may I help?'

'Hello, it's George Tiltman. I didn't think you'd be working today. I was going to leave a message to let you know that at last the police have released Carol's body. I've arranged for her funeral to be held at Hastings Crematorium at eleven o'clock Wednesday morning. I wondered if, by any chance, you might be free to come?'

He knew the poor man would need all the support he could get.

'It's good of you to let me know, Mr Tiltman; yes, of course, I'll most certainly be there. Is there anything I can help you with regarding the arrangements?'

'Thanks for the offer, but I think everything's organised. I don't expect many will be there, but I've arranged for a buffet lunch back here at Whitegates after the service for those who do come... I'll see you on Wednesday, then. Bye.'

Russ replaced the receiver and made a note in the diary of the funeral arrangements. He put the files in the cabinet, had a brief tidy up in the office, and decided to lock up and return to the cottage.

After a sandwich lunch, he spent the first part of the afternoon in the garden, mowing the lawn and weeding the flowerbeds. Satisfied with what he'd done, he made himself a mug of coffee and took it outside to the wooden bench on the patio. He was a reluctant gardener, and although he did it only out of necessity, he did enjoy the sense of contentment that came from a job well done.

He then turned his attention to domestic chores, which he disliked even more than gardening. An hour and a half later, the guest room had been prepared for Duke, the cottage had been cleaned and the beer was in the fridge. He took a shower, changed his clothes and settled down on the settee with the latest Jack Reacher novel.

Duke arrived at seven on his T-Bob. By eight, they were next door, seated at a table in an almost empty Smugglers pub. Over the meal, Duke gave a run down on the Millwall game; apparently the Lions had won and avoided relegation. Glen's son, Alan, had thoroughly enjoyed himself, and was now the proud owner of a Millwall scarf Duke had bought for him from the club shop.

Russ recounted the conversation he'd had with Hannah on their way back to Folkestone, and of the family reunion.

The look on Duke's face betrayed his unease. 'I know you've fulfilled your obligation to the Drews with Hannah safely back home, and we've given the SCU all the information we had, but I can't let it go. I keep wondering how many other young girls are being subjected to the same treatment as Hannah. I've no doubt that right now, somewhere in London, depraved bastards are causing such pain to these young kids – destroying their lives.'

Russ nodded and took a sip of his beer. 'Maybe....Once we've caught this serial killer...Maybe we could start dismantling some of Provone's business set-ups.'

Duke smiled. 'Count me in.' He paused, 'You know, it reminds me of something I read years ago about a guy they called "the Star-fish Man."'

Duke related how a guy who lived and worked in a town on the East coast of America would spend his lunchbreak each day, walking along the beach, rescuing stranded starfish. Apparently, by some quirk of nature, the waves of the sea would wash thousands of starfish onto the beach, which would then get burnt to death by the scorching sun. Each day, this guy would spend his lunch-hour walking along, picking up starfish and tossing them back into the sea. A work colleague met him on the beach and pointed out the hopelessness of the situation. As he looked at the thousands of starfish, he asked the guy what difference he was making by rescuing just a few. The guy picked up a single starfish. "It makes all the difference in the world to this one!" and threw it back into the sea.

Russ smiled. 'Hey, that's good, says it all, really.'

A pretty young redhead came to their table and took away the empty plates.

Russ went to the bar and came back with two more pints. 'I've been thinking about our possible serial murderer. I'm not convinced Carol Tiltman was his first victim; he's been too clever. My gut feeling is that he's killed before and honed his perverted skills. No doubt Baillie will have checked with HOLMES2 for even the slightest comparison with unsolved murders in the UK, but I doubt he'd have checked with Interpol. Do you think Em might do us another favour?'

Duke took out his mobile. 'Worth a try; hang on a sec.' He pressed a keypad for speed dial.

While he chatted to his sister, Em, Russ made a quick visit to the Gents. As he returned to the table, Duke gave him the thumbs up.

'No problem. She'll get on to it first thing tomorrow. She and Val send their love.'

'Thanks. You never know; we could be lucky.'

They finished their drinks and went back to the cottage. Russ gave Duke spare keys to the cottage, the office and his Capri, and suggested they had breakfast together at seven in the morning. Duke decided to have an early night and went up to his room, while Russ sat in the lounge and watched the news on TV before he too went up to bed.

The alarm clock woke Russ at six. After a brief visit to the bathroom, he quietly made his way down the stairs. In the kitchen, he left a message on a Post-It note, telling Duke he'd gone for a run and would be back at seven. He slipped out of the cottage and ran toward the nature reserve. He had almost reached Winchelsea Beach when he met Duke running towards him. So much for the tiptoeing and the note!

They returned to the cottage at seven, showered, and enjoyed a leisurely breakfast before driving to the office, Russ in the Capri and Duke on the T-Bob.

By eight thirty, and with some clever manoeuvring, they managed to leave just enough space for Sue's Mazda in the parking area and, as if on cue, she turned from the High Street into Market Road.

When she came to a stop, Duke walked to the car and opened the driver's door for her. 'Morning, Sue, you're looking as lovely as ever.'

She got out of the car and he gave her a bear hug. She kissed his cheek.

'Now, that's how every girl should be greeted when she arrives at her work-place. Hello, Duke, it's so good to see you.'

Extricating herself from his arms, she turned to Russ and gave him a light kiss on the lips. 'Morning, Boss, the A-Team's reporting for duty.'

She unlocked the boot of her car and took out a briefcase, a bunch of flowers and pointed to a large cardboard box. 'Perhaps one of you would be kind enough to carry that up for me?'

Duke grabbed the box as Russ took the briefcase and flowers. Sue locked the car and led the way up stairs to the office.

Duke offered to make the coffee, while Sue took a glass vase from the cardboard box, filled it with water and arranged the flowers, placing them on the coffee table.

Duke brought in the coffee and mugs, and placed them on the small table. He and Sue occupied the clients' seats, and Russ pulled the desk chair around to the front of the desk.

Sue listened in disbelief as Russ and Duke detailed the chain of events in Hannah Drew's rescue.

She was incredulous. 'I can't believe you did all that! You could have been killed!'

Like most people, she knew such things went on, but to hear of it first-hand made her nauseous. She picked up on the mention of the warehouse and snuff videos and asked what *that* meant. Duke looked at Russ. *How do you explain such depravity?*

Leaning forward Russ said, 'Sue, it's too horrific to describe. I know it's hard to believe, but there are evil creatures who set up video cameras and film themselves sexually and violently abusing their victims until they die.'

She was clearly shocked. 'But why? How could anyone do such a terrible thing?'

'For money! There are perverts who will pay an enormous amount for a video like that.'

Her eyes filled with tears. 'It makes me feel sick'.

The phone rang. Russ picked up the receiver. 'Good morning, Walker Investigations – how may I help you?'

In spite of the background noise of traffic, he recognised the voice immediately.

'Hello, Russ, it's Em. I don't know if you can hear me; I'm outside the office in Victoria Street. I ran a check for you with Interpol. Guess what? Just over twelve months ago a thirty-seven-year-old woman called Martina Fischer was murdered in her home at Bielefeld in Germany and the perp was never caught. The MO is not identical to the Carol Tiltman killing, but there are enough similarities to suggest it could be the same killer. The officer in charge of the investigation is Kommissar Juergen Roeseler at Bielefeld Police Headquarters. I don't know if I'll be able to get a copy of their file, but I'll try. If you decide to follow this up, for Heaven's sake keep me out of it.' She gave him the address and telephone number of the Bielefeld Police Headquarters.

His heartrate increased; this might be just the break they needed.

'Em, you're fantastic. I really appreciate this - but be careful; don't worry about the file. Please don't take any more risks; you've given us plenty to go on. By the way, your big brother's here – would you like a word?'

'I'd better not; I've got to get back to the office. Tell him "hi" and give him my love. Bye for now.'

Duke was grinning at him as he replaced the receiver. 'So, what has little sister come up with?'

Sue was looking more composed as she refilled the coffee mugs. Russ repeated what Em had said about the unsolved murder in Bielefeld.

He turned to Duke. 'That's three too many! He's got to be stopped – but it's information we need. Duke, if you could make a start with Elaine Knightley's murder, I'll see what I can get from Kommissar Roeseler about Martina Fischer's death.'

He stood up and handed Duke the file on Carol Tiltman's murder. 'Have a look at this; my notes about Elaine Knightley are at the back.'

He turned to Sue. 'Could you find out about flights to Bielefeld for me? I'm going to pop to the newsagents; be back in five.'

'No problem; it'll only take a few minutes.' She went to her desk and booted up the laptop.

Russ bought a map of Germany from the newsagent and some Euros from the local Bureau de Change.

On his return to the office, he found Duke feverishly making notes, while Sue, with a smug look on her face, sat playing with a pencil. 'All done; the city of Bielefeld is half way between Dortmund and Hanover and the nearest airport is Paderborn. You'll have to get a train from there to Bielefeld. Air Berlin have daily flights to Paderborn from Stansted at six in the evening; the return flights leave Paderborn at three thirty in the afternoon. Most of their passengers are British Army personnel and their families, as there are three British military camps based at Herford near Bielefeld, and one in Bielefeld itself. There are still some empty seats on today's flight and on tomorrow's return. There's a small, inexpensive hotel in the centre of Bielefeld, about two hundred yards from the Police Headquarters; they still have vacancies for tonight. '

He looked at Duke. 'Can you believe this woman? Intelligent as well as beautiful. I think we're on a winner here.'

She picked up an eraser and threw it at him. 'Don't patronise me. Would you like me to book a seat on the flights and accommodation at the hotel, or not?'

Grinning, he caught it and placed it on the desk. 'Please, Sue. I'll nip back to the cottage for my passport and an overnight bag, and call in here before I set off.'

Within half an hour, Russ was back in the office and ready to leave. Duke had already left. She gave him a sheet of paper with the addresses of the Police Headquarters and the hotel, plus the electronic tickets for the flights that had been emailed to the office. As he put them into his bag, she got up from her chair, walked round the table and looked up into his face.

'I'm so happy to be here; thank you for last night.'

She inclined her head. The kiss lasted for several minutes until he raised his eyes and, over her shoulder, he noticed the blonde woman at the George Hotel watching them.

He pulled away. 'I'd better make a move. Hopefully I'll see you tomorrow evening. Be good.'

Chapter 16

She gave him one last peck on the cheek. 'Have a safe journey. I'll ask Duke if he'd like to have a Chinese meal this evening; it'll save him having to cook.'

It took Russ just over an hour to get to the Dartford Tunnel. Traffic had been surprisingly light on the M25 and there had been no hold-ups. He made a pit stop for coffee and the toilet at the Thurrock Service Station before continuing north on the motorway. Twenty minutes later, he turned onto the M11 heading for Bishop's Stortford. This was the first time he'd flown from Stansted, and he was surprised at the size of the terminal car park. He approached the entrance and pulled up at the barrier. After three attempts at getting the machine to accept his credit card, the barrier finally lifted, and he went in search of an empty parking space. He made a note in his scribbling pad that he'd parked in row 5 of Zone J, close to a shuttle-bus picking up point. Five minutes later, he was in the bus on his way to the terminal.

Entering the terminal concourse, he was astonished at the size of the building and the large number of people milling around, or in queues waiting to check in. He joined a short queue at the Air Berlin check-in. His passport and electronic tickets were inspected, and he was given a boarding pass. He was told he could keep his holdall as hand luggage, and was directed to the shuttle train that would take him to the appropriate departure lounge.

The flight to Paderborn took just over an hour, but as Germany is an hour ahead of the UK, the plane landed at eight fifteen continental time. Paderborn is a small airport and, unlike most of the passengers who had to wait by the carousel to collect their luggage, he was through Customs clearance in no time at all. Outside, he took a taxi to the railway station, where he caught a train for Bielefeld.

Three quarters of an hour later, he arrived at Bielefeld Railway Station, and from a kiosk on the platform, he bought a map of the city. Unfolding it, he located Hermann Strasse where the hotel was situated, and estimated it would take some fifteen to twenty minutes to get there on foot.

The street cafés and pubs were filling up with young people; he guessed many were probably students from the City University. There was an air of healthy innocence and fun, and not a hoodie in sight.

Eventually he found the Police Station in Niederwall, a busy crescent-shaped road. It was a large, modern concrete building that could easily be mistaken for a college or a municipal building, were it not for the large sign 'Polizeiwache' over the main entrance. Just past the police station he saw Heidi's Restaurant and Bar. His stomach rumbled, reminding him he hadn't eaten since breakfast. As he entered the Restaurant, the maître-de' welcomed him and took him to a table for two by the window. He ordered steak and chips, plus a German beer. As he waited, from his inside pocket he took out the sheet of paper with the address of the hotel. Sue had booked him into the Hotel Dieter in Hermann Strasse, which according to the map, was literally round the corner from the Police Station.

After an enjoyable meal, he left the restaurant, and within a hundred yards, he was at Hermann Strasse. He booked into the hotel and was given a twin-bedded room on the first floor. He undressed and took a shower before calling Sue on his mobile. Rather than exploring the city on his own, he decided to get into bed and watch satellite television before having an early night.

The next morning, a little disappointed that a full English breakfast wasn't on the menu, he tucked into the bread rolls and slices of cheese and meat.

He left the hotel at nine, and made his way to the police station. There were three people in front of him at the enquiry desk, and an attractive and polite young police woman behind the glass window attending to them.

Eventually it was his turn. She smiled. 'Guten Morgen. Kann ich ihnen helfen?'

He shrugged his shoulders and gave her his best helpless expression. 'Good morning. Do you speak English?'

She smiled, and made a rocking movement with her hand. 'Only a little, I'm afraid.'

He smiled back and handed her his business card. 'Would it be possible for me to speak to Kommissar Juergen Roeseler, please?'

She studied his card and looked up. 'Why you wish to speak with him?'

'Please tell him I have come from England to speak to him about Martina Fischer.'

'One moment.' She picked up a telephone and punched in three numbers. When it was answered, she spoke very quickly and glanced at Russ once or twice during the conversation.

She replaced the receiver, and pointed to a chair by the wall. 'You sit down, please.'

Within two minutes, a tall, thin man in his early thirties, wearing jeans and a green sweatshirt, came through a side door into the reception area. He had a serious expression on his face as he approached Russ and held out his hand.

'Good morning. I am Officer Gerhard Moltman.'

Russ stood up and shook his hand. 'Good morning. My name is Russ Walker.'

The detective nodded to the door. 'This way, please.'

The door led into a corridor. Halfway along, they went up a flight of stairs to the first floor. He was shown into an interview room sparsely furnished with a brown formica-topped metal table bolted to the floor, and three wooden upright chairs. Although there was a large "No Smoking" sign on the wall with the words, "Rauchen verboten" the room smelt of stale cigarette smoke.

'Mr Walker, please sit down. I apologise we have to use this room; it is the only one we have available at the moment. I understand you wish to speak to Kommissar Roeseler about Martina Fischer. He is very busy at the moment; perhaps you could tell me what you wish to discuss with him.'

He had expected he might have to negotiate with subordinates before getting to see the Kommissar, and chose his words carefully.

'Officer Moltman, for a number of years I was a senior detective in the Metropolitan Police in London. I am no longer a policeman, but am now a private investigator. I have been hired to investigate the murder of a woman in England, and have reason to believe that this murder might be connected with the murder of Martina Fischer here in Bielefeld. I understand Kommissar Roeseler is the officer in charge of the Fischer investigation – that's why I would like to see him.'

Officer Moltman made a note in his pocket book. 'I will pass this on to the Kommissar, but I need to know how it is you are aware of the murder of Martina Fischer, and why you believe there is a connection between these murders.'

'It was through a comparison check with Interpol that I discovered the modus operandi is very similar, and the evidence suggests we are looking for the same killer.'

Moltman raised his eyebrows and stood up. 'Please wait here, Mr Walker. I will see if Kommissar Roeseler is free to meet with you.'

In next to no time, he was back. 'Please, follow me.'

Russ was led along the corridor to the Kommissar's office.

Roeseler greeted Russ warmly with a handshake. He was a blond haired handsome man, aged about fifty. He wore a black suit with an open necked white shirt, and black slip-on shoes.

'Welcome, Mr Walker, come and sit down. Would you like tea or coffee?'

Russ opted for a black coffee and sat in a metal-framed upholstered chair. 'It's good of you to see me, Kommissar. I'm relieved that you speak such good English.'

Roeseler laughed. 'My English is not very good. We have all to learn English at school, but it was a long time ago now. We have a lot of English and American films on the television, and many times I have been on holiday in England. I get by.'

Officer Moltman brought two mugs of coffee into the office and left, closing the door behind him.

Russ picked up his coffee and began to explain the reason for his visit. In an attempt to establish a rapport, he spoke of his own police background and then went on to talk about Carol Tiltman's murder. He put the coffee mug on the floor beside him, unzipped his document case, and took out copies of the reports on the autopsy and forensic evidence, plus photographs of the crime scene. He handed them to Roeseler, picked up his coffee and sat back quietly while the Kommissar studied them.

Roeseler was clearly excited. 'Mr Walker, I am thinking you may be correct. There are many similarities to the case we are investigating.'

'Kommissar, there is more. A week ago, there was another murder in England. The victim's name is Elaine Knightley. She was killed only fifteen miles from where Carol Tiltman was murdered. I don't have all the details, but I have been told by the detective in charge of the investigation that the MO is almost identical. It suggests that both murders were committed by the same person. It appears we are looking for a serial killer.'

Kommissar Roeseler stood up, moved the papers about Carol Tiltman to one side, and went to a filing cabinet against the wall to his left. From the second drawer, he pulled out a thick file and placed it on the desk.

'This is part of the records we have on the murder of Martina Fischer, aged thirty-seven. She was murdered on 17th June last year, in the evening between the hours of six and ten. She was not married; an agency nurse, living in a ground floor apartment in a suburb of Bielefeld called Bethel; her address was apartment 82 Weissdornweg, Bethel.'

He handed Russ three photographs. They were in colour and had been taken from different angles. Sadly, it was all too familiar - the body of a naked woman lying spread-eagled on her back on a double bed. Russ could hardly believe it. Her hands and feet were tied to the castors at the four corners of the bed just as Carol Tiltman and Elaine Knightley's had been. Instead of duct tape on her mouth, she had been gagged with what appeared to be a scarf. Unlike Carol Tiltman, there were a number of bite marks on both breasts and between her legs. As this victim had no pubic hair, the close up of the vaginal area clearly showed signs of severe bruising. A small piece of red material – probably her panties - was protruding from the vagina.

As Russ looked at the shocking photographs, Roeseler said, 'It was a vicious, sadistic attack. Her death was caused by strangulation. It is the same culprit who did this, and the murders in England, yes?'

He handed the photographs back. 'Yes, Kommissar, it has to be. Did you have any suspects for this? Did you arrest anyone?'

Roeseler shook his head. 'No-one. The culprit left traces of semen on her face and in her vagina. It was enough to give us a DNA profile, but it didn't match any in our national database. Our scientific team found no trace of hair, skin or fingerprints other than that of the victim. Like the English victim, she was covered in oil, and had no defensive injuries. We found no evidence under her fingernails. We interviewed all her male friends and known sex offenders in the area without success, and our door-to-door enquiries and appeals for witnesses were also without success.'

'Did she keep a diary, and what about her telephone records?'

'No diary, just a calendar in the kitchen. The only thing she had written on it was the date of her menstrual period.' He looked at his notes, 'That was on the 5th of December, and the word "Agent" which in English means "Agency" on the 15th - two days before she was murdered. We checked her telephone calls and found nothing to help us.'

Roeseler and his team had obviously been as thorough as their English counterparts, but now there were new possibilities to consider. Russ and the Kommissar spent the next half hour considering the questions raised by this new information. Was the perp an Englishman who had spent some time in Germany but was now back in the UK? With the close proximity of British Army bases, it was possible he had a military connection. There again, perhaps he was German, but now living in the UK. Clearly the Kommissar and DI Baillie were going to have to work closely together on this. At least they now had DNA evidence that could be checked against the UK register.

Roeseler pointed to a map on the wall behind him. 'I think perhaps I should explain. Bethel is an area of the city with its own identity. It is unique; almost like a small town within the city. The name Bethel is a biblical word; it means "House of God". In the latter part of the nineteenth-century there were approximately 42,000 people with epilepsy living in Germany. Very few received any help with their affliction until, in 1872, a great philanthropist and Lutheran Pastor, Friedrich von Bodelschwingh, became the director of an institution dedicated to the care and treatment of epileptics. Over the years, various clinics, work therapy units, schools and residential homes were built, and it has developed into the biggest Institution for the treatment and research into epilepsy in Germany. People with epilepsy come from all over the world to find help at Bethel. In addition, there are centres for treatment, therapy and care for those who have psychological problems or mental disability. Martina Fischer was a nurse helping these unfortunates.'

Russ wondered why he had never heard of Bethel. 'You mean it's more than one large hospital on its own site?'

Roeseler laughed. 'You need to see it, my friend, if you have time. It is like a separate town. Because it is a Christian foundation, many of the buildings and roads have biblical names. In the early days, most of the nursing and administrative work was done by members of two religious orders – the Diakonissenanstalt Sarepta – that is an order of deaconess sisters – and the Diakonenanstalt Nazareth, an order of male deacons. There were many hundreds of them. Today, you will still see many of the nuns in their habits, but the men wear civilian clothes.'

Russ had every intention of seeing it, especially the road where Martina Fischer lived. But before he left, he wondered if Roeseler might be persuaded to let him have a copy of the SOCO's report.

'Kommissar, I'm grateful for all you have shared with me. You will obviously want to be in touch with the officer in charge of the investigations into the English murders; I've written his details on one of those sheets of paper. Before I leave, I wonder if it would be possible for me to have a copy of the report from your Scene of Crime Officers, and perhaps your own report?'

He smiled as he shook his head. 'I'm sorry, my friend; you know I cannot allow that.' He pulled out the two reports. 'These are the reports, but I cannot copy them for you. However, I think you will forgive me, for I must leave you alone for ten minutes while I go to the cloakroom.' He placed them on top of the photocopier at the right side of his desk. 'I will be back in ten minutes.' *What a hero!*

As soon as Roeseler left the room, Russ got up and began to copy the reports. There were about thirty pages in all, and he wondered if ten minutes would be long enough. It was a slow machine, and by the time he'd copied the last page, he was relieved to see he still had about two minutes left. He quickly made a copy of the crime scene photographs and the telephone records, and replaced the papers where the Kommissar had left them. He sat down again and put the copies in his document case, which he was zipping up as Kommissar Roeseler came back into the room.

Russ got to his feet and shook his hand. 'Thank you for the time you've given me. We are all anxious to arrest this killer before he does it again. I wish us all good luck.'

The Kommissar gave Russ a pat on his back. 'You have done some good for us. Thank you. I will come with you to the door.'

He led Russ down the stairs and out into the reception area. Once again they shook hands.

'Auf Wiedersehen, Mr Walker.'

Russ walked back to the hotel to collect his holdall and hand in his key. As he left the hotel, feeling slightly disorientated by the traffic roaring past on what, for him, was the wrong side of the road, he noticed a ubiquitous Starbucks across the road. He decided to play it safe and use a pedestrian crossing some fifty yards away to his right.

He bought a coffee and carried it outside to an empty table on the pavement. He took out the map of Bielefeld; the area called Bethel – pronounced 'Beetle' by the Kommissar – was not far away on the southern side of the city. He estimated it would take around thirty minutes for him to reach Weissdornweg, the road where Martina Fischer had lived.

He finished his coffee and set off for Bethel. Crossing Kreuz Strasse, he followed the pedestrian signs for Bethel, and within ten minutes he was passing clinics, therapy units, and hospitals, all with Biblical names - Gilead, Nazareth, Nebo, Patmos, Gilgal and Kidron. There were shops, schools and cafés. On the pavements, carers pushed disabled patients in wheelchairs, or walked hand in hand with epileptic patients wearing protective headwear made of leather. Russ noticed that throughout all the streets and roads of Bethel, the speed restriction for vehicles was the equivalent of fifteen miles per hour.

It took him longer to reach Weissdornweg than he had anticipated. It was a quiet residential area on the outskirts of Bethel. Apartment 82 was in a purpose built block of flats at the end of a cul-de-sac. The building backed onto a wood of Tannenbaum trees, which would have given plenty of cover for the perp to slip away unnoticed.

There was no point in asking the present occupier if he might have a look over the apartment; he just wanted to get a picture in his mind of the location of the crime scene.

He walked back into the centre of Bethel and took a taxi to Bielefeld railway station. Once he'd bought his ticket, it was only a ten minute wait before he caught a train back to Paderborn. He arrived at the airport at one thirty and had two hours to while away before the flight back to Stansted. This gave him plenty of time to have a snack in the restaurant and purchase two giant Toblerones at the Duty Free Shop for Sue and Duke.

Chapter 17

The Boeing 737 touched down at Stansted at a quarter to six UK time. Half an hour later, he was back on the M11, heading for London. Traffic was reasonably light until he hit the M25 and the rush hour traffic. It was stop and start most of the way to the Dartford Crossing, but once over the Thames and through the toll, he made good progress for the rest of the journey back to Rye Harbour.

It was nine fifteen when he arrived at the cottage. Sue's Mazda was parked beside Duke's T-bob in front of the garage, and so he left the Capri by the harbour wall.

He unlocked the front door and called out, 'So, where's the welcoming committee?'

There was no reply. On the kitchen table he found a note – "Hey super sleuth, welcome back! The A-Team's next door at The Smugglers."

Russ took his holdall upstairs and deposited it in his bedroom. After a quick visit to the bathroom to freshen up, he went down the stairs and out to The Smugglers. He found Sue and Duke in the pub lounge, sitting at a corner table, midway through their meal.

Sue jumped up and gave him a chilli – flavoured kiss. 'Guten arbend, mein Herr.'

Grinning, he pretended to wipe traces of her meal off his mouth. He reached over and shook Duke's hand.

'Hey; good to see you.'

He went to the bar and ordered a pint and a mixed grill. He took his drink back to the table and while he waited for his meal, he told them their suspicions had been confirmed; Martina Fischer had certainly been a victim of their serial killer. He gave them a detailed account of his conversation with Kommissar Roeseler, and of how he'd generously allowed him to make copies of some of the documents in their file.

Duke continued eating as he listened. Putting his knife and fork together on his cleared plate, he wiped his mouth with a serviette. 'Do we know anyone who could translate the reports into English for us?'

Sue said, 'My friend Julie at Ashford read modern languages at Uni, – she's fluent in German. I'm sure she would do it.' She looked at Russ. 'Do you want me to ask her?'

'Yes please, Sue. Tell her it's confidential and you'd better warn her it will be pretty gruesome.'

'She'll be okay. If I take them with me, I'll get them to her before I come into the office tomorrow morning.'

Russ passed her the reports. 'Oh, that reminds me, Sue. It's Carol Tiltman's funeral tomorrow morning. I'd appreciate it if you'd come with me and discreetly take some photographs. I know it's a longshot, but it's not unknown for a murderer to attend the funeral of their victim. In their warped mind, it can be a turn on. I'd like a photo of everyone there, and later, hopefully George Tiltman will be able to identify them.'

A waitress brought Russ his meal, with a knife and fork wrapped in a paper serviette.

'So, how did you get on with the Elaine Knightley case?' Russ asked Duke.

'I called on her sister Catherine at lunchtime; the poor woman's still in a state of shock. It took a bit of persuasion, but eventually she agreed to let me have a look in her sister's house.'

Russ was surprised. 'Were the SOCOs still there?'

He shook his head. 'No, thankfully they'd gone. I had a good nose round and took a few photographs. Elaine was pretty much a loner; not much of a social life. There was a diary beside the telephone in the hallway, but hardly anything in it. Apart from functions at the school where she taught – parents' evenings or concerts – she didn't seem to go anywhere. Most of the pages were blank, with the exception of an occasional appointment with the dentist or a hairdresser. But wait for it; on the day she was killed she had written "4pm BO".'

Russ punched the air. 'Yes! We have a connection!

A couple sitting four tables away looked across at him and smiled.

Russ lowered his voice. 'Baillie said she was killed between four and six. This "Bo" has to be our man! According to Wadsworth, Carol had met someone who was into S & B, and the matron at the retirement home said Carol Tiltman had mentioned a possible sex partner called Bo - but who the hell is he?'

Sue looked confused. 'What do you mean, S & B?'

Russ smiled at her. 'You dear, sweet creature; it's "sadism and bondage." Some people find giving or receiving pain heightens their sexual pleasure!'

She let out a breath. 'Whoa!'

Duke gave a slight nod of his head. 'I asked Catherine if she knew anything about Bo, or if Elaine had ever mentioned the name. She said Baillie had asked the same question, but she hadn't a clue – the name meant nothing to her. I searched the house and her car but there was nothing to indicate who he might be.'

There was excitement in Russ' voice. 'Duke, this is the break we've been looking for. BO could be initials, or maybe a shortened name for a Boris, Bob, or whoever.'

Sue offered, 'I wonder if she gave private tuition to anyone with that name or initials.'

Duke looked at his pocket book. 'Yes, that occurred to me too. I went to her school and spoke to the secretary. Needless to say, Baillie had already been there. Apart from an eleven-year-old pupil called Brian Osborne, no one else at the school has those initials - staff or students.'

'Did you find any porn videos or magazines to suggest she was interested in kinky sex?' Russ asked.

'No, nothing. I was going to rummage through her wheelie-bin but it was empty. Either the SOCOs took the contents or the refuse collectors had called that day. One thing did surprise me – she was an intelligent woman, but didn't have a daily newspaper. Bearing in mind the subject she taught, I would have thought she needed to keep abreast of current affairs. The only papers I found, were freebies, the one's full of advertisements.'

Russ was quiet for a moment. There was something stirring at the back of his mind. If only he could access it. He closed his eyes in concentration. Suddenly it clicked. 'When I searched Carol Tiltman's car, it was spotless – not even a sweet paper. The only thing I found was in the glove compartment – it was a free newspaper! It didn't occur to me at the time, but why did she keep it? Why did Elaine Knightley keep those freebies? Advertisements! Maybe they both met Bo through an advertisement!'

Duke straightened in his seat. 'As far as we know, neither of them had a satisfying sex life, and those freebies have loads of adverts from people looking for relationships. I think we're onto something!'

Russ concurred. 'After Carol's funeral, I'll collect the paper from her car when I go back to the house. If you get the papers from Elaine Knightley's house, maybe we'll be in luck.'

They stayed in the pub until closing time and then went back to the cottage for coffee. Sue decided to pass on the coffee and, with the German reports, left for Winchelsea.

Duke spread himself out on the settee, while Russ went into the kitchen and brewed up some coffee. He brought the mugs into the lounge, handed one to Duke, and sat down in an armchair. 'Tomorrow night I'm going to Harbour Rocks; do you fancy coming? Elmo will be there.'

Duke laughed. 'I'd like to see Elmo, but I outgrew Shakin' Stevens about twenty years ago! I think I'll give it a miss. I want to pop back to Shooters Hill tomorrow afternoon, make sure Glen's okay. I'll stay the night and come back Thursday morning.'

Deciding it was time for bed, Duke went upstairs to his room, while Russ washed the coffee mugs and set the table in readiness for breakfast the next morning.

Russ and Duke were in the office by eight thirty. Duke went to the kitchen to make coffee while Russ began to update the Tiltman file. Thirty minutes later, the door opened and Sue walked in, wearing a navy blue trouser suit and white blouse. She had dressed for the funeral and had brought a bag of jam doughnuts, which she gave to Duke.

'Hi! Sorry I'm late. I've been to see Julie; she's more than happy to help with the translations; she hopes to have them finished by tomorrow morning at the latest.'

Russ reached for the player and lowered the volume of Buddy Holly. 'Hey, thanks. I hope you warned her about the content.'

Sue nodded. 'She said she has a strong stomach.'

She moved to the player, turned it off and removed the disc. From her bag she took another CD, inserted it and pressed play.

Russ took its case from her hand and read the cover. He looked across and met Duke's eyes. 'Oh good, it's Vivaldi's "Four Seasons."'

Duke smiled but said nothing as he helped himself to a doughnut.

Sue declined the offer of a coffee and sat opposite Duke.

Reaching for the player, Russ lowered the volume. 'Duke's going to Elaine's house and hopefully bringing back any free papers he finds. I'll get the one from Carol Tiltman's car after the funeral. Then we'll have to plough through them to see what we can find.'

Duke raised an eyebrow. 'What about DI Baillie? How much are you going to tell him?'

Russ thought for a moment. 'I imagine he'll be at the funeral. I'll tell him about the murder of Martina Fischer in Germany, but I think we'll keep our suspicions about Bo to ourselves. Let's see what develops.'

It was quarter to eleven when Russ pulled into the crematorium car park. As it was full, he followed the signs for the overflow car park.

Sue was incredulous. 'I can't believe it! Look at all those cars; they can't *all* be here for Carol's funeral, surely?'

'Pretty unlikely. They're probably attending the one before Carol. Could be it was a local dignitary, or perhaps a young person.'

Russ locked the Capri and they made their way to the chapel entrance, where some twenty mourners were waiting outside the main doors. He recognised Jeremy Wadsworth talking with Janice Austin and two other women. Jenny Pierce stood to one side with a grey-haired man in his sixties, wearing a black suit. Thirty feet away to the left of the group were DI Baillie and DS Askew; they appeared to be reading some of the memorial plaques at the edge of the lawn.

Bailey turned and gave a nod of his head as Russ and Sue approached. He almost smiled as he held out his hand.

'Morning, Russ, not much of a turn out for the poor woman. I think one or two are from the village... The rest are probably from his firm at Bexhill.'

Russ shook the hand warmly. 'Morning, Alex.'

Askew made no attempt to shake Russ' hand, but smiled as he nodded his head at Sue.

'Sad, isn't it?' Russ gestured towards Sue. 'You remember my PA, Sue Westbrook.'

Baillie turned on the charm. He gave a hint of a bow and offered his hand. 'My dear, it's a pleasure to see you again.'

Russ quickly scanned the car park, the driveway and the gardens. 'It doesn't look as if the perp's going to show up.'

Baillie responded. 'I guess that was too much to hope for.'

At that moment, the cortege appeared. The hearse, followed by a black limousine drew up outside the chapel doors.

As they walked towards the mourners, Russ lowered his voice. 'Perhaps we could have a word after the service. I don't know if you've heard from Germany, but I've some important information about another murder.'

Baillie stiffened. 'A what? I haven't been into the office this morning; what are you talking about?'

They stopped while Sue and Askew continued walking towards the entrance. Russ dropped his voice to a whisper.

'Carol Tiltman wasn't his first victim. He killed a woman in Germany six months before her. Same MO.'

The bearers had the coffin on their shoulders and were leading the procession into the chapel. 'We'd better join them. I'll give you the details after the service.'

As they entered the chapel, the organist was playing "I know that my Redeemer liveth" from Handel's "Messiah." The coffin was placed on the catafalque while the funeral director ushered the mourners into their pews. George

Tiltman was clearly distressed, wiping his eyes with his handkerchief. He occupied the front pew with a younger man and woman – presumably his brother and sister-in-law. Baillie, Askew, Sue and Russ slipped into the pew at the back.

The bearers made their reverential bow to the coffin and, with military precision, marched slowly down the aisle and left the chapel. The officiant was a priest in his seventies, a portly grey-haired man with a kind face. Russ presumed he was a retiree, supplementing his pension by undertaking what was known as "Rota Duty". He had a caring attitude and a gentle voice. He began, 'I am the Resurrection and the Life, saith the Lord .....'

This was the first funeral Russ had attended since Becky's, and he wasn't prepared for the emotional effect it was having. As he fought back the tears, Sue slipped her arm through his and gave it a comforting squeeze.

The service progressed with a hymn and a reading and then it was time for the homily. Here was an experienced priest who was no stranger to ministering in tragic situations. Avoiding clichés and pious platitudes, he spoke gently and sympathetically, making eye contact with his congregation. He ended the address by reading words of comfort he attributed to another priest, a Canon Scott-Holland, who had been on the staff at St Paul's Cathedral in London at the turn of the last century. He read, 'Death is nothing at all; I have only slipped away into the next room. I am I and you are you. Whatever we were to each other, that we are still. Call me by my old familiar name; speak to me in the easy way you always used...'

Several of the mourners were blowing their noses; Baillie included. Russ hoped the words would help George Tiltman; but to the perpetrator, it would mean something else. Death *was* nothing at all... to him!

At the end of the service, the mourners were led out of the chapel through a side door. The floral tributes had been spread out on a paved patio to be viewed by George Tiltman and his family.

Baillie touched Russ' arm. 'I won't be going to Tiltman's home; I have to get back to Hastings. Can we go for a walk in the grounds? I need to hear what you have.'

Russ told Sue he would meet her back at the car, and he and Baillie made a discreet exit. They found a wooden bench in a secluded area of the garden, where Russ explained how a check with Interpol had led to the discovery of the unsolved murder of Martina Fischer. He told him of his meeting with Kommissar Roeseler and gave details of the murder.

Baillie put his hand on Russ' shoulder. 'I won't ask you how you managed a check with Interpol, but well done! Bloody hell; that's three victims, but thank God they have his DNA... At last!'

Russ looked Baillie full in the face. 'Alex, one of us is going to nail that bastard, and I don't mind which of us does it. Just remember, I'm not working in opposition to you. When – or if – I get something concrete to help in the investigation, I'll pass it on to you.' He paused, and as if it was an afterthought, he said, 'By the way, have you made any headway in your search for Bo?'

Baillie shook his head and grinned. 'How the hell do you know about that? No, nothing yet. I think Bo's the perp, but as they say, we're following various lines of enquiry. To be honest, we haven't a bloody clue.'

Baillie got to his feet, and Russ followed. 'I have to go. Thanks for this chat.'

Baillie joined Askew in the Mondeo and they drove off.

The Capri was the only vehicle left in the carpark. Sue was scrolling through the photographs in the camera as he slipped into the driver's seat.

She switched it off, reached over and squeezed his hand. 'You okay?'

'Yeah, fine thanks. The old boy did a good job, didn't he?'

She smiled. 'He was a real pro; pitched it at just the right level. George Tiltman held up well, considering... Poor man. Hey, I think I've got an admirer; DS Askew asked if I'd like to have a drink with him sometime.'

Russ flinched. 'So what did you say?'

'I thanked him, but said I already had a significant other in my life.'

They caught up with the procession of cars just before they reached Whitegates. Russ left the car on the grass verge at the side of the road and they walked up the drive to the house.

Tiltman had hired caterers to provide a buffet lunch, and as they entered the hallway, a waitress holding a tray offered them a glass of white wine.

In the sitting room, George Tiltman looked composed as he moved around the room, making small talk and thanking people for coming. From across the room, Russ caught

Jeremy Wadsworth's eye – he gave Russ a venomous look and turned his back.

While people were helping themselves to the food, Russ asked Tiltman if he might have a word in private, and was shown into his study. Russ told him about the murder of Martina Fischer, and of the DNA evidence. He asked to borrow the key to Carol's Mini and slipped out to collect the free paper from the glove compartment.

Chapter 18

They arrived back at the office at two and found Duke attempting the *Times 2* crossword.

'Hey dudes.' He tossed the paper onto the coffee table. 'You're both so enthusiastic about this thing, I thought I might be missing something, but it leaves me cold... Made me realise what sad little lives you must have.'

Sue groaned. 'Don't push it, Duke; you're outnumbered. How about making coffee for the boss and his PA?'

Duke laughed. 'His what?'

'Russ introduced me to DI Baillie; he said I was his personal assistant. From dogsbody to PA in just two days; not bad, eh?'

Duke shook his head in mock disbelief, levered himself out of the chair and went to make the coffee.

He returned with three mugs and a packet of chocolate Digestives.

From his inside pocket, Russ pulled out the free newspaper from Carol's car, and gave it to Sue. 'The last four pages... I reckon there must be at least five hundred ads. Think of yourself as a sexually frustrated middle-aged woman looking for some fun. You're married, and you don't want to put that in jeopardy - but there's no sparkle anymore. So you're not looking for a long term relationship – just a bit of discreet sexy fun.' From the desk drawer, he took out a red felt pen. 'Highlight the ones you think might interest you.'

Duke produced two similar papers. 'These were in Elaine's kitchen; her sister doesn't know I've taken them.' He passed one to Russ.

For several minutes they sat quietly, reading the ads. Every so often, Duke broke the silence with 'Good Lord' or 'I don't believe it!'

'Yes! I've found it!' Sue shouted triumphantly. 'It's in the section marked "Adult Contacts". Just listen to this; "Gigolos 4U. Male escorts available for discerning ladies. Spice up your life with a young athletic, attractive male. All tastes catered for. Satisfaction guaranteed: Absolute discretion assured: Clean and safe. Client's choice of venue. Hire a beau by phoning this number...." It looks like a mobile number.'

Russ snorted. 'Hire a beau! Yuck! So that's why he calls himself Bo! Well done Sue.'

'Yeah, there's a similar one here too!' Duke exclaimed. 'Same advert but a different mobile number.'

Russ shook his head. 'It's not in this one.' He compared the date of publication with Duke's copy. 'Yours is the most recent edition. Mine is a month old.'

'Hey, wait a minute.' Russ got to his feet and took the Tiltman file from the cabinet. He placed it on the desk and flicked through the pages. He extracted a sheet of paper. Three days before she was killed, Carol phoned an agency. I assumed it was the nursing agency.' He looked at Sue. 'What was the number for Gigolos 4U?'

She repeated the number.

Russ checked his notes. 'It's the same!'

He picked up the phone and dialled the number. The continuous tone indicating the number was unobtainable. It was the same when he dialled the number from Duke's paper.

'I didn't think it would be that easy. Presumably he dumps the phones after the murders.'

Duke took out his mobile. 'I'll see if I can sweet talk someone at the publishers. They should have a record of the person who placed the adverts.'

Russ picked up his address book. 'It's worth a try. I'll see if I can get Les Sawyer to help.'

He found the number and dialled. It was answered almost immediately. 'Hey, Les, it's Russ Walker; I'm looking for a favour. I've two mobile phone numbers that are no longer in use, and I need to know who they were last issued to.'

'Russ, how're you doing? Boy, are you missed. Is it right you've changed your name to Philip Marlow?'

'Oh, very droll. Les, this is important; I'd really appreciate your help.'

'Come on, Russ, you know I can't do that.'

'Les, if I promise to take you and Sal to that steakhouse in Stratford...'

'Yeah, you said that last time, and we're still waiting.'

He looked across at Sue. 'No, I mean it, and I've an extremely beautiful woman I'd like you and Sal to meet.'

'Hey, now that's different. Sal would never forgive me if I passed up on that. Come on then, give me the numbers.'

Russ read them out, sent his love to Sal and disconnected.

Sue was grinning. 'So, who was that?'

'He's a great guy; he works for the security services, a specialist in computers and communications. He has a lovely wife called Sal. She and Becky were close friends.'

Duke disconnected his mobile and closed his notebook. 'That was a waste of time! The head office is in Eastbourne; according to their records, it was a John Brown of Sussex University who placed the adverts. He paid in cash. When I asked if anyone would remember dealing with him, the woman just laughed.'

Sue picked up the freebie again. 'Some of these adverts are from agencies recruiting men to become escorts.' She pointed with her finger. 'There are two here that not only give their telephone numbers, but their Internet websites. I'll log on and see what I can find.'

Russ got up from the desk and exchanged seats with Sue. 'Hey, you're thinking like a sleuth already.'

Sue booted up the laptop and connected to the internet. She sat back looking at the screen. 'They've got to be scams. Both sites claim to have lots of single women who need escorts to parties, the theatre or just for company. It says escorts of all ages can earn up to a hundred pounds a session. To register as an escort, all you have to do is give a brief description of yourself, plus your credit card details as there's a one off registration fee, and then just wait for the calls.'

Duke pulled a face. 'I wonder how many losers fall for that?'

Russ picked up the phone. 'Let's try one of those numbers.'

She handed the paper to him and he dialled. A recorded message kicked in. 'Welcome to Male Recruitments! Are you looking for adult fun and an opportunity to earn easy money? We have hundreds of single women from all over the country, looking for men to escort them to various functions or for other services – men, just like you. If you are 18 or over, you could earn up to a hundred pounds a session, any day of the week, tax free. For further information and to register with us, go to our website at www.....'

Russ disconnected, then dialled the second number and heard the same recorded message. As soon as he replaced the receiver, the phone rang.

Sue picked it up. 'Good morning, Walker Investigations. How many I help you?' She passed the receiver to Russ. 'It's for you.'

'Hi Russ, it's Les Sawyer. Those two numbers were pay-as-you-talk mobiles, bought over the counter at a shop in Hastings by a John Brown of Sussex University. They were cash transactions.'

'Hey, thanks Les, you're brilliant! I've got two more numbers for you – these are in current use. Could you tell me who they're registered to?' He read out the numbers.

'Like I've got nothing else to do. Come on, Russ, don't push it!'

'Sorry Les, but it *is* important – just this once, please?'

'You smooth talker; I'll call you back.'

Russ put the receiver on its cradle. 'Well, we're no further forward. The numbers in Bo's adverts were registered to the same John Brown of Sussex Uni.'

All three of them considered the meaning of this, but it was Sue who gave voice to it. 'Unless he advertises again, there's no way we can trace him.' She paused, then added,

'There are four other advertisements – two offering male escorts and two male or female escorts. I could phone and ask if Bo is available for a session – he might be on their books! And if that doesn't work, I could put an advert in the paper, something like – "Bo, I don't have your number, but do you still make visits? Would love to meet you", and give my mobile number and a false name.'

Silence fell between them until finally Duke spoke. 'It's a longshot, but it might be worth a try. There again, he might suspect someone's onto him - what do you think, Russ?'

For a moment he faltered; the last thing he wanted was to warn the perp that they knew his name or, more importantly, put Sue at risk.

'That's not a bad idea, Sue. If Bo is connected to any of them, you'd have to give my cottage as your address, and arrange to meet him there where Duke and I would be waiting. If that doesn't work, we could think about plan B and place the advert for next Thursday's edition.'

The phone rang again, and Sue picked up the receiver.

It was Les Sawyer for Russ.

'Les, thanks for getting back; any joy?'

'Hi, Russ. Both numbers are registered to a Clive Frost, 17 Wicks Road, Ashford in Kent. He's had these numbers for about two years.'

'Thanks, Les. I'm really grateful. Love to Sal.' He hung up.

Russ shared the information with them. 'All these so-called agencies could be run by the same bloke. Let's wait and see if Sue strikes lucky with any of them before we pay Frost a visit.' He turned to Sue. 'Over to you, Sue; see if you can get a date with Bo for tomorrow morning.'

Duke got to his feet. 'I'm going to make a move. I'll see you tomorrow about nine. Good luck, Sue.' And he left.

Sue took out her mobile and dialled the first number on her list; it was answered by a woman. 'Male Escorts. How can I help?'

Russ noticed Sue's hand was shaking slightly as she held the phone to her ear. 'Oh, hello, I live at Rye Harbour in East Sussex. Do you have any escorts that cover this area?'

'We certainly do, dear; what do you have in mind?'

Sue swallowed. 'I've never done this before, but I'm feeling lonely and I'm looking to have some fun with a broad-minded man in his twenties or thirties... but he must be discreet and trustworthy.'

'Don't worry dear. Our escorts are hand chosen; you'll be perfectly safe. We guarantee discretion and satisfaction. The charge is a £150 for an hour and a half session, payable in cash to the escort when he arrives. Would you like to make a booking?'

She sounded nervous. 'Well, the thing is... I don't think I want just anyone. A friend of mine had an escort called Bo, and she said he was wonderful. Does he work for you?'

The woman paused, and then said, 'I take it you've never met him?'

'No, I haven't. It's just that I'm a bit scared of having a total stranger come to the house. My friend said she felt safe with Bo.'

'I can understand that, dear; Bo's a lovely young man. When would you like him to call?'

'Oh, that's wonderful – you mean he's one of your escorts?'

'Yes, dear. Do you want to make an appointment?'

Sue looked at Russ and put her thumb up. 'Yes, please. I shall be on my own tomorrow morning. Could he come at eleven?'

'I need just your first name and the address?

'It's Ann, and I live at Fishermans Cottage, The Stade, Rye Harbour. It's next to the Smugglers Pub.'

'Right, Ann. Bo will be with you at eleven; and in case you have nosey neighbours, he'll be carrying a briefcase to make it look like a business call. Have fun; bye.'

Sue disconnected. Her face was flushed. 'Phew! I wasn't sure I could do it!'

Russ went round the desk and pulled her to her feet; she was trembling slightly. 'Ann, you were brilliant!' He kissed her lightly on the lips. 'Now, I think it's time I bought you some lunch. Let's go along to the Mariners.'

When they returned to the office at two, the light was flashing on the answering machine. There was one message from a Paul Cavanah of Buckle and Cavanah, a firm of solicitors at Ashford, asking if Walker Investigations would be interested in undertaking investigative work for them.

Sue returned the call and made an appointment for Russ to see Mr Cavanah at Ashford at three that afternoon.

Chapter 19

It was a half an hour journey to Ashford. Russ left his car on the market place and walked to the solicitor's office in Church Square. The square was inaccessible to motor vehicles, and had the appearance of a cathedral close. On either side of the narrow paved footpath were cobblestones. The medieval buildings surrounding the ancient parish church were mainly private dwellings. He identified the solicitor's office from the brass plaque on the door, pressed the intercom button on the panel beside the oak door, and was buzzed in.

A plump, hard-faced receptionist wearing a loose-fitting chiffon trouser-suit, rang Cavanah's extension and announced Russ's arrival. He was asked to take a seat in the clients' waiting area.

Almost immediately, Paul Cavanah appeared in the doorway and smiled as he offered his hand to Russ. It was a confident, firm handshake.

'Mr Walker, it's good to meet you; shall we go to my office?'

Russ followed him up the carpeted stairs and was shown into a large, cluttered office on the first floor.

Cavanah gestured to a wing backed chair, positioned at an angle in front of his large desk.

'Please, have a seat.'

Cavanah went behind the desk and sat in a swivel chair. Russ noticed he had smiling eyes.

'From time to time, we find it necessary to engage the services of a private investigator, but unfortunately the local man is somewhat unreliable. I believe he's overly distracted with his own personal problems at the moment. Last night I was at a drinks party and found myself talking to Detective Inspector Baillie. I happened to mention the problems we've been having and he suggested I ought to make contact with you. I understand you've only recently moved to Rye?'

Russ wondered if Baillie was being altruistic, or had he welcomed an opportunity to divert his time and attention away from the Tiltman case? Either way, he didn't mind. He was glad to have made this contact.

'That's right; just over three weeks ago. I ought to make it clear I'm not interested in providing evidence of infidelity for divorce proceedings, unless criminal activity is involved, but if I can offer help in other ways, then I'd be happy to consider them. That's assuming we can agree the appropriate fees and expenses.'

Russ outlined his charges, but Cavanah showed no interest in quibbling over money and readily accepted the proposition Russ offered.

'I have a delicate situation I need help with. My client is a local Councillor who has been selected by his local association to stand as a candidate in the next parliamentary elections. He and his brother are partners in a retail business, supplying aids to the disabled. Three months ago, one of his employees claimed to have slipped on an uneven floor in the storeroom of their premises, and damaged his back. Unfortunately, there were no witnesses to this, and he's been off work ever since. He claims he's unable to work due to the pain, and is threatening to sue my client for negligence unless he's prepared to settle out of court for £30,000 in damages.'

Russ took out his notebook. 'Isn't that something for the insurance company to sort out? Presumably your client is covered by employers' liability.'

'Yes, he is, but this employee is a nasty piece of work, and is aware that adverse publicity could scupper my client's chance in the elections. My client is anxious to avoid court action, but he can't afford to shell out that amount of money to keep him quiet.'

'That sounds like a nice little case of blackmail to me.'

'Quite so, but for obvious reasons my client would prefer not to involve the police. This is a marginal seat, and a delicate situation like this could make a difference to the outcome.'

Russ would have preferred to hold back from accepting this assignment until he'd caught Carol Tiltman's murderer, but it shouldn't be too difficult to obtain a few photographs of this employee participating in activities that would be impossible for someone with a bad back to engage in. After all, they were a team of three now.

Russ clicked his ballpoint pen. 'If you'd like to give me the name and address of this poor sick employee, I'm sure we can sort this out sensitively to your client's satisfaction.'

Cavanah got up from his chair and handed Russ a sheet of paper. 'I think all the information you need is there. I hardly need to remind you that this is strictly confidential. Thank you for your help.'

Russ returned to the office just as Sue was about to lock up and leave.

'Hi, gorgeous. I think our contact with Buckle and Cavanah could be useful. I know we're preoccupied with nailing this killer, but we have to think ahead. Cavanah offered us a small assignment which I decided to accept. It shouldn't take too much time to sort out, and hopefully he'll want to call on our services in the future.'

'That's great, and there's some more good news. The head of security at a pharmaceutical company wants to talk to you. He was very cagey with me, but they've obviously got a serious problem, and for some reason don't want to involve the police. I told him it might be a day or two before you could get back to him, but he said that wasn't a problem. I've put his name and number in the diary. Things are really looking up for Walker Investigations.'

Russ grinned. 'Hey, who knows – I might even start earning enough to pay you the going rate! Now, about tomorrow and our date with Bo... If you come straight to the cottage – say about ten – park in front of the garage. I'll ask Duke to leave his car with mine further along the Stade. We can have coffee together before this character turns up. But you're not to worry. You only have to answer the door to let him in; Duke and I will take over from there. You won't be in any danger, I promise.'

'To be honest, I'm not really anxious; if anything, I'm excited. Just think – this time tomorrow it will all be over and this evil creature will be in custody.'

'If he turns up and really is Bo, yes.'

The next morning, Duke arrived at the cottage at nine, having left his car by the harbour wall, and at five to ten Sue pulled into the parking space in front of the garage. Over coffee, it was decided that when the escort arrived, Sue would answer the door and invite him into the lounge. Russ would be out of sight in the kitchen with the door slightly ajar; Duke would be in the dining room.

He was on time. It was exactly eleven when the doorbell rang. Russ and Duke took up their positions while Sue answered the door. He was in his mid-thirties, dressed like a businessman in his light grey suit and black leather briefcase. He was clean shaven, medium build, about five ten with closely cropped blond hair.

There was something about his smile that sent a shiver down Sue's spine. He held out his hand.

'Hello, you must be Ann; my name is Bo. I think you're expecting me?'

Nervously, Sue shook his hand. 'Oh, hi; yes, do come in.'

He followed her into the sitting room, placed his briefcase on the settee and sat down beside it. 'You look nervous, Ann, but you needn't be. I was told this is your first time with an escort.' His eyes scanned the room. 'Nice place you've got. I take it there's no chance we're going to be interrupted?'

Trying to hide her nervousness, she sat in the armchair, and tucked her trembling hands under her thighs. 'I have the house to myself; my husband's in London all day – he won't be back until this evening. You really are Bo, aren't you?' she said with a hint of anxiety.

'Of course I am. Look, don't worry – I'm here to do whatever you want.' He paused, glanced at his watch and then fixed his eyes on her breasts. 'You're a beautiful woman, Ann, and I like what I see.' He smiled and looked into her face. 'We've got an hour and a half to have some real excitement, but if we could just get the business of the fees out of the way, then we can forget all about it and get down to the fun.'

She got to her feet. 'Yes, of course. I'll just get my purse.'

Moving past him on her way to the door, it almost threw her when he leaned forward, reached out with his hand and squeezed her bottom. She immediately tensed and had to force herself not to slap him.

She reached the hallway where Duke was waiting. He gave her a reassuring grin and a thumbs-up sign, then indicated for her to wait upstairs. He entered the lounge, closing the door behind him, as Russ appeared at the door from the kitchen. The poor sucker was visibly shocked; the colour drained from his face. Panic-stricken, momentarily he froze, like a rabbit caught in the headlights of an oncoming car. Then reality kicked in; he was in deep trouble. He grabbed for his briefcase and leapt to his feet, but Russ quickly stepped forward, put a hand to his chest and thrust him back onto the settee.

Duke wrenched the briefcase from his hand as he and Russ stood over him.

'Okay, lover boy, just listen carefully. We don't want to hurt you, but if we have to, we will. Now nice and slowly put your hands on top of your head and link your fingers.'

The man was terrified and did as he was told. 'What the fuck's going on? I haven't done anything wrong; she asked me to come.'

Russ took a step back. 'I want you to stand up slowly, keeping your hands on your head.'

He struggled to get his balance and did as he was told. Russ patted him down. There were no weapons, but he took the man's wallet from the inside pocket of his jacket.

'Right, now, drop your trousers.' Duke ordered.

'No way! What the hell are you talking about?' he answered.

Duke put his hands together and cracked his knuckles. 'I said drop your trousers, and I won't ask you again.'

Lowering his hands, he unbuckled his belt, undid the top button and slowly pushed his trousers to his ankles.

'Now your boxers, and lift up your shirt,' Duke continued.

He slid his underpants down to his knees and pulled up his shirt, exposing his genitals. Above his small, limp penis was an untrimmed bush of blond pubic hair. Duke glanced at Russ and gave a slight shake of his head. This pathetic creature was no serial murderer. Clearly he wasn't worried about leaving DNA evidence.

Russ pushed him back down onto the settee. 'So, what's your real name, sunshine?'

He covered himself with his shirt. 'Laurence Norman. Look, I've been stitched up – what's this about?'

Duke opened the briefcase, tipped the contents onto the floor and began to separate the items with his right foot. 'Close your mouth and speak when you're spoken to. So what have we got here? A vibrator, KY jelly, condoms, digital camera, aromatherapy oils, and what's this? A packed lunch! Man, you're really prepared for a hard day at the office!' This was a disappointment, but not unexpected; no baby oil, rope or duct tape.

Russ inspected the contents of the wallet. The UK driving license with an unflattering photograph confirmed he was Laurence Norman, with an address in a village called Chartfield, near Hastings. The credit cards and RAC membership were all issued to the same person.

'Right, Laurence, so why are you calling yourself Bo?' Russ demanded.

'I work for an escort agency; they told me a woman wanted to hire an escort, but was nervous and wanted someone called Bo. The Agency doesn't have anyone using that name, but as she'd never met him, I pretended to be this bloke.'

Duke reached over and took a white business card from Russ' hand. 'It says here, "Mr and Mrs L. Norman," and there's a telephone number – perhaps we should ask Mrs Norman to confirm his identity?' He took his mobile from his pocket.

'Oh, for God's sake, please don't. She'll go berserk! Look, if she ever found out I've been doing this, she'd divorce me - and we've got three young children; please don't.' His lower lip trembled; he was on the verge of crying.

Russ raised his eyebrows and gave a slight nod of his head to Duke. He lowered himself into the armchair nearest Norman, and Duke sat in the chair opposite.

'Alright, Laurence, pull your trousers up – and then you can tell us about the escort business.'

Norman quickly got to his feet, pulled up his underpants and trousers, tucked in his shirt and sat down again. From his jacket pocket, he took out a handkerchief and blew his nose. He was anxious to get this over with.

'I've only been doing this for three months. I used to work for Rother District Council, but was made redundant. We've got a big mortgage, but I couldn't get another job. I went on a course to learn how to do aromatherapy and reflexology, but I've been struggling. It takes time to build up clientele.'

Duke cut in. 'So, how did you get into male prostitution?'

His shock had turned to embarrassment. He looked down at his hands. 'I saw an advert that said men could earn hundreds of pounds a week as escorts, and I enrolled. I did it online on my computer.'

'I take it your wife never knew?' Duke asked.

'Good Lord, no!' he replied sheepishly. 'Thankfully she doesn't know how to use the computer. The Agency sends me bookings by email; sometimes it's two or three a week, sometimes more. I get a hundred quid each time, and they get fifty. I send them a cheque each month.'

'So, who runs the Agency?' asked Russ.

'It's called Male Recruitments and I send the cheques to a Post Office box number at Ashford. I don't know anything else about them.'

Russ stood up. 'Okay, Laurence, you can go, but if you want your marriage to survive and your children to be proud of you, I guess it's time for a change of profession.'

Norman nodded but said nothing, and quickly replaced the tools of his trade in his briefcase. He was in such a hurry to get to the door, he almost tripped over his own feet. Russ stood on the threshold and watched him run the length of the Stade.

Duke called up the stairs to Sue. 'Hey, Ann, lover-boy's gone; sorry, but he wasn't Bo. Come and join us.'

When she came into the room, they told a disappointed Sue what had happened.

She said, 'I was so worked up, I hardly slept last night. I really thought we were going to get him.'

Duke encouraged her. 'You played your part to perfection; well done. I guess we'll have to think about plan B and put our own advert in the paper – see if we can flush him out that way.' He turned to Russ. 'In the meantime, how about we have a drink and a bar-snack at the Smugglers, and then you and I could go to Ashford and have a word with Mr Frost?'

Chapter 20

It was about two when Russ and Duke set off for Ashford in the Capri, and Sue returned to the office in Rye. According to the map, Wicks Road was on the outskirts of the town, close to the William Harvey Hospital. The houses on both sides of the road were large three-storey semi-detached dwellings, built somewhere around the turn of the last century. Number 17 was halfway along on the left. A black BMW was parked outside. Russ pulled into a space two houses along.

Frost's house looked neglected – the front door and sash-window frames were badly in need of a fresh coat of paint. There were grey-coloured net curtains at the windows. They entered an alcove that couldn't have seen the bristles of a broom for at least a year, and Russ pressed the bell-push on the red-brick wall beside the door. Through the stained glass window above the door they saw the hall light had been switched on. The door was opened by a slim, heavily made-up middle-aged woman. Her bottle-blonde hair had been backcombed, reminding Russ of an archetypal pub landlady. The top three buttons of her pink nylon blouse were unfastened, revealing a deep wrinkled cleavage, and her ample breasts strained the remaining buttons. Her short denim skirt would have had more appeal on someone twenty years younger.

She looked at each of them in turn, and hesitantly asked, 'Yes?'

Duke smiled at her. 'Good afternoon; we'd like to have a word with Mr Frost, please.'

'What about?'

'Perhaps you would be kind enough to tell him Mr Walker and Mr Windsor would like to speak to him about Male Recruitments. It won't take long.'

Her eyes narrowed, 'I'll see if he's free.' She closed the door.

Duke turned to Russ. 'I don't fancy yours. I think I'll go for Clive!'

Frost opened the door. He too was in his mid-fifties, about five ten and heavily built, wearing a garish short-sleeved summer shirt, knee-length beige shorts and sandals. He made no attempt to conceal his irritation.

'I'm Clive Frost. What do you want?'

Duke held out his hand. 'Good afternoon, Mr Frost, I wonder if you could spare us a few moments – it's about your business, Male Recruitments.'

Frost ignored the hand. 'What about it?'

Duke made to step over the threshold, but Frost blocked his way.

Russ smiled. 'It's all right Mr Frost, we're not from the Inland Revenue; we're private investigators and believe you could help us with a case we're working on.'

Frost didn't return the smile. 'I think you've got the wrong address. I don't know what you're talking about.'

He stepped back and began to close the door.

Duke pushed against the door and forced his way into the house, Russ followed. Frost moved away from them.

'What the fuck do you think you're doing? I didn't invite you in; get out!'

Russ closed the door behind him. 'That's not very friendly, is it? We just want to ask a few questions. Let's find your office, shall we?'

Frost hesitated; he was well able to look after himself in a fight, but it was obvious he was no match for these two.

'Look, I don't want any trouble. What's this about?'

'If you take us into your office, I'll explain. It shouldn't take long.'

He led them into what, for most occupiers of houses of this design, should have been a sitting room. The room reeked of cigarette smoke and fried bacon. The light was on and the curtains drawn. There were two large old-fashioned armchairs facing the empty fireplace, beside which was a widescreen television set showing an episode of 'Judge Judy'. Between the chairs stood a tea-trolley which held two coffee mugs, a plate holding a half-eaten bacon sandwich, an ashtray in need of emptying and a copy of the *Daily Mirror*. Against the wall on the other side of the room was a large office table and swivel chair. On the table were two laptop computers and a printer. Only one of the computers was in use.

Beside it was a smaller table and office chair. A large desk diary lay open on the table, and a cordless telephone sat in its cradle.

There were two large filing cabinets against another wall, and two wooden dining-chairs.

Russ looked at the woman. 'And you are...?'

'Shirley Temple – but what's it to you?'

Duke pointed to the desk chair in front of the computers. 'Why don't you sit down, Clive?' He positioned the other swivel chair next to it. 'And you, Shirley Temple, can sit here.'

Frost nodded to her and they sat down. Russ and Duke sat facing them on the wooden dining-chairs.

'So, what can you tell us about an escort who uses the name Bo?' Russ asked.

The woman frowned, looked at Frost then back at Russ. 'We don't know anyone with that name. What's this about?'

Duke cut in. 'You arranged for an escort to visit a woman at Rye Harbour this morning. You told her his name was Bo, but he turned out to be a turd by the name of Laurence Norman. All we want to know is how we can contact the real Bo.'

Frost answered. 'We don't know anyone who uses that name. The woman said she'd never met him, so we gave the job to Norman. Did he fuck up, or something?'

Russ pulled a free newspaper from his pocket. 'Apart from a bit of deception, no!' He held it up. 'In here, there are several advertisements for escort agencies, and we know at least two of them are yours. How many others do you run?'

'They're all ours. We provide male *and* female escorts. It's all above board - nothing illegal. Sometimes there will be an advert from someone pretending to be an agency, but they don't last long.'

I'll bet you make sure of that!

'Do you run them all from here?' asked Duke.

'No, we have several offices.'

'When you say we, do you mean *you* own the business, or do you work for someone else?'

'We're not the owners. We work for a company called Alpha Associates. They cover most of the south of England.'

Frost picked up a cigarette packet from the desk, took out a cigarette and placed it between his lips. He searched unsuccessfully in the pockets of his shorts for a lighter. The woman reached behind him to the desk and produced a lighter which she handed to him. He lit up and dropped the lighter, into the breast pocket of his shirt.

'I guess it's quite a lucrative business. So where's the head office of Alpha Associates?' Russ asked.

'It's in London,' said the woman, 'but why do you want to know? We've told you, we don't know anyone called Bo.'

Duke eyeballed Frost. 'If a Tom finds another woman on her patch, her pimp soon moves the newcomer on; so how do *you* move someone on if they advertise themselves as an escort? My guess is you phone for an appointment and beat the shit out of them when they turn up. Am I right, or am I right?'

Frost curled his lip. 'I dunno what you're talking about.'

Russ decided to test their reactions. 'Not long ago, there was an advertisement that purported to be an agency: "Gigolos 4U: Hire a beau", it said. Did you put him out of business?'

The woman glanced quickly at Frost, and although his face remained impassive, Russ noticed he'd stiffened a little.

233

Frost stood up. 'I haven't a fucking clue what you're on about, dickhead! It's time for you to leave.'

He turned his back on them and began to make for the door.

Duke leaped up behind him, forced his right hand between Frost's legs and grabbed his testicles, while his left arm snaked round his throat. Frost went up on his toes and gave a high pitched scream.

'I get really angry when people call me dickhead; don't do it again. Now, tell us about Gigolos 4U – who is he?'

The woman swore and lunged at Duke, but Russ pulled her back and restrained her. Frost was in agony and remained perfectly still.

'Tell him, Clive; just tell him,' she shouted.

Duke squeezed and Frost screamed again. 'All right, all right,' he gasped. 'We were going to teach him a lesson, but it turned out to be the boss' son.'

Duke released Frost, who collapsed on the floor. 'So, are you going to tell us who he is, or do I have to force it out of you?'

Russ let go of the woman and she knelt down beside Frost. 'Tell them, Clive, and they'll leave us alone.'

'You know I can't; it'll get us both killed.'

Duke went down on his haunches. 'Listen to me, Clive. Tell me his name and where I can find him, and maybe I won't have to mention where I got the information. Failing that, I'm going to take the hard drive from your computer and any other records you have to give to the police, then squeeze your balls so hard they'll never work again.'

'Alex, Alex Provone. His old man kicked him out of the business; doesn't have anything to do with him. He lives somewhere in Brighton.'

'Where in Brighton?'

'We don't know his address; we only had his mobile number.'

'So how did you find out who he is? Russ asked.

The woman answered. 'We reported to our head office that we'd seen the advert, and they asked me to answer it, booking a session with him at my flat at Hastings. They sent two men down from London to keep the appointment and rough him up a bit... One of them recognised Alex and told him to get back to Brighton and behave himself.'

Duke nodded in encouragement. 'You're doing well, Shirley, but not well enough. We want his Brighton address.'

'Even if I knew it, I daren't give it to you – but I honestly don't know. We were told to keep our mouths shut about him being the boss' son, and to forget any mention of Brighton.'

Clive got to his feet and still nursing his testicles, half-fell into one of the armchairs. He shook his head. 'You don't know who you're dealing with. Why don't you just drop it and go away?'

Russ was tired of playing games. He gripped Frost's face and turned it towards him. 'You'd better believe me, Frost; we know who we're dealing with. But tell me this – why doesn't Old Man Provone have anything to do with his son Alex?'

'I don't know. There's a rumour that his old man rejected him, because there's something wrong with him; I dunno what it is – that's all I know.'

They took their leave of Frost and Shirley Temple and headed back to Rye.

Russ was grinning. 'What do they call it, the Law of Karma? "What goes around, comes around". Bloody hell, we're back with Provone – or at least his murderous son.'

Back in the office, over coffee, Russ filled Sue in about Alex Provone, aka Bo.

'All we've got to do is find him.' He got up and went to the filing cabinet. 'I kept a copy of Provone's file when I left the SCU.'

Spreading the papers on the desk, he shared with Duke and Sue the brief background of Marcus Provone. 'Aged forty-nine, wealthy owner of an import/export business based in Canning Town. Personal address, Jade House, a large detached property in Stonewell Road on the Isle of Dogs. To the public at large, he's Mr Decent, a pillar of the local community. He's donated generously to a number of community projects on the Isle of Dogs, funded the setting up of a Family Care Centre in Telford Street, where counselling and support is available to deprived and struggling families, is an active Trustee of the Centre, often seen chatting to both paid and volunteer staff. He also sits on a couple of local school Governing bodies.

In spite of his public persona, intelligence suggests his import/export business is a cover for a growing empire dealing in drugs, pornography, prostitution and money laundering. Behind his respectable facade, there is a hardened criminal, the head of one of the largest crime syndicates in the south of England! Believed to own a number of London nightclubs including two in Limehouse. Appears to think himself untouchable by the law. His wife's name is Francesca; an attractive blonde, who it's believed has no involvement in Provone's business affairs. They have two children, Amy, aged 27 and Alexander, aged 25.'

He looked and smiled at Sue, 'Guess what? They both went to your Alma matar, Nottingham University. Amy was a medical student and is now a Junior Doctor at St. Thomas' Hospital, London, and Alexander read Business Management. No other info on him. The intelligence we had was that Provone's wife and children appear to be a normal family, and probably think he's a legitimate and successful businessman.

'The SCU have no doubts that Provone – or at least his 'employees' acting on his orders – were behind the bomb that killed Becky. Plenty of circumstantial evidence but nothing that would be admissible in court.'

. 'I wonder why the son was rejected by his father? And if he's believed to be living in Brighton, how do we find him?' Sue asked.

Duke frowned. 'Frost said there was something wrong with him. I wonder if it's a health problem. As for finding him, he's probably using an assumed name.' He pulled out his mobile. 'I'll ask Em to run a check with the DVLA and HM Revenue and Customs, but I don't hold out much hope.'

While Duke talked to his sister, Sue made a fresh cafetiere of coffee and brought it into the office.

'Nottingham University would have an address for him, but it may not be his present one, and I doubt they would give it to us anyhow - data protection and all that. How about I try his sister; pretend I'm organising a reunion for alumni of his years at Uni?"

"It might work; give St. Thomas' a ring. If she's still there, it's possible she could be on duty."

Duke came off the phone. 'I knew it couldn't be that easy. There's no record at the DVLA of an Alexander Provone ever registering a vehicle, and HM Revenue and Customs only have his parents' address.'

Sue found St. Thomas' number on the internet and dialled the number. Amazingly, Dr Amy Provone was on duty and the receptionist paged her. After a couple of minutes' wait, she picked up a phone and was connected to Sue. In a casual and relaxed voice, Sue explained the reason for her call, and the difficulties she was having in tracing a number of the students, Alex included. Amy happily gave her Alex's address, apologising that she couldn't remember the post code. Sue thanked her and rang off.

Grinning, she looked up; Russ and Duke were staring at her in astonishment. 'Flat 20, Harmony House, Downs Avenue, Kemp Town, Brighton.'

Chapter 21

She looked up and smiled as he entered the utility room. 'Hello! The other one's free.' She was bending down, loading the larger of the two washing machines.

He smiled back. 'No, it's okay; I did mine yesterday.' He said, 'A bulb's blown on the top landing and the damn trip-switch has gone again.'

He turned to the large wooden box on the wall behind the door, and pulled down the hinged front panel. Beneath the row of trip-switches was a fuse box connected to the alarm circuit for the emergency exits. He glanced back; she was busy spooning in the washing power. He flicked the switch to silence the alarm, and closed the panel.

'I'll leave you to it – bye' he said, as he opened the door to leave.

He knew the old man was having him watched. On several occasions he'd seen the goons in the doorways opposite or sitting in cars, pretending to read newspapers. Amateurish idiots! It was so easy to slip out the emergency exit at the rear of the block, over the low wall and into the adjoining road. As long as he left the light on in his room, he could come and go at his leisure, and they were none the wiser.

He put on his helmet, and sat astride the 250 cc Yamaha Virago. He liked this bike – shame he would have to get rid of it soon. His damned epileptic condition prevented him from getting a licence to drive or ride a bike like this, even though the acetazolamide he'd been prescribed had kept the seizures at bay for the last five months. Yes, he was attached to this bike. He'd stolen it a week ago in Eastbourne, and changed the plates to those of an identical one he saw in Rye, trusting that if a cop car with number plate recognition equipment were to flag him, it would come up as being taxed, insured and MOT tested and he wouldn't get pulled over. It was a trick he'd pulled many times before.

With the gear in his backpack, he pulled away from the kerb, excited at the prospect of an hour's undisturbed pleasure. She'd said she'd be alone all evening, and was definitely into bondage.

Duke was concerned. 'So, how do we play this? Are you going to share it with Baillie, or do *we* get to him first?'

The images of Carol Tiltman and Elaine Knightly flashed into Russ' mind. There was no hesitation; he stood up. 'Let's go and find him. Sue, we'll leave you to lock up.'

'Of course, but please be careful and keep in touch.'

It was early evening when they arrived in Brighton. Duke grinned as they passed The Royal Pavilion on their left.

'Always reminds me of a cross between the Kremlin and the Taj Mahal.'

The Royal Pavilion, designed by the famous English architect John Nash, was built in the style of an Oriental Palace in the late-18th and early-19th century as a seaside retreat for George, Prince of Wales who became the Prince Regent and later still, King George IV. As a Prince, he used it as a discreet location to enjoy liaisons with his long-time companion and socialite, Maria Fitzherbert.

Stopping at a BP garage, they picked up a street map of the city and made their way west along Marine Parade to Kemp Town. Historically, this area of Brighton was popular with artists and actors, and is known to have a sizeable gay community. Over the years, many of the large Georgian properties had been converted into flats and bars. Acacia Trees lined both sides of Downs Avenue. The large detached houses and modern apartment blocks had an air of affluence. There were limited parking spaces, restricted to local residents displaying permits in their car windscreens. Harmony House was set back from the road with its own garages and parking area. Opposite were several small shops with a lay-by for customers' vehicles. Russ drove slowly past and two streets away found a small Pay and Display carpark. He pulled in to a parking bay and switched off the engine. From the glove compartment, he took a small roll of black fabric and a laminated card. Grinning, he unrolled the fabric to reveal a priest's clerical collar sewn into the top.

'It's authentic, it's called a Bib Stock.' He put the collar round his neck securing it with velcro tabs, and smoothed the black fabric down his chest, tucking it into his jacket.

Clearly impressed, Duke linked his hands together. 'Bless me, Father, for I have sinned.'

Russ mimicked a parson's voice. 'Sorry, my son, I'll need a month or more if I'm to hear your confession.' He reverted to his normal voice. 'Flat 20 has to be on the third or fourth floor; presumably there's a fire escape at the back, but if we use that, we'd draw too much attention. I guess it has to be the direct approach. I'll park in the bay reserved for residents and we'll take it from there.'

He started the car, drove back to Downs Avenue and turned into the parking area reserved for residents of Harmony House. As he placed the laminated card which read 'Priest on Call' on the dashboard, he saw an elderly woman with a Zimmer frame slowly approaching the main entrance.

'Give me a minute; I'll get inside then let you in.'

Duke hoisted his small rucksack onto his left shoulder.

Russ reached the door as the woman inserted her key in the lock. She turned and smiled. 'Hello, Father. You must be the new priest at St. George's; my friend goes to the church. She says they've been looking forward to your coming.'

He smiled. 'Me too. Here, let me hold the door for you.'

He waited until she had shuffled her way along the corridor and turned the corner before opening the door for Duke. Ignoring the lift, they took to the stairs. On each landing there were direction signs for the numbered flats. 20 was on the fourth floor, round a corner at the end of the corridor. After pulling on latex gloves, Duke stood to the side and nodded. Russ rang the doorbell and waited. They heard it ring inside the flat, but there was no response, so he rang again. Duke unzipped his rucksack and took out a small tyre iron. Jamming it between the door and the frame close to the lock, he wrenched it back sharply. There was a dull crack of splintering wood, and the door swung open. He rushed into a small hallway, Russ close behind. He checked the bathroom, kitchen and two bedrooms as Russ entered the lounge. Provone wasn't home, but he'd left the wall lights on.

242

The flat was clean and tidy, and expensively furnished. In the lounge, gold velvet drapes were tied back at the windows; a luxurious beige three-seater settee and matching armchair were angled in front of a large flat screened TV. A laptop attached to a printer was open on a small oak table by the window.

Aware that Provone could return at any moment, time was of the essence. Russ checked the bedrooms. Apart from porn magazines and videos, he found no incriminating evidence. Confirmation that they were at the right address came from a cupboard under the kitchen sink, where he discovered two bottles of baby oil and a coil of blue nylon cord, which he left in situ. He returned to the lounge to share the good news with Duke and found him sitting at the table looking at the laptop.

'Hey, Father, I'm not sure a man of the cloth should see this. The twisted bastard had left it switched on. I didn't need a password – I just touched the mouse and this filled the screen.'

It was a website for devotees of sadism and bondage, offering any number of images and videos that could be downloaded, plus a forum for like-minded people to chat to each other, and links to other bondage sites.

Beside the computer was a hands-free telephone charging in its cradle and a writing pad and ballpoint pen; several pages had been torn from the pad, leaving a clean top sheet. Russ picked it up, held it close to his eyes and angled it to a wall lamp.

'There are indentations from whatever was written on the last page to be torn out.'

'Here, allow me.' Duke took a pencil from his backpack and lightly shaded over the imprints. 'It looks like a shopping list and then... Bloody hell! Look at this - the sicko's out on a date! It's a bit faint ... But there it is ... Today's date, 'brutalbarbs25', 7.30 to 8.30pm Basement flat, The Firs, 29 Station Road, Benwick, Bexhill.'

Russ checked his watch; it was 7.45pm. 'There's no way we can get there before he leaves.'

He took out his mobile and speed-dialled Baillie. It rang seven times before going to an answering service. 'Alec, this is an emergency – it's Russ Walker. We've located Bo. Please phone my mobile as soon as you hear this – there's no time to lose.' He ended the call. 'Sod it, I'll have to call CID at Hastings.' He got as far as keying in the area code when his phone rang.

It was Baillie. 'Sorry, Russ, I was in the shower; tell me what you've got.'

'I'm in Brighton with a colleague and there's no time to explain, just trust me - this is kosher. Bo's real name is Alexander Provone, and at this very moment he's in Benwick, near Bexhill, having sex with a woman who calls herself "Brutalbarbs". He'll only be there until 8.30pm.'

He gave Baillie the address and promised he and Duke would be at Hastings Police Station in a couple of hours with a full explanation. Before hanging up, he suggested Baillie contact Brighton CID to secure Provone's flat, as it had already been broken into.

Duke vented his frustration with a few expletives. 'It should have been us collaring Provone. Let's hope Baillie and his team don't fuck it up.'

'He won't – he's a good cop. Let's see what else we can find before we leave.'

Duke concentrated on the laptop, printing copies of anything he considered significant. Russ made a note of the telephone number, and scrolled through the records of incoming calls and dialled numbers. He listened for any stored messages on the answering service. There was only one; it was a man's voice.

'Hey it's me; thanks, but I can't make it.' It had been made from a public call-box.

Among papers lying on a pouffe, there was no personal correspondence, just a few invoices from utility companies addressed to Mr A. Provone.

They were running out of time. 'Come on, Duke, let's get out of here.'

Duke left the laptop still showing the bondage site, stuffed the papers he'd printed off in his rucksack, and was ready to go.

They pulled the door to behind them, and saw no-one as they left the building.

Throwing his rucksack over to the backseat... Removing the clerical collar, Duke got into the drivers' seat. Russ called Sue on his mobile to update her on the situation. Wary of traffic cops and speed cameras, Duke pressed down on the accelerator as often as he could, maintaining a good pace.

It was a little after 10pm when they drew up outside Hastings' Police Station. Russ asked the officer at the reception counter to let DI Baillie know they had arrived.

An eager looking DS Askew appeared behind the glass screen and called for them to go through a side door. He pressed the lock release button. He met them the other side and vigorously shook their hands.

'Well done! We got him! The governor can't wait to talk to you.' He led the way up a flight of stairs to Baillie's office.

As they entered the room, Baillie was standing at the window behind his desk, talking into his mobile. He turned and grinned, gesturing with his free hand for them to take a seat. There were three padded chairs against the wall in front of the desk; Russ and Duke sat down. Askew closed the door but remained on his feet.

The telephone conversation ended, Baillie came round the desk greeting them with warm handshakes. He looked at Askew.

'See if you can rustle up some coffee and sandwiches for our friends.' With a nod of his head, Askew left the room.

'We've got a lot to discuss, not least how in God's name you identified him, and knew where we'd find him; but we'll come to that. I guess you're dying to know how we arrested him. After your tip off, we took a team of ten officers to Benwick. With the front and rear covered, we stormed into the flat and caught the perp literally with his trousers down. They were both naked and covered in oil; "Brutalbarbs" tied to the bed just like the others, and he on top of her.

'She was scared shitless, but not of him – of us! She insisted what they were doing together was consensual and not against the law. He didn't resist arrest and made no comment before or after being cautioned. He was allowed to get dressed, then cuffed and brought back here. The woman was in a state of shock once she realised why he'd been arrested, and how close she'd been to being his next victim. We left a liaison officer to look after her.'

Russ ran a hand through his hair. 'That's a great result, Alec. Presumably he had his paraphernalia with him.'

'Oh, yes.' He ticked them off on his fingers.' Baby oil, blue rope, a vibrator, a riding crop, an IPhone and a motorcycle helmet. We haven't located the bike yet, but we are looking for it.'

There was a tap on the door. Askew had returned with coffee, sandwiches, and a half dozen bottles of lager.

'Sorry, there's no champagne.' He placed the tray on Baillie's desk.

Baillie stood up. 'Help yourself, gents – then it's your turn.'

Over coffee, Russ explained how they had identified Provone through the classified ads in the free papers, and through applying pressure to an escort agency, they discovered he was living somewhere in Brighton. He told of his knowledge of the Provone family, and how they duped his sister into revealing his address.

Duke took over by describing how they had gone to Brighton and discovered his flat had already been broken into, and how a brief search of the property led them to finding the details of Provone's date with "Brutalbarbs".

Elated with the result, Baillie was happy to call it a day, and sent Russ and Duke home.

It was just after nine the next morning when they all arrived at the office. Sue brought in the cafetiere and mugs and placed them on her desk next to a vase of red roses. 'You deserve champagne and medals for what you've done. I'm so proud of you both. I'm looking forward to hearing all about it.' She depressed the plunger and poured the coffee. 'Like my flowers? Just after you left yesterday, I had a visitor who won't take no for an answer, DS Askew. He asked me out again, but I gave him short shrift; he insisted on leaving the flowers. I felt guilty; it was quite sweet of him, really.'

Russ made no attempt to hide his irritation. 'Maybe I should have a word with Baillie.'

She smiled. 'Forget it; it's not a problem.' She tapped a key on her laptop and swivelled it round towards them. 'Take a look at that.' Duke leaned closer to Russ for a better view.

On the screen was a film clip of a middle-aged man, stripped to the waist, laying large concrete paving slabs at the front of a semi-detached house. He was obviously making a new path of about fifteen yards in length from the pavement to the front door of the house. The clip moved to him lifting several more slabs from the back of his estate car and placing them in a pile in the front garden, and then cut to him laying them.

Duke straightened up. 'Oh, very nice, Sue. If that's what turns you on, come up to London next week and I'll let you film me in my jockeys putting out the rubbish bins.'

She laughed, turning back the laptop. 'Don't be such a smart-arse.' She looked at Russ. 'While you were in Brighton, I was worrying about both of you. I couldn't just sit about doing nothing, so I had a look at the notes you'd made after your visit to the solicitor, Paul Cavanah at Ashford. I found the address of the employee who claims he has a back injury and is threatening to sue his employer, and there he is, strong as an ox, lifting and laying concrete slabs. He didn't see me. I shot that as I sat in my car. Would you like me to send it as an attachment to Mr Cavanah?'

'Great work, Sue, I'm impressed. Yes please – his client will be delighted.'

The doorbell rang. Discovering it was DI Baillie, Sue pressed the release catch button.

He entered the office, looking dishevelled as if he'd been up all night, eyes bloodshot, face needing a shave.

Russ stood up. 'Hi, Alec, have a seat before you fall over.'

Sue made for the door. 'I'll be down at Patsy's if you need me.'

Baillie sat down. 'I'm on my way home to get a couple of hours shut-eye and wanted to keep you in the loop. Provone used his one permitted phone call to speak to his mother. She persuaded his father to hire a top-class lawyer in London, and we had to wait for him to arrive. In short, Provone denies he murdered Carol Tiltman and Elaine Knightley. He admits he visited them for consensual sex on the days they were murdered, but claims they were alive and well, though still tied to their beds when he left them. He'd left the back doors unlocked and someone else must have entered their homes and killed them. When asked why he'd shaved his head and exfoliated his body, his bloody lawyer advised him to say nothing more.'

Russ shook his head. 'What did he say about Martina Fischer in Germany?'

'We haven't mentioned her as yet. Kommissar Roeseler from Bielefeld will be arriving this evening to interview him, and he's bringing the DNA results, hoping for a match. DS Askew's organising door to door enquiries in Benwick, praying someone may have seen or heard something.' He got to his feet. 'By the way, the SOCOs are at his flat in Brighton. Are they likely to find anything that might incriminate either of you?'

Duke shook his head. 'Nothing that can't be explained, don't worry.'

'Good; I'll be in touch.'

Chapter 22

Baillie's visit had unsettled Russ. Was it really possible anyone would believe Provone's story? Could a clever defence lawyer raise doubts in a juror's mind? After all, no one witnessed the actual killings. Provone freely admitted to having visited the victims for kinky sex, but was there enough evidence to convict him? A match to the DNA samples from Germany would be enough to prove he'd had sex with Martina Fischer, but it wouldn't prove he actually killed her.

'I don't like it, Duke. Is the circumstantial evidence enough? Obviously everything points to Provone as the perp, but if he insists they were alive when he left them, could a top defence lawyer persuade a jury of reasonable doubt?'

'I'm with you; I don't like it either, but murderers are often convicted solely on circumstantial and hearsay evidence, and sometimes without even a body. If we could just find something to prove that he's lying. At his flat in Brighton, you said there was a short message left on his phone. Remind me – what did it say?'

Russ checked his note book. 'It was a man's voice, "Hey it's me; thanks, but I can't make it." It had been left at 2.30pm yesterday from a public call-box, but it could mean almost anything. Maybe Provone had arranged to meet someone for a drink or something. Maybe he'd invited a fellow pervert he'd met online to have fun with "Brutalbarbs" after he'd finished with her! His lawyer will have a field day with this.'

Sue returned to the office with three ham and cheese baguettes and made some fresh coffee. Over lunch, they brought her up to date on all that had happened, including their conversation with Baillie and their unease about the situation.

'Will the stuff you found on his computer or his telephone records give any clues?'

Duke concurred, 'That's what we'll have to work on; it's all we've got.'

Lunch over, Russ began typing out the list of calls and numbers found on Provone's telephone. Duke gave Sue the website address displayed on the perp's computer. She typed in the URLs and up it came. She let out a shriek.

'Oh my goodness, I feel sick!'

The homepage displayed numerous explicit scenes of tortured women. At the top were links to a forum, a chatroom, other bondage sites, and for specialist interests. She clicked on the chat room link; up came a list of people with weird usernames who were 'in the room', typing messages to each other. Sometimes they would ask each other if they wanted to have a private chat, and their names would disappear. There was obviously a facility for one-to-one intimate chat.

Duke started reading through the material he'd printed from Provone's laptop. There were several prosaic emails sent and received from friends or acquaintances, but the ones that caught his attention were to and from people using anonymous names - "themistress36", "plasticdemon," "wolfman38," "ringrider", "freaker10" and "gropeman." They were all using a free email service. Provone's user name was "hustler202". The messages were quite inane, bordering on the realm of fantasy; mostly descriptions of sex play they had indulged in or hoped for. "Wolfman38"'s messages were more personal than the others, giving the impression that he and Provone had known each other for a long time. Occasionally there were brief references to previous phone conversations. Duke wondered if it was his message left on the answering service.

An air of gloom seem to have settled; the atmosphere in the room felt heavy. Breaking the silence, Russ suggested they share what they'd discovered so far. Sue began by describing her shock and revulsion of the website, and detailed the contents of the chat room. Russ asked her to compile a list of all the user names she could find. Duke spoke about the emails, drawing particular attention to the ones from "Wolfman38." Russ explained that in the phone's memory store, there were records of all calls made and received, including missed calls; but there were hundreds, far too many for Les Sawyer to work on.

Duke pulled a face. 'Presumably Baillie will have the techs working on the laptop. Hopefully they'll identify "Wolfman38" and the others. The same with the phone records, but it could take several days, if not longer.' He rubbed his chin, deep in thought. 'She might need persuading, but I could ask sister Em for another favour. Maybe the Yards Cyber Crime Unit could tell us who "Wolfman38" is.'

He took out his mobile and went out to the landing, closing the office door behind him.

'When Duke's finished out there, I'll make a cuppa. Unless there's anything you want me to do, I think I'll head off home. There's a meeting at ChristChurch Uni at 8pm for all who've expressed an interest in working for an MA.'

'Of course you must go. There's not much else you can do here for the moment. I hope the meeting goes well. It's all very exciting!'

Duke came back into the office. 'Em didn't mind at all. As long as it was a single email address, she didn't think there'd be a problem.'

After coffee, Sue picked up her bag and keys, kissed them both, and left.

'I guess there's not a lot of point in both of us just sitting around here either. I was thinking of driving over to Hastings to see what progress Baillie and his team are making. Fancy a ride?'

'I don't think so, thanks. If on the way you could drop me off at Rye Harbour, I'll pick up my car and pop back to the shop and check Glen's okay. I'll probably stay the night and come back tomorrow morning.'

With Duke on his way up to London, Russ continued on the A259 to Hastings, resisting the temptation to drop in on Sue as he passed through Winchelsea. It was 5pm when he entered the police station. An attractive young woman at the reception desk asked him to wait while she phoned through to CID. A few minutes passed before a uniformed policewoman came into the reception area from a side door. She introduced herself as WPC Garrett and led him through the door and up the flight of stairs to Baillie's office. Baillie, in shirtsleeves, sat at his desk studying a file in front of him, his jacket draped over the back of his chair. He stood up and reached out to shake hands. The WPC left the room, closing the door behind her.

He gestured for Russ to have a seat. 'Provone's still insisting the victims were alive when he left them. He says he'd had sex sessions with both of them several times previously. Judging by the weirdos he was in contact with via the Internet, we can't dismiss the possibility he could have agreed or planned to let one or more of them take over where he left off. He denies that, of course, but maintains he'd left the back doors to both properties unlocked.'

'You obviously have people looking at his laptop and phone. Have they found anything that might support that theory?'

His voice betrayed the strain he was under. 'I keep pressurising them, but they argue it's a slow process and urge me to be patient. As you know, I can only hold him for another four hours before I ask the chief for an extension of twelve hours, and if that's not long enough, I'm not overconfident that a Magistrates Court will agree to any further detention.'

Russ could empathise; he'd been in similar situations during his time in the SCU. He asked if Kommissar Roeseler had any success when he questioned Provone.

'He came out with the same defence. He wasn't bothered by the DNA sample. He admitted he'd had consensual sex with Martina Fischer and insisted she was alive when he left, leaving the door unlocked. It turns out Provone suffers with epilepsy and had been at Bethel in Germany from mid-January to the end of July last year, receiving treatment at a specialist centre for the study and treatment of epilepsy. If Provone isn't lying, where the hell does that leave us? If – and I'm not saying I'm ready to believe him – but if he's telling an edited version of the truth, we could be looking for one, two, or God forbid, three murderers!

'I've sent DS Askew to Brighton for a couple of days, working with their CID, trying to dig up what they can from friends, neighbours, etc. He doesn't buy Provone's version of events, and I'll give him his due, he's almost hyper – never seen him so determined to nail a suspect.... And as if the poor bugger hasn't got enough on his plate, his wife's kicked him out of the house, and has changed all the locks. He's in a B&B at the moment. She keeps phoning the station asking to speak to me, but I've said I'm not available. I can't get involved and in any case; I know bugger all about marriage guidance counselling.'

Russ got to his feet. 'Alec, if there's anything I can do to help, officially or unofficially, you've only got to ask.'

'Thanks, Russ, I appreciate it.' He hesitated. 'Just a thought – perhaps I shouldn't say this, but if you found an opportunity to "unofficially" have a discreet word with Askew's wife – her name's Margaret – it might get her off my back.'

'Tell me where she lives and I'll call in on my way back to Rye.'

It was a detached white clapboard cottage on the High Street at Ware, a village to the west of Hastings. A picket fence and gate bordered the small front garden. Russ found a parking space two doors along.

He rang the doorbell, and as he waited admired the neatly-kept garden. It was small and compact, full and brimming with flowering cottage garden plants. Hollyhocks, poppies, cornflowers, and honeysuckle were beginning to bloom, as was the well-established wisteria surrounding the door frame. He heard bolts being drawn back before the door opened as far as the security chain allowed. Only half of the woman's face was visible.

'Who is it?' she asked brusquely.

Russ smiled. 'Hello, my name is Russ Walker. Is it possible to have a word with Mr Askew, please?'

The smile hadn't softened her. In an offhand voice she told him he no longer lived at this address, and could be contacted at Hasting Police Station where he worked.

He was thinking on his feet now. He handed his card through the gap.

'Actually, I'm a private investigator working with the police. Would you mind if I had a word with *you* instead?'

'If you've come about the evidence he keeps on about, provided you're alone, I'll give it to you – but I'm not having *him* in the house.'

He had no idea what she meant by "evidence". 'Yes, I'm alone. I can take it if you like. Save him bothering you, if that's okay.'

Closing the door, she unhooked the security chain and reopened it. He guessed she was in her early forties, but was not at all as he'd envisaged her. She was short and fat with brown curly hair and a round face that showed bruising near the left eye. She stood to one side, allowing him to enter and then closed the door, re-bolting it.

'It's about time someone came for it. I've phoned the station dozens of times, but I can never get hold of Inspector Baillie.'

Still unaware of what she was referring to, Russ tried to mollify her. 'Yes, I'm really sorry, Margaret, but he's incredibly busy at the moment.' He looked directly at her face. 'Hey, poor you; that's a nasty bruise you have. I guess it's pretty painful.'

She touched the side of her face, her eyes filling with tears. 'He did it; but he'll never do it again! I'll never let him back into the house. Last Wednesday, while he was at work, I changed all the locks on the doors, and as the windows are double glazed, there's no way he can get in. I left a text on his phone telling him what I'd done, and that I'd left a suitcase with his toilet bag and clothes outside the front door. I said if he tries to break in, I'll call 999 straightaway.'

'Good for you. Was this the first time, or has he hit you before?'

As if defeated, she slumped into an upholstered chair and pointed for Russ to take the settee. Grateful for the opportunity of a listening ear, she told him of the several years of physical, mental and sexual abuse Askew had inflicted on her. She explained how everything seemed to change once he'd been promoted from uniform to CID. Police work was all he was interested in. He no longer had any time or interest in her or their three children, who were now at her mother's home in Dover. She blamed Baillie for the long hours Askew had to put in. She said he was never at home, and when he was he'd spend hours in his study in the cellar, working on his computer or sorting out evidence for the cases he was involved with. When he came to bed, he was crude and demanding, and often hurt her if she resisted. She pointed to the bruise on her face.

'That's nothing compared to what he's done to my body. Three nights ago, he raped me. I can't take it anymore.'

Russ could feel the hackles rising on his neck. Trying not to let his disgust and anger show in his voice, he reached over and took her hand as she wept.

'I'm so sorry, Margaret. I really think you ought to talk to your doctor; take some photographs of your injuries while you can still see them, and then you should go and see a solicitor. No-one should have to experience what you've just described.'

She pulled a tissue from her sleeve and wiped her eyes. 'Will you take his work files and whatever evidence he has?'

'Of course, just show me where it is.'

Margaret stood up, led him into a dining room and pointed to a door. 'That leads to the cellar; it's all down there. None of us are allowed into his study; it's all confidential police work. Call me when you've got it.'

She flicked the light switch on the wall to the left of the door.

He opened the door, and had to bend slightly to avoid hitting his head as he cautiously went down a short flight of steps. The small carpeted room smelt musty; not enough ventilation. The only furniture was a small wooden table and a swivel office chair. Two wide shelves were screwed to the cellar wall. On the table were three manila files, a laptop computer and printer. The shelves held three cardboard boxes, and various items of stationery. Weight-lifting apparatus had been placed against the opposite wall.

Troubled by Margaret's mention of the existence of police evidence, he took a box from the shelf and placed it on the desk. On the lid was written, "Confidential - Evidence re-ongoing cases (Clean)". Inside were several unsealed A5 brown envelopes, all marked with different initials on the address labels. In each of them he discovered a woman's thong or panties. He presumed the ones with "CT" and "EK" belonged to Provone's murder victims. Putting them back into the box, he returned it to the shelf. He took down a second box labelled "Confidential - Evidence re-ongoing cases (laundry)". Again, it contained brown envelopes, each marked with initials. Unsurprised, he discovered women's unwashed underwear, presumably taken from laundry baskets; among them he found envelopes marked "CT" and "EK."

What the hell was Askew doing with this stuff? Baillie would go ballistic when he hears of it, and rightly so. Putting the box and its contents back on the shelf, he took down the third box. It was labelled "Confidential Evidence" and contained 15 CDs in clear plastic cases, each marked with initials. He flicked through until he found the one marked "CT". Switching on the laptop, he put the CD in the disc player.

He recognised Carol Tiltman immediately, naked, spread-eagled... and alive! The camera had been positioned to the right at the foot of the bed. A person wearing a SOCOs white hooded coverall and latex gloves appeared at the right side of the bed. He pulled off his right glove and began to stroke her pubic hair. Turning his face to the camera, Askew pulled back the hood and smiled.

Russ retched, the bile rising in his throat. He swallowed it back and ejected the CD. Replacing it in its cover, he made a hurried search in the box for the ones marked "EK" and "MF". Putting them in his pocket, he pulled out his mobile; there was no signal here in the cellar.

As he rushed up the stairs, he shouted for Askew's wife to quickly pack an overnight bag. She stood in the dining room, confused. He urged her to hurry, telling her she was in danger.

'Trust me, Margaret, there's no time to lose. You need to get out of the house now! Is there a friend you can stay with just for tonight? If not, we'll find a hotel. Hurry – I'll explain why – once I know you're safe.'

Seeing the anxiety in his face, she quickly ran upstairs.

He checked his mobile; the display showed the signal was strong, that he'd missed a call and had a voicemail message from Duke. He pressed the play button. 'Hey, Russ, it's Duke. Just had a call from sister Em. They've traced him, "Wolfman" is a cop - DS Askew.'

Without waiting to hear the rest of the message, he cut it off and speed dialled Duke.

He picked up straightaway on his hands-free. 'Hey, Russ, are you there yet? For God's sake, be careful. I'm at the Brenzett roundabout. Probably take another twenty minutes to get to you.'

Russ cut in excitedly. 'Hey, Duke, he's definitely the murderer; he filmed himself and I've got the discs. I'm going to drop them off to Baillie.'

'Sod Baillie; is Sue all right?'

'What do you mean? What are you talking about?'

'Askew's at Sue's flat right now. Get moving; I'll call you back in a minute.'

Margaret entered the room carrying a holdall. Russ grabbed her arm. 'I'm sorry, but I've got another emergency. I have to go. Can you get yourself to a friend or neighbour, and just stay there? This is deadly serious; give me your mobile number. I promise I'll phone later and explain everything. Please, you have to trust me.'

The tone of his voice convinced her. She scribbled the number on a Post-It note and gave it to him.

'I'll go to the vicarage; it's just down the road, they'll look after me. Please phone as soon as you can.'

Locking the front door behind them, she turned right heading for the vicarage; Russ ran to his Capri. Burning rubber as he pulled out from the curb, he was back on the A259 within minutes. His phone rang; it was Duke.

Duke explained, 'Sue told me just before I left that Askew had been in touch again; phoned her mobile and asked if she could spare him about half an hour this evening around 6.30pm. He said he was carrying a heavy burden and desperately needed a sympathetic ear. Apparently he talked her into it, but she told him she had to be in Canterbury by 8pm. She begged me not to mention it to you, didn't want you to be jealous.

'I'd stopped for a meal at the service station at Farthing Corner on my way back to London when Em phoned with the information about "Wolfman". I manoeuvred my way back onto the southbound carriageway and tried to phone Sue to warn her to leave the flat, but I couldn't get through. I phoned you and was put through to the voicemail service. I've been driving like a bat out of hell. Look after her, Russ; I'll be with you soon.'

Attempting to drive at speed in a built up area is always a hazardous undertaking. From Hastings to Winchelsea, the road winds its way through several villages, offering few opportunities for overtaking slower vehicles. Negotiating the twists and turns, and at the same time putting a call through to DI Baillie, was sheer madness, but the seconds were ticking by. Sue's life was in jeopardy; he had no choice.

Chapter 23

She'd turned him on the first time he met her. With the faintest trace of make-up, her exquisite eyes, the sensuous smile, the tailored trouser-suit hugging her shapely figure, he was captivated. There was an aura of sweet innocence, almost naivety about her, as if she was genuinely unaware of her natural beauty and the sensuality she exuded. When he'd asked her out, she crushed him with her refusal. She was giving herself to "a significant other". It had to be Walker, the interfering bastard. He'd covered all bases, Provone would take the rap. Walker should have kept his meddlesome nose out of it.

Tonight she was his, not Walker's. Soon she would play the star roll; he would caress her, taste her, violate her. She'd regret the hurt and humiliation she had caused by turning him down.

He parked as close to the entrance as possible; pressed the button for flat 2, and through the intercom announced his arrival. There was a buzzing sound as she activated the door release. The door to her flat was open. He breathed in, savouring the faint aroma of perfume wafting from the hallway. She came to the door wearing a floral three-quarter length summer dress. She smiled and invited him in.

He apologised for his appearance, explaining that he'd come directly from a crime scene and hadn't had time to get out of the white coveralls or latex gloves. He held up his bag. 'My clothes are in here.'

She led him into her small sitting room. 'Have a seat, I'm just making coffee.' She turned and left the room.

He didn't sit. He put his bag on the settee, and felt in his pocket. There was a slight twitch of his mouth as his fingers curled round the syringe. Following the noise of the electric kettle, he silently made his way into the kitchen, a slight smile on his face. She had her back to him, spooning instant coffee into two mugs. His index finger eased off the needle cap and he gently took the syringe from his pocket. Turning to reach for the kettle, she jumped with fright as he grabbed her from behind, his left arm trapping both arms as it circled her waist. She was too shocked to scream as she felt the prick of the needle in her upper arm.

She tried to shout as she struggled to free herself from his hold, but her voice became a whisper; a numbing sensation began to sweep over her body. Her legs gave way, but she remained upright, held in his grasp.

He laid the syringe on the work surface and, with both arms, carried her through to the sitting room, placing her in a sitting position next to his bag on the settee. He took a cushion and slid it behind her head for support. Returning to the kitchen he retrieved the syringe, capped the needle and brought it back. He unzipped a side pocket in his bag and slipped the syringe inside.

He smiled as he knelt in front of her. 'Sue, my precious, we're going to have some fun. We've plenty of time, there will be no interruptions; your friends think you're going to Canterbury.'

She knew she was conscious; she could see him, hear him, but couldn't respond. It was as if her body and half her brain had been anaesthetised. She wanted to scream, to kick out, to get up and run. Tears ran down her face, but she was mute and completely paralysed.

From his bag, he took out a camera and tripod, and held them in front of her. 'I'll set this up in the bedroom. I'm going to make you a star.' He laughed. 'A porn star! You'd like that, wouldn't you?'

He got to his feet and went out of the room. He called out, 'What a lovely bedroom, a perfect location to shoot a film. Oh, and if you are wondering about the phone, it's disconnected – as is your mobile here on the dressing table.'

With the tripod and camera in position, the duvet and pillows removed from the bed, he went back to the living room. 'The scene is set, all we need now is the starlet.' He began to remove her clothes.

His Capri was never intended to rival a Ferrari 458 Italia. The tyres screeched, giving off blue smoke as Russ turned into the residents' car park. He cut the engine as Duke's Skoda pulled up beside him. They leaped from their cars – no time for greetings – and ran to the main entrance. Russ pressed the call button marked "Tradesmen". There was a click as the door lock released.

He looked at Duke, 'Great security!'

Duke held the tyre iron he'd used to get into Provone's flat. When they reached Sue's door, he heard Russ say, 'Go for it'. He jammed the iron between the frame and the door and wrenched it back. The door flew open, and Russ rushed into the hallway. All the inner doors were closed. No matter; he knew which was her bedroom. He pushed on the handle but the door had been bolted from the inside. Duke shoved him aside and threw his bodyweight at the door. The hasp offered no resistance and his momentum carried him into the room. He dove to the right, taking a crouched position. Russ, close behind, did the same to the left.

In all, it had taken less than two seconds. The ceiling light was on, the curtains at the window drawn closed. Askew stood at the far side of the bed, the fly zip of his coveralls open, his partially sheathed erection in his left hand. On the bed, Sue, wearing bra and panties, lay on her back, unrestrained but motionless.

Clearly shocked by their intrusion, it was like a reflex action as Askew grabbed the knife lying beside Sue's head. He held it to her throat.

'Make one move, either of you, and I'll slit her throat.'

Russ saw a trickle of blood where the tip of the knife pricked her skin. He straightened up, lifting his hands in surrender. 'For God's sake, Askew, take it easy. Put the knife down; we can sort this out.'

'Is that what you'll do, sort it out? The fucking Lone Ranger and Tonto sorting everything out.' He looked at Duke. 'Stand up slowly, keeping your hands where I can see them.'

Easing himself up, he adopted a deferential approach. 'You're a damn good copper, Askew. You're smart, too. Don't let this get any worse. Sue admires you, you know. Don't hurt the only woman who just wanted to be there for you. You don't want that on your conscience.'

'It's true,' said Russ. 'You've been under a hell of a lot pressure but you've got him. There's overwhelming evidence, Provone's going to go down. Don't crack up now. Throw the knife on the floor.'

In his peripheral vision, Duke saw a sign of movement. Without moving his head, he concentrated. He saw it again – yes, there was someone in the hallway out of Askew's line of vision.

From behind the curtains there was a loud crash, as something shattered the window pane. Instinctively, Askew turned his head, his attention drawn to the billowing curtains. Russ knew this was his only chance. Like a wild animal, drawing on every ounce of energy, he pounced, launching himself over the bed, to ram his body into Askew's. In the split second before the impact, Askew's face turned and he thrust the blade into Russ. The force of the collision knocked Askew off balance and against the wall as Russ staggered backwards, pulling the knife from his chest.

In that instant, avoiding Sue, Duke leapt across the bed. Askew was skilled in self-defence, but he was no match against Duke. Deflecting the punches, his hands went for Askew's throat. With his thumbs on the windpipe, he began to apply pressure, restricting his air flow. Askew stopped struggling and his knees began to give way. Duke removed his hands and Askew dropped to his knees, coughing, gasping for breath. With his foot, he pushed Askew into a face down position, pulled plasticuffs from his belt, and secured Askew's hands behind him.

'It's okay, Windsor, we'll take it from here.' Baillie and a uniformed officer had appeared. They dragged Askew to his feet and manhandled him round the bed and out of the door.

Oblivious of the blood soaking his shirt, Russ had climbed onto the bed and was cradling Sue in his arms. She was alive but unresponsive.

'The bastard's drugged her.' His voice was slurred. 'Duke, she needs an ambulance.'

'So do you, my friend.'

From his mobile, Duke phoned for two ambulances. Extricating Sue from Russ arms, he gently laid him beside her, and ripped his shirt open. Taking a handkerchief from his own pocket, he pushed it into the wound in an attempt to stem the blood flow. He took Russ' hand and put it on the blood-soaked cloth. 'Press hard on this, buddy; it's going to be okay.'

His eyes swept the room for Askew's bag. It was on the floor at the foot of the bed. Opening it he found what he was looking for - duct tape. He cut off several strips, removed the handkerchief from Russ' chest, and stuck them over the wound, effectively sealing it.

He squinted – the light hurt his eyes, too bright. There was a dull ache in his chest. The blurred image above him moved in and out of focus, then a vague flash of recognition.

'Duke? What's going on? Where am I?'

'Hey, bro, welcome back! You're at the Conquest Hospital. You've had surgery for a knife wound and you're just waking up.'

Russ closed his eyes, trying to assimilate what he thought he's heard. It made no sense. He opened them again. 'Knife wound? I don't know what...'

His voice trailed off; he was drifting in and out of consciousness.

'It's okay, bro, don't try to talk. Go back to sleep. We're staying with you. We'll be here when you wake up.'

Miraculously, the knife had missed his vital organs, but caused serious damage to the sternum and in the inner cavity of the chest. Following surgery and three days in intensive care, he had been transferred to a private ward.

It was another six hours before he opened his eyes again.

Duke gently squeezed his hand. 'Hey, Russ, how are you doing?'

'A bit sore. How long have I been asleep?'

'Not long – just three and a half days.'

'Ever the comedian, you...'

He suddenly stopped. His body tensed. It was as if his brain had just clicked into gear. The reality of the situation began to dawn on him.

He shouted, 'Sue! What's happened to Sue?' Oh dear God! Duke, what happened to Sue?'

Someone was stroking his other hand. 'I'm here, Russ.' She was in tears. 'Thanks to you two, I'm alright.'

Ward Sister Clare Pepper eased passed Duke to check on the saline drip, and to take Russ' blood pressure. 'Good afternoon, Mr Walker. You're looking so much better. I've told your friends they can have ten minutes with you, and then they'll have to go. We need to change your dressings, and the doctor wants to examine you.'

She then pressed a button which electronically raised the top half of the bed, elevating him into a slightly more upright position.

As soon as the Sister left them, Sue leant over and lightly kissed him. 'How are you, Russ? I've been so worried. Duke and Inspector Baillie told me what happened. Apparently Askew drugged me with Rohypnol, a date rape drug, and I was hardly aware of what was going on. I'll never be able to thank you and Duke enough for...' She began to cry.

Duke, who was never one for showing affection, kissed Russ' forehead. 'You had me scared, bro. When I saw Askew put the knife in, I thought that was it.'

Duke and Sue sat on opposite sides of the bed, each holding one of his hands. Duke explained that Askew was in custody. Baillie had taken the incriminating CDs from Russ' pocket and the SOCOs were still at Askew's house, gathering evidence. Police station records showed that Askew had either been on annual leave or on a rest day when he committed the murders. He'd told his wife he had gone to Germany on a "stag weekend" with colleagues, as one of them was about to get married at the time of Martina Fischer's murder. It appears he and Provone had made contact with each other on the bondage website two years ago and made their arrangements by email and phone. Both had now been charged with three counts of murder.

Sue pointed to various floral arrangements and "get well" cards. 'You're a popular man. The big display's from George Tiltman. The one next to it is from Elaine Knightley's family. The smaller sprays are from Inspector Baillie and Janice

Austin, and one with a small card attached with just the letter 'D' on it.'

Sister Pepper popped her head round the door. 'Time's up, I'm afraid.'

Sue and Duke reluctantly got up to leave, promising to be back in the evening.

Grinning, Russ said, 'Hey, deconstruction is a great occupation.'

Duke and Sue looked quizzically at each other. Duke shrugged his shoulders. 'I don't know what he's on about either!'